THREE GIRLS GONE

BOOKS BY CAROLYN ARNOLD

Remnants

On the Count of Three

Past Deeds

One More Kill

DETECTIVE MADISON KNIGHT SERIES

Ties That Bind

Justified

Sacrifice

Found Innocent

Just Cause

Deadly Impulse

In the Line of Duty

Power Struggle

Shades of Justice

What We Bury

Girl on the Run

Her Dark Grave

Murder at the Lake

Her Buried Past

Prequel: Life Sentence

SARA AND SEAN COZY MYSTERY SERIES

Bowled Over Americano

Wedding Bells Brew Murder

MATTHEW CONNOR ADVENTURE SERIES

City of Gold

The Secret of the Lost Pharaoh

The Legend of Gasparilla and His Treasure

CAROLYN ARNOLD

THREE GIRLS GONE

bookouture

Published by Bookouture in 2025

An imprint of Storyfire Ltd.
Carmelite House
50 Victoria Embankment
London EC4Y 0DZ

www.bookouture.com

The authorised representative in the EEA is Hachette Ireland
8 Castlecourt Centre
Dublin 15 D15 XTP3
Ireland
(email: info@hbgi.ie)

ISBN: 978-1-83618-071-5
eBook ISBN: 978-1-83618-070-8

PROLOGUE

They got away with it before, and they would again. Besides, the choice was made, and it was too late to turn around now. Like a car careening down an icy road, there was no point in resisting. They ended up where they were supposed to be, just like destiny had intended.

They glanced in the rearview mirror. The girl was nestled on the backseat, her blond hair fanned out beneath her head. For now, she was sleeping, but soon her eyes would shut for the last time.

Until then, they intended to savor the journey. It had been far too long since the last one. Somehow, they had forgotten the rush that came with snatching a child from under the world's nose.

Taking advantage of her vulnerability and exploiting her trust was heady. First, by convincing her to get into the car. Second, getting her to sniff the rag soaked in chloroform. All they had to say from the driver's seat was, "Does this smell funny to you?" and hold it through the console. She had leaned in right away, took a deep inhale, and knocked herself out.

Easy, peasy.

The recollection brought a smile, a sense of pride and power. They bravely took a stand to transform the world into a better place, and were righting future wrongs while they were at it. If this girl was allowed to grow up, she'd become like the rest. Selfish and needy, manipulating and hurting those who loved her the most. She'd chip away at their pride until there was nothing left but an empty shell.

That couldn't be allowed to happen. They'd teach her. And once the girl's tiny body was put on display, the world would pay attention. People would be horrified and fearful. More chaos would follow. But what they couldn't predict was that the hunger was back.

This child wouldn't be the last.

ONE

Amanda Steele accepted there were more tragic endings than happy ones. A sad fact of life. A viewpoint gained from experience as a homicide detective with the Prince William County Police Department. While she lived in the small town of Dumfries, Virginia, a rather sleepy place fifty minutes from Washington, DC, she was stationed at Central District in Woodbridge. It was less than fifteen minutes from her hometown, but it was more populated and spread out. It also boasted the famous Potomac Mills mall, and offered quick access to Interstate 95. Both made traffic a nightmare at times. But the town wasn't without its green spaces and trees.

She was loaded in the passenger seat of a department car while her work partner, Trent Stenson, drove them to one such place. Heroes Memorial Park. A girl's body had been found on the carousel in the playground and was rumored to be six-year-old Hailey Tanner. She'd disappeared after her weekly ballet lesson at a local dance studio just three days before. Something so routine had turned into every parent's worst nightmare. Amanda refused to think about where the girl had been all this time and what she had suffered. If there was any mercy, death would have been swift and painless.

When her boss had called, Amanda had been wrangling her nine-year-old daughter, Zoe, into getting ready for school. She ended up dropping her off at her aunt Libby's, but not before squeezing her so tightly that Zoe claimed Amanda was suffocating her. She let Zoe go with some reluctance. There were parents who would never hug their daughter again. It was for them and the girl that she was on the move.

Trent turned into the parking lot, free to visitors, and was waved past by a uniformed officer. He was one of many posted in the area, and several cruisers peppered the lot. No civilian vehicle was in sight. Earlier guests would have been escorted out and any new arrivals turned away. No sign of the news media either. Yet, anyway. She didn't expect that to hold out.

The flashing lights and the police activity played out in stark contrast to the otherwise typical, beautiful May day. The air was warm, and the sky was clear.

Amanda got out of the department car with Trent. She shook her shoulders, willing the tension out. With every step, she braced for what she was about to see.

Two uniformed officers were standing side by side, facing them. They stood in front of a makeshift tent that blocked the view of the scene and eliminated the risk of any potential lookie-loo with a cell phone.

"Hey." The often exuberant greeting was watered-down and solemn. It had come from Officer Brandt. Officer Wyatt, who was next to him, dipped his head and gestured to the opening.

Amanda stepped inside.

Time slowed down. All the surrounding chaos quieted. Chirping birds fell silent.

While Amanda had seen Hailey's photograph at the station and in the news, nothing prepared her for this. Here the flesh-

and-blood reality smacked against the grim truth that all the public petitions hadn't worked.

Her small body was set on the carousel, posed loosely in a fetal position. She was dressed in a pale-pink ballerina's tutu and slippers. A chiffon scarf, in a matching shade, adorned her neck. Her sweet, pale face was turned upward, eyes open. They were speckled with petechiae, evidence of oxygen starvation. Mascara was caked on her lashes and a bright-pink lipstick stained her rosebud lips.

"It's definitely her," Trent said, sounding dejected.

Amanda found it hard to take her eyes off the girl. The cosmetics made the scene even more unnatural, unsettling. "Hailey Tanner." Amanda uttered her name, feeling it would be disrespectful otherwise.

The sound of coins jingling together had her stepping out of the tent. She came face to face with a man she hadn't met before. Salt-and-pepper hair, in his late forties, early fifties. He was dressed in a suit jacket, slacks, and tie.

Amanda blocked the doorway. "This is a crime scene. You'll need to leave." How he got this far was unsettling.

In a swift move, the man lifted his jacket to expose the badge clipped to his waistband. "Detective Lloyd McGee with Missing Persons. Stationed at East." He didn't wait for Amanda to react, but sidestepped her. He came to a standstill upon seeing the girl and said nothing.

That explained why she didn't recognize him. While Eastern District Station was also in Woodbridge, she had no reason to go there. "That still doesn't explain why you're here."

He turned around, but the movement was slow and appeared painful. "I heard it come over the radio and had to know if it was her. Hailey was my case."

She couldn't fault him for wanting to be here, but there was a lot she held against him. Like why Hailey's case hadn't been escalated to Homicide. "And now she's ours. My partner and I will keep you informed."

"And you are?"

She stiffened. "Detective Steele," she offered, choosing not to offer her given name.

"Detective Stenson," Trent piped in.

"Why didn't you hand this over to Homicide? A little girl was taken, endangered," she said.

"First of all, I have superiors who I answer to, and they make the decisions."

So he doesn't like to shoulder any responsibility...

"And second, the parents are wealthy. Considering the evidence, everything pointed to it being a kidnapping for ransom. That falls within our purview to handle. We never thought that she would be—" He closed his mouth and shook his head. "Not that I need to explain myself to you. We're where we are. Nothing we can do about it now."

"Really? That's your take on this? Simple acceptance?" she said, thinking he was letting himself off easy.

"Listen, if I knew we'd land here, of course I would have fought for the case to be reassigned. Unfortunately, I wasn't equipped with a crystal ball."

Maybe McGee was shielding himself from regret, but his callous sarcasm had her temper flaring. Crystal ball or not, the PWCPD had failed Hailey. Herself included. When Amanda had first heard about Hailey Tanner, she never expected a happy ending, but she didn't insert herself into the investigation. She could justify this decision because of her heavy caseload. After all, the other victims she fought for deserved her focus. But look where that had gotten the girl. Where it had gotten all of them. They were too late to save her. And now, they had to hunt a killer.

TWO

Amanda had a hard time prying her gaze from the child. So small, so innocent, so fragile, so very dead...

"I'll need to notify the girl's parents," McGee said.

The detective's words pulled Amanda from her reflection. "Oh, no, you won't. That's our job." Some child abductions were orchestrated by the parents, whether it be for financial reasons or otherwise. She and Trent needed to gauge their reactions.

"Her parents aren't in on this, if that's what you're thinking. Trust me."

"No offense, Detective, but I don't know you or the Tanners. Stenson and I will deliver the news. You can join us." One concession she was willing to make.

"Whatever you'd like." He flailed an arm.

The detective was clearly dealing with his own issues, but this was about Hailey and finding her killer. There wasn't time to waste on personal feelings or perceived slights.

"I just thought since I have a relationship with them already, it might be easier for them to hear it from me."

His concern for the Tanners' feelings suggested his hardened demeanor was a wall he hid behind. She might have judged him too soon. "I get that, but nothing will make hearing about their daughter's murder easier for them."

"You might have a point, but are we going to head out?" McGee jacked a thumb toward the lot.

"Not quite yet," Amanda told him.

"You want her parents to wait longer?"

"It's not about that," Amanda said. "Right now, the Tanners have hope. Once we show up, that's gone. There's no way I'm doing that until I have something more to say than their daughter is dead."

McGee held up a hand. "Fine, but it would be tragic if the Tanners heard about their daughter from someone else."

"Like the media?" she said, and McGee nodded. "I agree with you there."

"Well, I worry how long it's going to take to get some answers. I don't even see the medical examiner on scene to give us cause or time of death."

Officer Wyatt popped his head into the door opening. "Everyone's been called. I'm sure they'll be here soon."

Crime Scene and the Office of the Chief Medical Examiner were stationed in Manassas. Not accounting for traffic, it was a thirty-minute drive away. And that had no bearing on whether there was available manpower.

Amanda leaned closer to the girl. "There is petechiae in her eyes."

"Starved of oxygen. Maybe the scarf was used," McGee suggested.

Amanda passed Trent a side-glance and shared another observation. "She's dressed up as a ballerina with the tutu and the slippers. The makeup is done, as if she's in a performance. But the scarf doesn't fit. Ballerinas don't wear them. And it looks much too large for a child."

"I'd say it belongs to a woman," Trent put in.

"But if the scarf is the murder weapon, why leave it with the body? It could give us prints and DNA," McGee said.

Us... But the reason a killer would risk that wasn't encouraging. "This person might not be in the system, which means leaving a trace isn't a concern for them. The scarf may serve another purpose. To hide bruising? The killer may have wanted her to look serene."

"Was she taken in a tutu and slippers?" Trent asked, looking at McGee.

The detective shook his head. "When she left the dance studio after her lesson, she was back in street clothes. There was a tutu and slippers in her locker at the studio."

"The studio stored them there?" It sounded unusual for a child to have their own locker.

"They offered that to Hailey because her parents donated a lot of money to the studio," McGee said. "But the style of this tutu is like the one in the girl's locker and others in her closet. I searched both when I was confirming her last moves."

Chills rolled over Amanda's arms. Was there more to this? "She has other tutus in her closet?"

"She did, yeah. Don't ask me how many. Accounting for her wardrobe wasn't my focus. It was just something I noticed while searching her room. It's not like I had any idea that..." He stopped talking as his eyes drifted to the small body.

Were the similar tutus a coincidence? Or was Hailey dressed in one of her own? If so, was the killer someone close to the Tanner family? Someone who Hailey had trusted?

THREE

Amanda stepped out of the tent. "We need to speak with the person who found her," she told the officers.

Wyatt directed her attention to a woman sitting at a picnic table with her back to them. Officer Traci Cochran was taking her statement.

"Her name's Susan Butters," Officer Wyatt told her, and Amanda led the way over to the picnic table. Officer Cochran watched them approach and stood up once they got closer. Susan Butters turned around. Her skin was blotchy and eyes bloodshot from crying. Adrenaline wasn't doing its job and shielding her from the jolt of what she'd seen.

"Ma'am, if you'll excuse me a moment." Cochran hopped up from the table's bench and walked about ten feet away with Amanda, Trent, and McGee in tow. She studied McGee, her forehead creasing. "I don't think we've met before."

"Nope. Detective McGee with Missing Persons, and you?"

"Missing Persons? Sadly, I guess your job here is over," she said. "I'm Officer Traci Cochran. So here's what I know..." She filled them in on Butters's statement, which they'd verify and build on. "And she's got a clean record," Traci added.

"Thank you," Amanda told her.

"I assume you want to have a chat now?"

"We do," Amanda assured her.

They walked over to Susan, and Traci made all the introductions without specifying McGee was with Missing Persons.

"Is that Hailey Tanner? Did I find Hailey? No one will tell me." Susan rubbed her cheeks, grinding her palms into the damp flesh.

"Did you know Hailey?" Amanda had to assess whether Susan's shock was genuine or a performance. It was too soon to conclude if the killer was a man or woman. If anything, the woman's scarf and how Hailey was lovingly arranged suggested the latter.

"Yes. Well, from the news. Not in person. She was taken last week."

Since Hailey's predicament was widespread knowledge, Susan's assumption was understandable. Amanda would still ask Hailey's parents if they knew Susan Butters.

"So it is her?" Susan pressed.

"We're not at liberty to confirm that," Amanda said. "I also request that you refrain from telling others what happened here today until the parents of that child have been notified. Have you spoken to anyone, texted or called?"

"No. My fingers didn't want to work to call nine-one-one. I just want to forget about all of this. I should have just stayed home like every other day. But, no, I had to get off my butt and out the door for a walk. And look where that got me." The latter bit came out like she was talking to herself.

"Then you don't walk every morning?" Trent asked, jumping in before Amanda got there.

"Do I look like I'm into exercise?" Susan gestured at her body, her face grimacing as if she were ashamed by the extra weight she carried. Amanda would never presume to gauge someone's lifestyle from their appearance. Everyone metabo lized differently. Some people could eat a carrot and run for an hour a day and get nowhere. Amanda loved that she could eat anything and stay lean.

"What made you come out today?" Amanda was skeptical because lots of villains portrayed themselves as heroes.

"My mother's skillful ability to guilt-trip me. She told me to stop feeling sorry for myself and get out in the fresh air. It would do me some good." She rolled her eyes.

"Are you depressed?" This blunt personal question came from McGee, and had Trent and Amanda locking eyes.

"Ah, yeah. But you would be too if you lost the job you had for a decade and your twelve-year-old dog in one week. I don't have human kids. Barnie was my fur baby."

Considering this, her mother's "encouragement" was rather harsh. "I'm sorry for your loss and that you're going through a rough time." Amanda's sentiment was sincere, but potential motives rolled around in her mind. Susan's health or other life circumstances might have made having children impossible. The trick was finding out that reason without crossing an ethical line. *Think, think, think...* "Well, kids are an enormous responsibility. But I've heard that as rewarding as having a dog might be, they're like having toddlers for their entire lifetime."

"Oh, they are that. Don't get me wrong, though. I'm not against kids, but I fear having them isn't in the cards for me. That's me. No job, no dog, no boyfriend, and now this." Susan clenched her jaw and shook her head. "Let's hope this is rock bottom. I don't know what else I could take. Though I can't see how it can get much worse."

Amanda passed another brief glance at Trent. He gave a slight nod of his head, which she took to mean he understood why Amanda had said what she did. Susan sounded bitter that she didn't have children. Had she abducted Hailey to become an instant mother? But then things took a sideways turn? Had Hailey's death been unintentional in a flash of rage? "Did you touch her or anything in the area?" Extending the benefit of the doubt was like playing Russian roulette in this line of work. Sometimes fatal.

"No way. It was clear she was dead."

"Sometimes people do things when they are in shock they wouldn't otherwise," Amanda said. "Even when they know it's wrong."

"I never touched her or anything near her," Susan repeated.

"Did you see anyone at the park this morning, leaving or at a distance?" Trent asked, drawing Susan's gaze to him. He had his notepad and pen in hand.

"The officer asked me these questions. Is it necessary to run through them again?"

"We're just verifying," Trent said.

"No one else was here that I know of, until the cops showed up. Though maybe I just can't remember right now." She touched her head. "Please, tell me who would do such a thing to a little girl."

The inquiry was innocent on the surface, but Susan might want to feed off their reaction to the scene. To her work. Amanda wasn't going to bite. "There's no explaining some people, ma'am. Just for elimination, Officer Cochran would like to collect your prints and DNA." Amanda bobbed her head, as if to encourage Susan's acceptance.

"Sure."

Amanda smiled at her. "Thank you. That will save us some time later. Call me if you think of anything once the shock wears off." She gave Susan her card.

"Okay."

"And remember, don't speak a word of this to anyone. We still need to notify the girl's parents," Amanda reiterated.

"I promise."

Amanda studied the woman's eyes, hoping she wasn't making the wrong call. She waved Officer Cochran over and told her to collect the samples from Susan. To Susan, she said, "After the officer finishes, you can go home, but please don't leave town in case we have more questions for you."

"I won't."

Amanda's attention was drawn to the parking lot. Vans belonging to Crime Scene and the medical examiner were there now. But unwelcome arrivals had also turned up. The news vehicles were parked on the street, aiming their cameras at the action in the park. She detested how the media had no boundaries and profited from tragedy. Hunger for catching an exclusive story outweighed human compassion.

"Sickening." Detective McGee flailed an arm at one news van. "The Tanners deserve to hear about their daughter from us, not them."

"Yep. We need to wrap this up as fast as possible, and get her out of here," Amanda said.

FOUR

Amanda breathed easier seeing that investigators Emma Blair and Isabelle Donnelly were assigned to the scene. They were thorough and showed respect for the victims. The two of them were inside the tent along with Medical Examiner Hans Rideout and his assistant, Liam Baker, when she slipped inside with Trent and McGee.

"What a shame." Rideout's words sliced through the impromptu moment of silence, even though the utterance was a fraction above a whisper. "Given the situation here, I'd like to move her out as quickly as possible. I'll process everything back at the morgue when I return and get started on her straight away."

"Good idea." Every police department in America was the subject of public scrutiny, the PWCPD included. People would demand swift answers.

Liam managed the ME's schedule and pulled out his tablet and tapped away, likely shifting things around to prioritize Hailey's autopsy.

CSI Blair was snapping pictures of the girl in situ and the immediate area around her. Then she expanded out, taking in more of the scene. She'd do even more once the girl's remains were taken and the blockade tent was removed. CSI Donnelly stood by.

A few minutes later, CSI Blair stepped back, letting her camera dangle from its strap and sit against her chest. "There. I'm finished, if you want to get in there."

Rideout signaled to his assistant, and they moved in to wrap the girl in a black bag.

"Any idea how long she's been here?" Trent directed at Rideout.

"Detective, I'm good, but not that good."

Rideout was being modest. Knowing him he was more concerned about being held accountable to his estimation. "No one's going to hold you to it. Just an approximate," she requested.

Rideout slid his gaze toward her. "Not playing today." He turned his attention back to getting Hailey tucked away. "Okay, maybe I will. She's well into rigor. This suggests the time of death was anywhere between four and ten hours ago."

Amanda pulled her phone to consult the time. "Since it's nine AM now, that would put TOD between eleven last night and five this morning." This also meant that Hailey had lived with her kidnapper for days. That could support her earlier theory that the person who took her never intended to kill her.

"And she was probably killed elsewhere and then brought here," Trent said.

"Lividity might help us determine that. I'll advise once I get to work on her," Rideout said.

Lividity was the name given to how blood pooled at the lowest points in the body after death. It provided insight into how the victim was positioned in the hours following death.

Trent made a good point. They would need to find the murder scene. Was it somewhere associated with Susan Butters? Or was Amanda desperate to see the woman as a killer to get swift justice for Hailey? After all, the tutu may have come from the girl's own closet, and they hadn't established a connection to the Tanners yet.

"Liam, stop!" Rideout rushed out, raising his voice a few notches.

Liam froze in place, his hands on the girl's body near her shoulders. One of his hands had tugged on the scarf and exposed the flesh underneath.

Amanda leaned in for a better look but stepped back at a pointed look from the ME.

"The petechiae in her eyes and bruising around her neck indicates strangling. I can't know if it was done by hand or with a ligature, such as this scarf even, until I get her back to the morgue. I won't conclude this as cause of death, but it seems quite likely."

A strangulation could be intentional or the result of someone lashing out. "We'll need the scarf tested for DNA."

"Absolutely," Blair said.

"Whoever did this created the image of a perfect princess or child star." CSI Donnelly's words came in an undertone and twisted Amanda's gut.

"The question is why," Trent said. "Was it remorse? Did they have genuine affection for the girl?"

Amanda looked at where the sweet girl had been, recalling her in the fetal position. The scene was staged, so why set it this way? Was it for the shock factor? Or was it what Trent said, to signify remorse? Had it been a woman who had set out the child with a loving, but misguided, hand? She may have taken the child after losing one of her own or, as she thought before, was someone who wanted kids but didn't have any. *Or* was this more about drawing attention to Hailey as a performer, as a star? She was a ballerina. Had she performed and attracted her killer's attention? She shoved all these thoughts aside. It was too soon to jump to any conclusions. "Let me know everything you find out, as soon as possible," she told Rideout. "And notify me immediately if there are any signs of sexual assault." Just voicing the request soured the coffee in her stomach.

"I will," Rideout said.

The ME and his assistant got Hailey zipped away into the body bag. When Amanda stepped out, more news vehicles were pulling up along the park.

Blair stood next to her. "It never gets easier."

"Nope."

Rideout and Liam came out with the body, and Blair went back inside.

There would be no more putting it off. The Tanners had the right to know what had happened to their daughter. She looked over her shoulder at McGee. "You can leave your car here and come with us. We need you to bring us up to speed on the way to the Tanners' house."

FIVE

As she walked toward the parking lot with Trent and McGee, Amanda made a quick call to her boss, Sergeant Malone, to confirm the body was that of Hailey Tanner. She also told him their next stop was to deliver the news to the girl's parents. When she got off the phone, she spotted a security camera in the lot. She pointed this out to Trent.

"I'll follow up on the footage," he said.

"Let's hope it gets us somewhere because there isn't any CCTV on the nearby streets."

They'd had some luck with doorbell cams in the past, but they weren't an option here without homes across from the park.

Trent sat behind the wheel of the department car, and Detective McGee got comfortable in the backseat. Amanda rode shotgun. Her vantage point afforded her a clear view of the *PWC News* van as it nosed into the mouth of the parking lot and was turned away. Diana Wesson was looking back at Amanda from the front passenger seat. As they passed, Wesson swiveled around and smacked the dash. Despite the horror

Amanda had just seen, that brought a smile to her face. She'd escaped the nosy, unscrupulous reporter. She checked her phone and made sure Wesson's number was still blocked.

McGee spoke up with directions to the Tanner house, and she looked back at him. "Tell us anything you think we should know before going in. Prime suspects in her disappearance, details of when she went missing..."

"You know she was taken after her dance lesson last Friday evening," McGee began. "No employee at the studio witnessed anyone suspicious or saw Hailey go off with a stranger. I also spoke to the parents of the other students. No one saw anything. No cameras outside the studio or neighboring buildings. As for suspects, the family, their friends, and relatives were ruled out. The primary focus has been on the Tanners' live-in nanny."

"Her name?" Trent asked while making a left turn.

"Mara Bennett. She's been with the family since Hailey was born and came home from the hospital. This was her second job as a nanny. She only left the first when the family had a change in their financial situation and had to let her go."

"Why suspect her?" Amanda imagined the woman would have a close bond with the girl.

"She usually drops Hailey at her ballet lessons and picks her up. Not last week."

"Why not?" Trent said, looking in the rearview mirror.

"And she didn't stick around while Hailey had her lesson? Was that normal? Hailey was just six years old." That was where her mind went first.

"I'm feeling a little tag-teamed here."

Get over it... That was Amanda's instant thought, but she censored herself. "Lots of questions are typical with a fresh case."

"I get that. As for Bennett not hanging around, that was encouraged by the studio. The thinking was it would be less of a distraction during the lessons. Sometimes Bennett would use that time to pick up groceries for the family. I verified that was the case last Friday."

"All right, then, back to Trent's question. Why didn't she pick her up on Friday?"

"She got a text from Jean Tanner. That's Hailey's mother. Only Jean was adamant she never sent it and the phone records from her provider backed that up. This text wasn't sent from her phone to Bennett."

"I don't understand," Amanda said. "Jean would have been in Bennett's contacts."

"And she is. But the sender ID'd themselves as Jean with a new number."

"I assume you forwarded this to Digital Crimes?" This unit of the PWCPD had detectives who specialized in technology. Her main contact, Detective Jacob Briggs, was a miracle worker.

"That's how I found out this much." Spoken on the defensive, like he took her question as an accusation he hadn't done his job. She hadn't made that assumption, but he hadn't earned her trust yet either. "That number is no longer in service," McGee added.

"It could still be tracked down," she pointed out.

"It was. All the way to a dead end. It was a prepaid number and came from a block serviced by Universal Mobile. Digital Crimes found out it was activated on the first of December and where it was purchased. It was some convenience store in town, but a trip there didn't net a thing. No video, and the owner has a strict cash-only policy."

Disappointing. "What else did this message say?"

"It was straightforward. Just that *Jean* was going to pick Hailey up from the dance studio on Friday."

"Getting Mara out of the way." Trent came to a stop at a red light. "Whoever took Hailey was familiar with her schedule.

But you said family and friends have been cleared. What about affairs, or coworkers? Were any of those considered?"

Family and friends... This time it stuck out to her. "It wasn't just her schedule they knew about. McGee, you said the tutu looked like ones Hailey had?"

"It did. Obviously, I can't say for sure."

"Fair enough," Amanda conceded.

McGee continued. "No affairs were uncovered. I told you the family was wealthy. Well, the father is in investments. He owns his own firm and focuses only on clients who have a starting amount of seven figures to invest. We considered a former employee, Nick Potter. He felt he'd been screwed over by Tanner in an investment deal. Potter lost seven hundred K."

Trent whistled. "That's a lot of money."

"To us mere mortals, but Potter is worth millions himself. But to make things worse between Tanner and Potter, Tanner dismissed him. For a moment, this guy was considered a suspect. I speculated he may have taken the girl to demand a ransom to make up some of what he lost. I released him from suspicion for a couple of reasons. One, his alibi checked out. And two, he didn't seem too affected by the shady business with Tanner either. Potter ended up opening his own firm."

"When did all this happen?" she asked, knowing that hurt feelings didn't always expire with time.

"November."

Amanda wanted to speak with Nick Potter herself. Alibi or not.

The light changed, and Trent went through.

"Turn right at the first street," McGee directed.

Trent did as he said, and soon after, McGee pointed out a large home. Trent parked at the curb out front.

The house was a statement of affluence. She understood how McGee may have become fixed on the ransom angle.

Amanda led the way to the front door. With each step, she

thought about the devastating news they had to deliver. She reached for the doorbell at the same time as McGee.

"Detective Steele, if you'd allow me." A hint of emotion bled into his voice.

She pulled her hand back. "Go ahead."

He pushed the button, and a melodious chime sounded inside the home and reached the step.

Footsteps pounded toward them, then stopped. Soon after, the door was opened. Jean Tanner stood there. Amanda recognized her from the news. As a rule, she avoided it in all its forms, whether it be print or digital. The job gave her enough of the sad, the bad, and the ugly. But the heartbreaking case of Hailey Tanner had still found its way to her prior to today, even outside of work.

"Mrs. Tanner," McGee said. "This is Detective Steele and Detective Stenson. Can we come in for a moment? We have news about Hailey."

"Ah, sure." She stepped back while appraising Amanda and Trent. Her straight and confident posture shrank, as if her innate sense was alerting her to what was coming.

Once they were in the entry, McGee asked, "Is Mr. Tanner home?"

"I'll go get him." Jean closed the door behind them. "Just sit in the front room, and we'll be there in a minute."

"Thank you, Mrs. Tanner." McGee wiped his shoes on the front mat before leading the way across the entrance into a space decorated with cream furniture. The formality made it hard to imagine a child playing in there.

Silver frames lined a dark cherry hall table against the wall. All the photographs were of a smiling Hailey. In one, she was dressed as a pumpkin for Halloween. In another, she was sitting cross-legged in front of a Christmas tree. The rest didn't appear to be taken for any specific holiday. A few showed Hailey in tutu and slippers. In every instance it was the same pale-pink dress that looked like the one she was found in, with a mesh sweetheart neckline and cap sleeves.

Jean stepped up behind Amanda and picked up a frame. "This one was taken before her performance in *The Nutcracker* last year."

"She's beautiful," Amanda said, turning to face the woman. Her mind repeated Donnelly's words from the crime scene. *A child star...* Amanda would inquire more about the show later, but it took place months ago. Was it even connected? But something else needed to be attended to first. It soothed her little that she wouldn't be the one delivering the news. She'd still be present to witness the Tanners' hearts being broken.

She left Jean and sat on the couch as Vincent Tanner entered the room. He was a striking man with blond hair and silver eyes. He was five or more years older than his wife, but neither of them looked over forty.

Jean returned the frame to the table and sat on a vacant chair near her husband. Both Tanners looked at McGee.

McGee straightened his tie and cleared his throat. "As I told your wife, Mr. Tanner, these are fellow detectives with the Prince William County PD. Meet Detectives Steele, and Stenson." He gestured toward each of them.

Vincent let his gaze linger on them. Then he stiffened. Like his wife, he must have sensed their presence meant nothing good.

"We're here because we have some news about Hailey," McGee began, and Jean gasped out.

Vincent became still, making it hard to tell if he was breathing.

McGee continued. "Unfortunately, her body was found this morning in Heroes Memorial Park."

"No, no, no..." Jean was sobbing and shaking her head.

The pain emanating from her was alive, as if an entity of its own. "We're very sorry for your loss," Amanda said, her empathy for them getting the best of her. But she'd been on the receiving end of such news before. Her husband and six-year-old daughter, Lindsey, had been taken from her. Not murdered, a car accident caused by a drunk driver, but gone, nonetheless. Same too for her unborn son and her ability to have children.

"What happened to her? Who did this?" Vincent's body language was stiff, and his voice raw, as he assumed a strong front.

"Wait," Jean intercepted, leveling a look at Amanda and Trent. "That's why you're here, isn't it? What unit are you with?"

"Homicide, ma'am." Trent told her.

"I guess it makes sense. You said she was found, but..." She shut her mouth and stared blankly across the room.

Being here to witness this couple's worst nightmare come to life burrowed an ache in Amanda's chest. As of this moment, all hope for Hailey's safe return had evaporated.

"Please tell us how she..." Vincent's voice petered out, but then he tagged on, "You said she was found in Heroes Memorial Park?"

McGee sat back and gestured toward Amanda.

Now, he passes the baton... "We don't have a lot of answers yet, but I assure you we will be working hard to get them."

"Did she... ah... suffer?" Jean hiccupped a sob.

"An autopsy will be conducted today, and we'll know more then." Amanda delivered that in an even tone, even as it drained energy from her soul. She'd do well to step back and detach, or this case would devour her sanity.

Jean touched her throat, and tears beaded in her eyes but didn't fall. She had retreated behind a protective layer of shock.

"We have some questions for you that might help us figure out who killed her." Trent put this as delicately as velvet, but Jean's mouth still opened in a silent sob.

Vincent glanced at McGee, then at Trent. "I don't know

what else we could say that we didn't already tell Detective McGee. We can't think of anyone who would have taken Hailey, let alone..." He paused there, but resumed speaking a few seconds later. "She was a happy kid, loved ballet, and being active."

"We can't imagine what you're going through right now." Though Amanda had an idea. But this wasn't about her. It was about the Tanners and their loss. Learning about Hailey was useful, and Vincent's offering teed up something Amanda wanted to discuss further. "Mrs. Tanner, you said that Hailey was in *The Nutcracker* last year?"

"That's right. Two weeks before Christmas she played the Sugar Plum Fairy, and she did a marvelous job. She outshone her classmates, but she is quite an advanced dancer for her age." Talking about her daughter in this sense seemed to have resurrected her spirits and shoved her grief aside, although Amanda noted the use of the present tense.

"Where did the show take place?" As she thought at the crime scene, it might have been Hailey's star quality that attracted her abductor and killer. Detective McGee had exhausted leads closer to the family. A stranger may have initially latched on to Hailey at the show. The similarity in the tutus a mere coincidence.

"At her elementary school," Vincent said and provided its name. "Most of Hailey's classmates danced around the stage without training. It was rather comedic." Despite his words, his expression was pinched with sadness.

"Were tickets limited to the families of the kids who attend there?" Amanda asked, but she had this horrible feeling rising in her gut.

Jean shook her head. "It was open to the public. The event was used as an opportunity to raise money for the school."

Meaning anyone could go... But that was five months ago. "Was Hailey in other shows or competitions more recently?"

"No more shows, and we don't let her compete," Jean said. "Vince and I don't want her around the negativity of competition and comparison."

So had Hailey's killer been in the background, stalking her, for months?

SIX

Talking with those at the school about the event was necessary. For now, Amanda would change direction. "Do either of you know Susan Butters?"

The couple looked at each other and shook their heads in unison.

"Who is that?" Vincent asked.

"She's the woman who found Hailey this morning," Amanda told them.

"We don't know her."

Trent stepped in and showed them Butters's license photo. Both Tanners said she didn't look familiar.

Amanda still wasn't convinced that Butters was innocent. She may have lingered on the periphery. Her claim she never went to the park a complete fabrication. Again, the similar tutu didn't mean it came from Hailey's closet. "Did either of you take Hailey to Heroes Memorial Park before?"

"No, but Mara might have," Jean said.

"That's the nanny," McGee said as a reminder.

There had to be some link between the killer and the park. Otherwise, why was Hailey placed in the playground there?

Had the killer watched Hailey playing there in the past? Possibly on the carousel itself? "We'll ask her about that," Amanda told the Tanners.

"Why though?" Jean spat. "Hasn't she been put through enough?" She shot a look at McGee. "There is no way Mara has anything to do with this. She's been here since the day Hailey was born. Our little miracle baby," she added in a softer tone and glanced at her husband. "How are we supposed to move on?"

"We tried several things to conceive, and it took us a few years to become pregnant," Vincent explained.

"Then the in vitro took. She was such a little princess right from the start. I swear she was born with a tiara on her head." Tears fell, and Jean wiped her cheeks.

"Pardon me for asking, but where did you go for the in vitro?" Another woman or couple not as lucky as Jean may have taken Hailey. But why wait six years? And how did that explain murder?

"It was a place in Washington called New Beginnings," Vincent said. "Jean's right, though. Mara was a terrific nanny. I saw her with Hailey. There's no way she's involved."

Jean snatched a tissue off a side table and blew her nose. "Mara loved Hailey as if she were her own child. Vince, we'll need to let her go now Hailey's gone."

Amanda, Trent, and McGee held the silence for a few beats. She was the first to speak.

"We understand Mara lives with you," Amanda said.

"She does, but she's gone to stay with her sister in town for a while."

"When was this?" Trent asked.

"Saturday," Jean said. "She said she wanted to give us some space."

That struck Amanda as odd considering Mara was being painted as one of the family. One would think she'd want to stay and support the Tanners. Unless another reason had sent her packing. "We'll need her sister's information. Did she leave that with you?"

Jean nodded. "Her name is Kendra Bennett." She gave them the address.

"I'm just finding it hard to accept all this," Vincent said. "We would have done anything to get Hailey back."

"Like pay a ransom?" Money as a motive wasn't ruled out. Something could have prevented the request from being made. Then from bad to worse, Hailey was killed.

"*Anything*," Vincent emphasized.

"We discussed posting a reward for her safe return but were cautioned not to do that." Jean looked at McGee.

"It's never advisable in abduction cases," McGee said.

"Hmph," Jean huffed. "Maybe things would have been different."

Amanda understood Jean's need to grasp an alternative, but she wasn't getting roped into that. Hypotheticals were a waste of time and energy without the power to change reality. But since the Tanners had money, they may have discussed their daughter being kidnapped. Rich people needed to take precautions the rest of the world didn't. "Did you and your husband ever discuss how you'd handle things if Hailey was taken?"

"What? Absolutely not," Jean said and calmed down when Vincent put his hand on her arm.

"Some people in your position do this. Unfortunately, there's a certain risk when a person has a lot of money." She put this as delicately as possible but was having a hard time. It was challenging to paint financial success as a liability.

"We never did that," Vincent confirmed. "Maybe if we were billionaires."

This conversation didn't eliminate Mara Bennett in Amanda's mind. Mara would know what lengths the Tanners would go to for Hailey's safe return. The plan could have turned from ransom, to presenting herself as a hero for a reward. Though it still didn't explain Hailey's murder. Amanda didn't see any advantage in laying this out to Hailey's parents. "Would it be possible for me and Detective Stenson to look in Mara's and Hailey's rooms?" She buried Mara's name because of how defensive the couple had gotten about her a moment ago.

"Ah, sure," Vincent said.

"I can take them up, if you'd like," McGee offered.

Vincent nodded. Jean was staring into space.

McGee led Amanda and Trent upstairs, leaving the Tanners alone with their grief.

They took a quick look inside Mara's room, rooting in drawers and the closet. No scarves or anything else that was blatantly incriminating.

"I told you I searched this room," McGee said.

"When Hailey was missing," Amanda responded. "Now that she's been murdered, we need to revisit everything."

"There's no way the nanny's behind this," McGee stated with confidence.

"Yet she volunteers to leave the Tanners' home the day after Hailey is taken. That didn't flag as suspicious with you?" Amanda served back.

"I think you're making too much out of her leaving. There was no reason for her to stick around. Her job was looking after the child. She was doing a kindness and giving the Tanners some space."

Amanda wasn't as trusting as McGee seemed to be.

"I'm with Amanda," Trent said. "Her leaving needs to be questioned. She could be caught up in this."

Amanda nodded and shared her earlier thinking. "She'd know how important Hailey was to her parents. That they'd have done anything and *paid* anything to get her back."

"Except one key thing. Hailey is dead," McGee said coolly.

"Sure, something went wrong." Even as she said that she hated how it sounded like she'd downplayed the situation.

"Okay, but the medical examiner said Hailey died just last night. If this was about a ransom, statistically the demand would have been made sooner," McGee kicked back. "Probably sometime on Saturday, but that didn't happen."

Yet they still never escalated Hailey's case to Homicide... "No answer on that, but was Mara around for that conversation about a financial reward?" Amanda asked.

McGee's cheeks flushed, and his nostrils flared. "She was, but—"

"*But,*" Amanda cut in, "it is possible then."

"If Mara took the girl, where was Hailey while Mara was here Friday night?"

"Mara might be working with someone," Trent suggested.

"I don't know." McGee groaned.

"Let's agree to disagree for now." She led the way next door.

Hailey's room was pink, pink, pink from the cushion on the window seat to the walls and the canopy over her bed with its gold stars. They likely glowed in the dark. The dresser, nightstand, bookshelf, and overflowing toy chest were white.

Amanda crossed to the window, and noted a wooden trellis beneath it, but took in the view it offered of a spacious backyard. It was surrounded by a six-foot-tall privacy fence made of cedar. An expensive choice, which again gave the message that the Tanners were financially comfortable. The playset, also cedar, offered a slide, climbing apparatus, small fort, and swings.

A mirror hung over a small makeup table and was bedazzled with stickers and drawings, likely made by Hailey. Amanda refused to dwell on that and opened the closet doors. It housed an organizational unit, but her interest was in the three tutus suspended from hangers. "They match the style of the one Hailey was found in."

A startled outcry came from the landing. Amanda shot out the door to find Jean standing there, wide-eyed.

"Mrs. Tanner, it might be best if you go downstairs with your husband," Amanda said softly. "We'll join you soon."

Jean shook her head. "I heard what you just said in there"—her eyes flicked toward Hailey's room—"about the tutu. She was found in one?"

This wasn't how she'd wanted to share this news with the Tanners. "She was. I see she must have loved one particular style. How many does she have?"

"Five. One was kept in her locker at the studio, then four here."

Amanda glanced at Trent, trying to do so without Jean noticing. But she rushed into the room and reached the closet before Amanda could stop her. She shuffled the hangers with the tutus along the rod, and then stood back, flailing her arm. "No, no, this doesn't make sense. There should be four. There's only..."

"Three," Amanda finished. "How many pairs of ballet slippers does she have?"

"Three. Two should be in here." Jean reached for a tote at the base of the closet, and Trent wedged in front of her.

"Please, Mrs. Tanner, let me." Trent stuck his gloved hands into the tote. He came out holding one pair of pink satin slippers.

"No, this can't be." Jean started quaking.

"Is there any way Mara has the tutu and slippers out getting cleaned?"

"I don't think so. They were all done two weeks ago."

Amanda met Trent's eyes. She thought of one explanation. The killer had been inside the Tanners' home. But was it a family friend or an intruder?

SEVEN

Before Amanda had McGee accompany Jean back downstairs, she'd asked if she had a pale-pink chiffon scarf. Jean said that wasn't her or Mara's style. After Jean left with McGee, Amanda and Trent discussed what the missing clothing from Hailey's closet meant for the case. "Well, there's no reason Detective McGee would have had to note the discrepancy," Amanda conceded. "Like he said earlier, he was concerned about a missing child, not her wardrobe."

"I'll give you that. And we don't know for sure if Hailey was wearing the clothing missing from her closet."

She angled her head to the side. "What are the chances she wasn't?"

"They still exist."

"Fine, but we still need to eliminate anyone who went into her room."

"I agree with you there, while also entertaining the possibility someone broke in."

"If they did, it wouldn't have just been for the tutu. It may have been a failed attempt to take Hailey right from her bed."

"Chilling thought."

"All of this is. For due diligence, we'll find out where Jean Tanner buys the tutus. The slippers look rather generic."

"You want to get started with the parents, I'll call this in?" Trent pulled out his phone. He'd get Crime Scene out to process Hailey's bedroom.

"Yeah. I'll head down. Join us when you're finished."

Trent nodded, and she headed for the stairwell. The upcoming conversation with the Tanners would be a tough one. To think you failed to protect your child outside the home was one thing, but within its four walls? That was another beast altogether.

When Amanda reached the sitting room, Jean was staring into space, while Vincent wore a confused expression.

Neither Jean nor McGee must have shared the discovery. "One of your daughter's tutus and a pair of ballet slippers are missing from her closet. It seems likely someone entered the room and took them." It was impossible to soften that news.

"I... ah, don't understand," Vincent said.

"Hailey was found dressed in a tutu and slippers, much like the ones she owns."

"Dear Lord," Vincent gasped.

Amanda glanced over at McGee, who didn't meet her eye. "We need to consider that a guest or an intruder is behind Hailey's murder."

"There's no way it's someone we know." Vincent was shaking his head. "And if it was an intruder, we'd have known."

Amanda appreciated why Vincent didn't want to entertain someone they knew being behind this. "Do you have a security system?"

"No, I... I messed up, not thinking it was necessary." Vincent glanced at his wife, but she wouldn't meet his gaze.

"You were being cheap, is what you mean," Jean said.

"Sure, blame me for this. It's always my fault, anyway."

"The only person at fault here is the killer," Amanda inserted. It was difficult seeing the Tanners turn on each other, but pain needed an outlet. Sadly, often those closest to us received the brunt of it. "Is it possible that someone broke into the home?"

"I suppose so," Vincent admitted. "Maybe when no one was home, but we noticed nothing out of place, unlocked doors, that type of thing."

"What about the window in Hailey's bedroom? Someone could have come in through there," Amanda pointed out.

"It's possible, but the yard's surrounded by a six-foot privacy fence. There's a gate, and it's always locked."

"It's possible someone climbed over or picked the lock." Amanda put that as delicately as possible, but Vincent still shifted as if preparing to get up. "Please, Mr. Tanner, it's important that we discuss this and investigate all the possibilities. Even the difficult ones. You should know that crime scene investigators will be here soon."

"My daughter's room is being treated like a crime scene." Vincent hung his head.

"I can't believe this is happening," Jean said. "That someone was in our home. In Hailey's bedroom."

"I appreciate this must be hard to accept," Amanda began. "But who could have accessed her room? Among family and friends?"

"Pretty much anyone who's been here," Vincent said.

Trent returned, tablet in hand, in time to hear Vincent's response. "We'll need a list of names." He perched on a chair, ready to record their response.

Vincent provided the names of family members, and his former employee, Nick Potter. He saw Trent raise his eyebrows at that, and added, "He was here Christmas week to drop off a gift for Hailey."

McGee had told Amanda their professional relationship fell apart in November. "Did you find that strange, considering that you had parted ways?"

Vincent shook his head. "That was between us. Business. Nick adored Hailey."

Goosebumps blazed a trail down her arms. She'd never cared for the word *adored* being used to describe an adult's feelings toward a child. The tutu and slippers could fit under a bulky sweater. Nick was there when the weather was colder, but Jean had said Mara had all the tutus cleaned two weeks ago. She hadn't mentioned any were missing. *Something else to check up on.* "We understand that *business* cost Nick several hundred thousand dollars."

"Trust me. His issue was with me, not Hailey."

"What if you're wrong?" Jean's voice was low, but a fire burned in her eyes. "You hurt him. This could be his way of getting back at you."

Vincent clenched his jaw, and a pulse tapped in his cheek. He didn't respond to his wife.

The lack of communication was telling, and the former employee earned himself a spot back on the suspect list. Alibi or not. "Did Nick go up to Hailey's bedroom when he came over?"

Vincent shook his head. "He'd have no reason."

"He did use the washroom upstairs," Jean inserted.

Vincent turned on his wife. "You honestly believe Nick did this?"

"I never said he did," she snapped. "I'm just saying..."

"You're tossing him at the police, or is this your way of blaming me again for what happened to Hailey?"

"You're not exactly a saint, doing what you did to him," Jean said in a low voice.

Trent cleared his throat. "What did happen?"

McGee gave them the basics in the car, but Amanda was also interested in more details.

"My husband here sold him on investing in this one stock. Only Vince pulled out but didn't warn Nick to do the same."

"He's a grown-ass man," Vincent huffed out.

Jean shook her head.

"That was what led you to parting ways professionally?" Amanda looked at Vincent.

"The trust between us was gone, so yeah."

Time to steer away from Nick Potter... "Is there anyone else who may have gone upstairs? Even just to use the washroom?"

"It could have been anyone if the main level bathroom was occupied," Jean said.

"And everyone would be on the list you provided Detective Stenson?" Amanda asked.

Vincent nodded.

"What about visitors to the home besides friends and family? A maintenance person or a maid?" Amanda asked.

"We're rather old-fashioned here. Vince works outside the home, and I clean it."

That was surprising, since she hired help for Hailey. "How else do you spend your time?"

"I'm involved with several charities."

"She goes to fancy lunches and gossips," Vincent pushed in.

The couple had a lot to sort out after they left. "It could be anyone who excused themselves from your sight. It would only take a moment to slip into her room."

"Thinking that someone violated her space..." Jean stopped there and rubbed her throat. "Actually, we had that dinner for our top-tier clients here a few weeks ago."

Vincent angled his head. "You can't seriously be bringing that up again."

Amanda looked at McGee. Was this something he'd held back on purpose, or had he not gotten around to sharing it?

"It was for high-value investors with portfolios worth tens of millions, and I have their names," Detective McGee said.

She'd be picking up this conversation when they left the Tanners.

"We're talking influential people with prestigious positions within the community," Vincent stressed.

From her experience, none of what he said meant they were innocent. A knock on the door, followed by the bell, prevented her from responding.

"I'll get that." Amanda left the room and swung the door open. Two female CSIs were on the step. Amanda wasn't familiar with them, but the credentials clipped to their light jackets and the collection kits in their hands gave them away. CSIs Blair and Donnelly must still be busy at the park. "I'm Detective Steele. Come in."

The CSIs stepped into the entry. Neither provided their names. One had a short, blond bob, and the other wore black-framed glasses. Detective McGee joined the party, but the CSIs didn't give him a second look.

"Point us where we need to go, and we'll get to work," Blond Bob said. "We were told it's a child's room we need to process."

"That's right. There might have been a home invasion." Amanda told her about the missing tutu and slippers from the closet.

"We'll look for evidence of that, prints, DNA. Are there any profiles we should eliminate?" Blond Bob asked.

Amanda was wondering if the other CSI spoke. "Prints and DNA belonging to Vincent and Jean Tanner, the girl's parents, and Mara Bennett, her nanny. And the lab should be getting samples from Susan Butters, as well. She found the girl."

"The others should be on file already," McGee told them.

"That makes it somewhat easier. The room is where?" Blond Bob pointed up the staircase and raised her eyebrows.

Amanda nodded. "Down the hall, third door on the right. Before you go, though, what should I call you? We've never met before."

"I'm Ruth Keller," the woman with the glasses said.

Blond Bob lifted her ID, making Amanda lean in to read the print. *Vanessa Stuart*.

"All good, then?" Stuart asked that with such bold arrogance that the back of Amanda's neck tightened.

"Yep." Amanda didn't move, though.

Stuart took the first step and looked over her shoulder. "We've got this under control. You can go back to what you were doing."

"Actually, two more things. One, you'll need to collect a tutu and the pair of ballet slippers from her closet to compare to what the girl was found in." They'd make sure the size, brand, and designer names matched.

"And the second?" Stuart huffed with impatience.

"Keep me posted." Amanda handed her business card to Stuart.

"Will do." She tucked the card into a back pocket of her black jeans.

Amanda returned to the group in the front sitting room but didn't sit down. She shared with everyone, "The CSIs are upstairs processing the room. They know the situation and what to look for."

Those words were enough to summon Trent to put his tablet away. He pushed it into the inside pocket of his coat and stood.

"Again, we are very sorry for your loss and wish we had come with better news," she offered the Tanners.

"I just can't." Tears pooled in Jean's eyes. "Until now, there was hope. Now, we'll be burying our miracle. How am I supposed to accept this?"

"One day at a time," Amanda said. "One breath at a time. Eventually it will get somewhat easier to put one foot in front of the other."

"You've lost a child." Spoken as more comment than question, but Amanda nodded.

"A daughter. Her name was Lindsey. Almost eleven years ago now." She rounded up, leaving out the month count even in her head. For years, Amanda broke it down to months, weeks, and days. She didn't like to think her grief was gone, as if it meant she no longer cared. It was preferable to believe it was just buried deeper down.

"I'm sorry for your loss," Jean offered.

"Thank you." Zoe had played a huge role in healing her. So had Trent. And to think that she initially resisted being partnered with him. But working with him reintroduced joy and purpose back to her career. In the accident's aftermath, her life was as fulfilling as a hamster wheel. Go to bed, wake up, work, go to bed, wake up, work... "One day, you'll look back and realize how far you've come and how much you've healed."

"I just can't see that yet."

"It takes time, and neither of you are alone in this. Just be patient with yourself and each other." She didn't have in-house support, and she'd turned her back on the help offered by her family. A decision she came to regret.

"We'll try," Jean said, taking her husband's hand.

"There are also professional therapists that can come and talk with you. I'm not sure if my colleague shared the number with you for Victim Services...?" Amanda looked at McGee.

He nodded. "They have the number."

"We'll be okay," Vincent said, though his voice wavered, exposing his claim as a lie.

"I appreciate you want to be strong for your family, but there's no shame in getting help. Everyone needs it sometimes, and no one should go through what you and your wife are alone," Amanda told him.

Vincent said nothing, but nodded.

Amanda got into the car with Trent and Detective McGee.

"Trent and I need to revisit the nanny and former employee, Potter, but I'm also interested in that client dinner party," she said.

"As Vincent told you, these people hold prestigious positions in the community," McGee said.

"I wouldn't care if one was the President of the United States." *Okay, that was a tad dramatic...* "Just because someone has a respected position doesn't mean they are innocent of wrongdoing. Did you question these people?"

"No, but I looked into them."

She shifted to face him in the back. "Which means?"

"Not a hard look."

"Right, so you saw who they were and gave them a free pass. Meanwhile, a six-year-old girl was missing, and they were in the family home in proximity to the girl. They would have been able to build up trust with her."

"I don't think you're hearing what I'm saying. These people aren't the type you accuse of anything, or even project a hint of suspicion toward, unless you have a solid case to start."

"We'll need the names," she said. "In fact, I'd like all your investigation reports sent over to us at Central."

"I'll do that, but I'm telling you that the investors at that dinner don't need your focus," McGee seethed.

"With respect," she said, not feeling any in this moment, "I've taken down people in high-ranking positions, those who should have been trustworthy mentors. Yet they committed some of the worst atrocities imaginable."

"You're referring to the sex-trafficking ring you brought down a few years back."

His knowledge of this didn't surprise her, as it had been big news. "Then you know I'm not easily intimidated. Neither is my partner here."

Trent looked at her and gave her a subtle nod.

"Well, I hardly think Mayor Beswick took Hailey Tanner and killed her."

He was probably right. But the facts remained that someone had abducted and killed a little girl, and Amanda would find that person. Witnessing the Tanners' grief had regurgitated her own, but cases involving children always hit hard. Lindsey would have turned seventeen next month.

EIGHT

Amanda was happy to see the back of Detective McGee when they dropped him off at Heroes Memorial Park for his car. Nothing personal, but she just needed a break from him. She might be projecting, holding him accountable for Hailey's fate. But maybe if he had done a better job, been courageous enough to ask tough questions, even of the bigwigs, Hailey may have been safely returned to her parents. *May have been...*

Trent was about to drive out of the lot when Officer Wyatt came trotting over, holding up a finger for them to wait. He went to the passenger side, and she put the window down.

He was panting. "Seeing as you're here, I thought I'd let you know that we've spoken to every civilian who has turned up at the park, and no one was here earlier this morning and can shed any light on who put the girl there."

She was thinking, *Thanks for the* non-*update*, but that was her bitter frustration talking.

"Also, one lock on the men's public restroom was broken from the outside," Wyatt added, earning her attention. "The CSIs are processing it, the door, and inside to see if there is any evidence that will assist the case."

Amanda had noted the Crime Scene van in the lot. As she'd suspected when CSIs Stuart and Keller showed up, Blair and Donnelly were still working here. "Interesting, but *one* lock?"

"There are two doors. One on each side of the building."

"Good to know, and thanks for that update," she told him.

"Don't mention it." Wyatt slapped the top of the roof and stepped back.

Amanda put the window back up and turned to Trent, shaking her head. "I'm not holding out high hopes, but it would sure be nice to catch the person behind this sooner rather than later."

"Agreed. They need to be held accountable. So where to next? The nanny or the former employee?"

"Or to speak to Susan Butters's mother."

Trent angled his head, as if her suggestion caught him off guard.

"The Tanners didn't know Butters, but she's still a suspect in my book. Her mother could provide more insight into Susan's mindset about children. If she was obsessed with not having one..."

"I think we should ask the nanny, Mara Bennett, if she knows Susan Butters before we take things that far."

"You think I'm getting carried away."

"I never said that. You've got impeccable instincts."

"But...?"

"You can get your mind fixed easier when the victims are children. Understandably so. They are hard cases for everyone."

No argument or defense could counter that. He was right. "Even so, Mara doesn't need to know Susan Butters by name or sight. She could have stayed in the shadows."

"It's possible."

She sensed his skepticism. "Okay, we'll bench Butters for now and talk with Mara Bennett. But we'll ask her about Butters."

"Your wish is my command." Trent smirked and got them on the road to Kendra Bennett's apartment.

Don't you mean your *wish...* He hadn't taken her theorizing about Butters seriously, so she'd keep her earlier suspicions about the fertility clinic to herself. There was even less cause to move forward on that front. With that decided, a sudden, intense sadness for Hailey moved in and bulldozed her. Trent's voice cut through, saving Amanda from giving in to the depth of the emotion.

"Did you want to grab a coffee or a bite to eat? We might not get another chance for hours." Trent flicked a finger toward the clock on the dash.

Noon right on the mark. It felt much later than that.

She wasn't that hungry, but with this job, one ate when the opportunity presented itself. "Something light maybe. Coffee? Definitely. Hannah's Diner too much to ask?" They were headed to Dumfries, the small town where she lived, ten minutes from Woodbridge. Also home to Hannah's Diner, which served the best coffee on the planet.

"Not at all, but coffee doesn't count as nourishment. Are you doing all right?"

"As fine as can be expected. You?"

"About the same. So there's no way to ask this but to come out with it. I noticed you asked the Tanners about the fertility clinic they used..."

So he noticed... "Is there a question in there?"

"I was just curious why."

She took in how pale he'd gone, and she wagered he thought it was motivated by personal reasons. "Oh, it's not for me," she rushed out. "I'm not... Yeah, no. Zoe and I are a good team." She offered a pressed smile. "Being a single parent to one child keeps me busy enough."

"I've heard one or two kids, it doesn't make a difference."

She laughed. "You should know not to believe everything

you hear. But does this mean that you and...?" Trent had been living with his girlfriend, Kelsey, for a few months now. And there were zero kids in the picture, unless...

"Hell—" Trent coughed, as if he had swallowed his spit the wrong way. When he composed himself, he said, "No, but I'm not saying no to kids forever. Just not right now. I'm not ready."

"I don't think anyone ever is."

"All right, so if it was about the case, what were you thinking?" He squinted as he studied her face.

She laid it out.

"That's a long shot. Six years have passed."

"That's why I didn't bring it up."

"Maybe if the case veers into a dead end, we can revisit. For now, we're not short on things to do."

"True enough." The first twenty-four hours of an investigation were always a whirlwind. Lots of information was being hurled at them, making it a game of duck or catch. Amanda also feared letting the wrong thing go, overlooking some crucial detail. But she'd grown up under the shadow of her father, the former police chief, who stressed looking under every rock and pebble. As he'd cautioned, it could never be assumed which one was hiding a vital clue. *Assumptions kill an investigation...* "Speaking of, we need to remember to reach out about the video footage from the park," she added.

Trent pulled into the diner's parking lot. "I'll do that. I've got the number for the municipality in my phone. You want to go in and grab our order?"

"Good thinking. That will speed things up. What do you want?"

"A coffee, and a turkey and Swiss on rye."

"You got it." She left him and went into the diner. For once, the place wasn't lined up out the door. Ever since Katherine Graves had joined her aunt, May Byrd, at the diner almost two years ago, the popularity of the place had skyrocketed. In little time, Amanda was handing over cash and heading back to the car with their coffees, Trent's sandwich, and a blueberry muffin for herself in a bag.

On the way out, she passed a group of chatty women going inside.

"They're saying it's that girl who went missing," one woman said.

Amanda stopped and turned. "Excuse me."

The woman who had spoken gave her a tight smile. "Yes?"

Small-town expression, without warmth. "I couldn't help but overhear you. Where did you hear that, about the girl? Hailey Tanner, I'm assuming?"

"Yes. It just hit the news. Heard it on the radio before I got out of my car."

Amanda stiffened but did her best to hide the reaction. "Thank you."

"Don't mention it."

The woman and her friends carried on to the counter while Amanda resumed her trek to the car. She passed the bag and coffees through the driver's window to Trent.

Trent stuck the cups in the console and was pulling out the food by the time she got into the passenger seat. "Guessing this is yours?" He held up the muffin, and she snatched it before he gave her some lecture about taking better care of herself. He still got out, "At least you opted for some food."

"There's more you should be concerned about. Word about Hailey is out."

"Oh, crap."

"Yeah." This investigation was about to take on a life of its own.

NINE

Amanda had taken a sip of coffee and Trent a few bites of his sandwich when her phone rang. "It's Malone," she said before answering on speaker.

"Tell me you've got some solid leads," Malone spat out the moment she picked up.

"We have a few things we're following up." She filled him in on the developments at the Tanner house, leaving out any of her speculations about Butters or someone from the fertility clinic.

"So either an intruder or someone the Tanners welcomed into their home," he summarized.

"That's the gist. We have a list of names, and Detective McGee with Missing Persons is getting more together for us. Apparently, the Tanners held a dinner for investors and Mayor Beswick was present."

Malone's end of the line fell silent, leaving her with the sound of Trent's chewing followed by him crumpling the wrapper from the sandwich.

"Sarge?"

"You can't honestly suspect the mayor's involvement in any of this."

"I never said that I did, but I thought you'd like to know." She'd been at this job long enough to know so much of it was about optics.

"Don't go near him unless you run it past me. Am I understood?"

"Understood."

"And whatever you do, work fast. The news is out, and the police chief wants to provide some answers ASAP."

No advantage would come from confirming scuttlebutt was already making its way around. She pictured Chief Buchanan all over Malone to provide him with updates. High-profile cases always put the department under a microscope. It was her and Trent's third such case in the last six months. "Trent and I will keep you posted, but that's all I can promise."

Malone mumbled something incoherent before ending the call.

"I don't envy him," Trent said as he got them on the road again.

"Me either. But is it just me or is the chief worked up more often these days?" When he first joined the PWCPD, he was a strong and fair leader who respected the team of people under him. In recent months, he wore his authority with more grit, putting her opinion of him in flux.

"Oh, he's more worked up all right, but there's also been a lot of cases garnering nationwide attention."

She had no response. It just put more pressure on everyone's shoulders. On *her* shoulders. "Tell me we'll have video from the park ASAP." He didn't have a chance to update her yet.

"I don't know about *ASAP*. The person I spoke with wasn't big into committing to a turnaround time."

"Stay on them."

"You can bet I will."

"Good. Now get us over to Mara Bennett."

. . .

Kendra Bennett's apartment building was only two blocks east of the diner, and Amanda and Trent reached it in a few minutes.

He knocked on the door for unit 405. A short time later, the peephole cover was slid over.

They held up their badges, and the deadbolt was unlocked and the chain undone.

A woman in her early thirties stood there in an oversized sweatshirt and black leggings. Her heap of brown hair was wound in a loose bun on the top of her head. A few strands cascaded at the sides of her face in curly tendrils. She tucked them behind her ears. "Hello?"

"Mara Bennett?" Trent asked her.

"Yes."

"We're Detectives Stenson, and Steele," he said. "We have questions pertaining to Hailey Tanner."

Mara's eyes filled with tears, but she nudged out her chin. "Where is Detective McGee?"

"Hailey's case is ours now. Could we come in?" Amanda asked.

Mara nodded, and the emotion playing out on her face told Amanda she'd seen the news or the Tanners had called.

"Okay." She backed up and let them inside the small apartment. The compact space was made to feel smaller by oversized furniture and hoards of bric-a-brac. Mara took them to the living room, which offered plenty of seating.

Mara took a chair, and Amanda and Trent sat at opposite ends of the couch.

"We understand this is your sister's apartment. Is she home?" Amanda wanted to know if they should expect any interruptions.

"Nah, she's at work. You never said what happened to the

other detective." Mara pinched the bridge of her nose, like she had a headache.

"I think you already know..." Amanda eased in.

Mara pressed her lips together, and tears fell down her cheeks. She swiped them away. "Jean called me. I can't believe it."

"You've had quite a shock," Amanda empathized, while not letting go of her suspicions toward the nanny.

"I just had this horrible feeling it would come to this. Jean told me to expect you. You're with Homicide?"

"We are." Amanda studied the woman. "Why did you have a horrible feeling?" She tiptoed into potential landmine territory. If Mara was guilty, she didn't want to spook her.

Mara's shoulders lowered. "I don't know. It's just I think whoever takes a child is a sick person, their heads not quite screwed on right. Do they not realize that a six-year-old is a lot of work?"

"People have kidnapped children because they couldn't have their own," Trent put in as he balanced his tablet on his lap.

"I guess so."

"What had you becoming a nanny?" Her answer could tell them a lot.

"I love children but have no interest in having my own."

"No interest at all?" Amanda wished for Mara to elaborate.

"Well, I'm not in any financial position to raise a child, for one thing. And to be honest, the whole birthing process freaks me right out."

Having a baby wasn't for the faint of heart, that was for sure. Amanda had endured fifteen hours of labor with Lindsey, and the pain scale went from excruciating to unbearable until the epidural sank in. But the first half of Mara's statement lodged in Amanda's head. Did she take Hailey for money?

"Do you have any idea who did this to Hailey?" Mara asked.

"We're following some leads," Trent told her.

"Jean said Hailey was found this morning in Heroes Memorial Park."

It was hard to read if it was a natural transition or an effort to steer the conversation. "That's right. Did you ever take Hailey to that park?"

Mara shook her head. "No need. The Tanners had everything a kid could want in the backyard."

Amanda remembered what she'd seen out Hailey's window and had to agree. "Are you familiar with a woman named Susan Butters?"

Mara chewed her bottom lip. "Never heard of her."

Trent showed her Butters's picture on his tablet. "Does she look familiar?"

Mara looked at the screen and shook her head. "I don't know how Jean and Vincent will ever recover from this." More tears made their way down the nanny's face.

"They told us Hailey was their miracle baby, that they would have done anything for her safe return." Amanda planted the bait and waited for a bite.

"Oh, they would have. They even talked about posting a reward to get her back."

Amanda wasn't sure what Mara's play was with sharing that. Had it been to get in front of it, to lessen suspicion against her? Or was she stating a fact? Amanda was having a hard time getting a read on the woman.

"You must have had a close bond with the girl yourself," Trent interjected. "This must be hard on you too."

"It's heartbreaking. I was with her from the beginning."

"Could you tell us a bit more about the day that Hailey was taken?" Amanda asked.

"Ah, sure. I dropped her off for her lesson at Tiptoe Studio, helped her change, and stayed until I saw her go into class. Then, I popped out to pick up some groceries Jean asked for. I was getting ready to make my way back to pick Hailey up when Jean texted me. She said not to worry about Hailey, that she'd pick her up. It wasn't a number I had in my phone, but Jean said it was a new one. I had no way of knowing it wasn't her. That someone was orchestrating Hailey's kidnapping."

"Of course not," Trent empathized, and Amanda resisted looking his way.

None of this cleared Mara. The sender could be her partner in crime. Amanda didn't enjoy regarding everyone with a critical eye, but the academy had drilled that into her. New recruits were warned not to take any situation at face value. "You said you helped her change for class, but you don't help afterward?"

"No, Candace, who owns the studio, helps, *helped*, with that."

They'd ask about this when they got to the studio. "Was it common for Mrs. Tanner to pick Hailey up after class?"

"No, I should have known something was up. I've been beating myself up about this ever since." A fresh batch of tears soaked Mara's cheeks, and she palmed them.

"It's common to blame ourselves when something tragic like this happens, but the only person who is responsible here is whoever took Hailey," Amanda leveled at her.

"I know you're right, but it's just hard."

"I imagine," Trent offered. "Did you ever see anyone hanging around, watching the girl? Anyone who you might have seen regularly on your walks? I assume you took her for walks?"

"I did. Just Nora, but she's eighty-two and lives three doors down from the Tanners. She makes the most delicious banana bread and loved spoiling Hailey. There's no way she's wrapped up in any of this. Her heart's going to break when she hears about her."

At least Nora didn't sound suspect. "What are your thoughts about Nick Potter, Mr. Tanner's former employee?"

"Nick? He seems like a decent guy, and Vincent struck me as remorseful for what happened between them. I take it you know about that?"

"We do," Amanda said.

"Why are you asking about him?" Mara let her gaze dance back and forth between them.

"We're trying to get a picture of the people in the Tanners' lives, and we heard he came by around Christmas with a gift for Hailey." Amanda would hold back about the missing tutu and slippers for now.

"He did, but there's no way Nick's involved in what happened to Hailey."

"You sound confident," Trent said. "Do you know the man well?"

Mara's cheeks flushed. "Well enough. We had a thing for a little while."

"By *thing*, you mean a romantic relationship?" Amanda sought clarity. It was possible that Nick Potter and Mara Bennett worked together.

"*Relationship* is too heavy a word to describe what we had. A tryst, a brief affair. Either of those would do it more justice."

"How long were you together?" Amanda censored herself not to say *couple*.

"Nick and I started up around Christmas and it lasted a week past New Year's."

"But things ended?" Trent looked up from his tablet.

"Just as fast as they started, but it was mutual."

"Was he ever over when the Tanners weren't around?" Amanda asked.

"Maybe once or twice, but please don't tell the Tanners. They didn't want me to have visitors over when they weren't around."

Amanda found that rule understandable even if a person didn't have a child. Factor in one age six, even more so.

"You took a risk. Hailey was old enough to talk and expose you," Trent pointed out.

"We were careful about that. He'd only visit when she was in school, and I had the house otherwise to myself."

"When was the last time Nick was there?" Amanda asked.

"January. Jean was out at some charity event or lunch with friends."

"Did you ever bring anyone else into the home without their knowledge?"

"No, I swear."

"No other lovers?" Amanda stressed.

"Absolutely not. I only let Nick in because I trusted him and the family knew him."

"Well, in most cases of child abduction, it is someone close to the family and the kid," Amanda pointed out.

"As I said, Nick's not responsible and neither am I, if that's where you're going with all these questions. Detective McGee made no secret we were suspects in Hailey's disappearance. Should I hire a lawyer?"

"That is up to you," Amanda said. "Right now, we're just talking."

"Well, I think it's time for you to leave."

A key jangled in the apartment's deadbolt hole but was promptly removed. The door swung open. "Mara? Why is the door unlocked?" a woman called out.

An older version of Mara peeked her head into the living room and brought with her the aroma of french fries and cheeseburgers. The source likely the paper bag stained with grease in her hand. Her expression of irritation deepened when she saw Amanda and Trent. "Police?"

"We are—" Amanda started but was interrupted.

"What are you doing here? Mara, you were supposed to

meet with that lawyer after that one detective came after you already."

"He cleared me. Kendra, these detectives are with Homicide." Mara's voice was small when she shared this news with her sister.

Kendra set the bag on an end table and crossed her arms. "Are you telling me that Hailey's dead?"

"Someone murdered her," Mara told her sister.

"Really?" Kendra turned on Amanda, let her gaze drift to Trent.

"You must not have seen the news. I believe it's already out there," Amanda said.

"No, not at all. It's been a day." Kendra dropped onto the couch and wrapped her arms around her sister. "Oh my God, Mara."

"Just one more question before we leave," Amanda said. Mara looked expectant while Kendra crossed her arms. "Were any of Hailey's tutus at the cleaners?" She'd leave the slippers out of the conversation.

Mara narrowed her eyes. "That seems like a strange question."

"Please just answer Detective Steele," Trent encouraged with a firm tone.

"I took them two weeks ago, but they should all be in her closet, except for the one at the dance studio."

Just as Jean Tanner had told them. But it wasn't so much about her answer, but Amanda being able to get a read on the nanny. Based on appearances, she was genuinely confused that Amanda had brought them up. "All right, thank you for your time. We'll see ourselves out."

She and Trent didn't speak until they were back in the car. Then Amanda broke the silence.

"Mara allowed visitors into the home against the Tanners' wishes. What other lines did she cross?"

"I admit that doesn't say much about her character, but it seems a leap from that to kidnapping and killing the child under her care."

Amanda would love to agree, but she'd witnessed too much human atrocity to dismiss the possibility.

TEN

Amanda saw Trent's viewpoint on Mara Bennett, but she wasn't ready to release her from suspicion yet. She had commented she didn't have money for children of her own. Had she taken Hailey, even worked with someone with ransom as the goal? Not a new theory, but McGee would have requested her financials having considered her a suspect himself at one point. He never mentioned why he'd released her from suspicion, but in his defense, Amanda hadn't bothered to ask. Her phone history couldn't have revealed any sinister plan to take Hailey with an accomplice or McGee would have pursued her. Amanda called McGee for more details on Mara, but had to leave a message. *Just one more person to wait on...*

The CSIs who processed Hailey's bedroom hadn't reached out yet. They should have finished by now. Amanda had left her card but was now wishing she'd gotten theirs too. If she didn't hear from them soon, she'd call the lab in Manassas or even CSI Emma Blair for their number. She'd like to convince herself no news was just that, but assumptions tanked investigations. She'd give them a bit more time before she followed up.

Trent parked in the long and empty driveway in front of

Nick Potter's house. It was a McMansion in a nice neighborhood.

"Let's hope his car is in the garage," he said and turned off the vehicle.

He beat her to the door, but her steps were slowed by the images forming in her mind. None of them were new, but they were crystalizing into clearer focus being here. Two people close to Hailey may have worked together and exploited the girl's trust. But if Mara and Nick were an item, money wouldn't be an issue if they headed off into the sunset together. Nick had enough to finance the trip. It was hard to consider this revenge for what Vincent had done to Nick, from Mara's perspective anyhow. She'd said that Vincent felt bad for what had happened. Though, that didn't mean that she excused his behavior. And the relationship between Mara and Nick could have been more serious than she let on. How that escalated to killing Hailey was unclear.

Trent knocked and followed up by ringing the bell right after.

The door swung open, and Nick stood there with his cell phone to his ear. "Listen, I've got to go." His voice petered out as he spoke, his gaze taking in the badges they were holding up. He almost had his phone in a pocket when it started ringing again. He held up his left index finger to them while he consulted the screen. "I really need to take this." He answered.

Amanda looked at Trent. *Unbelievable.*

"Yes, I know you need an answer on this today. Five minutes," Nick said and swept his phone from his ear to his pocket in a swift, fluid motion. "Yes, what can I do for you?"

"Detective Steele, and this is Detective Stenson," Amanda began. "You're Nick Potter?"

"I am."

"We need to talk to you about Hailey Tanner. If we could come inside..." She didn't present this happening as an option.

"Ah, sure." He fumbled backward to let them into the house. "Do you want water, coffee—" His ringtone cut him off, and he swore before removing his phone from his pocket and swiping left to refuse the call. "I'll set this thing to silent, or we won't get a minute of peace." He moved a finger around the screen. "All right, that's done. So, as I was trying to say, can I get either of you anything?"

"I'm fine," she said, and Trent declined the offer too. She'd normally accept as she found these concessions made the person being questioned more cooperative. But factoring in her suspicions, Nick might be trying to distract them with kindness.

"All right, then." He took them to the living room and told them to sit wherever they liked. He dropped onto the couch and said, "I haven't met you two before. I spoke with Detective McGee a couple of times over the weekend."

"The Hailey Tanner investigation is no longer a Missing Persons case," Trent said.

"I don't understand." His face pinched, and his eyes squinted.

If he was acting, he was good. "You haven't heard the news?"

"Just on the stock markets."

She somehow believed him. "We're sorry to bring you the unfortunate news that Hailey Tanner's body was found this morning."

"Her— What now?" Nick puffed out a deep breath and raked a hand through his hair, leaving strands standing up in his wake. "No, this can't... No, it's not possible."

"I assure you it is, Mr. Potter," Amanda said. "And we have some questions for you."

"Sure, I'll answer anything you ask. Wow. I'm just in shock." He popped to his feet and helped himself to a generous pour of amber liquid from the bar cart in the corner of the room. He took a few anxious gulps.

Amanda and Trent gave him a few moments, and in that time, he emptied the glass and refilled it.

"Mr. Potter," Amanda prompted.

"Ah, yes, sorry. I'm just in shock. And heartbroken." He dragged one of his hands under his nose and returned to the chair he'd been in before, with his drink. "I hope you don't mind." He met Amanda's eyes and lifted his glass.

It's your liver... But she was more interested in what had him reaching for the bottle. Was it grief? Guilt? A blend of both? Or did he fear he'd been caught? "If you need to drink, don't let us stop you."

"Well, I don't *need* to, but it will help me through this. I know why you're here." He slung back some booze.

"And why is that?" she asked.

Nick pointed at the tablet in Trent's hands. "You're not here for a friendly conversation. You think I'm involved somehow."

"Are you?" Hailey could have been held in this very house. McGee never would have gotten a search warrant with a verified alibi. Speaking of, they never got into what that was.

"Absolutely not." Nick tossed back the rest of his drink and wiped his mouth with his palm. "Can you not see how destroyed I am? That girl was a special light. There's no one else like her and never will be again." Silent tears fell.

Amanda braced herself. Letting her guard down and giving in to empathy wasn't an option. "Where were you on Friday, the day Hailey disappeared?"

"You now? You really think I *killed* her?" He looked at the empty rocks glass in his hand, as he balanced it on the edge of the chair arm.

"If you didn't, you shouldn't have a problem telling us where you were," Amanda said. "Though I'm sure I could look it up in Detective McGee's reports. But save me the trouble."

"I was here. Not exactly a rock-solid alibi, I know. But he

must have believed me. Can't you trace my phone? It would show I was here during the time Hailey was taken."

"That would only prove the device was here," Amanda said, thinking, *The Devil's in the details...*

"All I can say is you're wasting your time looking at me."

"But you see how you have motive?" She left that dangling, curious what he'd come up with.

"Are you referring to how Vince screwed me over? You think I killed Hailey over seven hundred thousand? Sometimes I make that much in a day. What ticked me off was the fact Vince betrayed me. He lost my trust when he didn't tell me to back out when he did."

"And then he fired you," Trent said.

"After I decked him and told him I quit."

Vincent left that part out. "Tell us about your relationship with Mara Bennett."

"I assume she told you we slept together for a bit?"

"She did," Amanda admitted, keeping it brief to encourage Nick to continue talking.

"It wasn't anything serious. It lasted less than a month between the end of December and into the start of January."

"When was the last time you were inside the Tanner home?" she asked.

"Just before the holidays. I brought over a Christmas present for Hailey. It was just after that Mara and I started seeing each other."

"And that was the *last* time?" She leveled her gaze at him. "You never went over since to hook up with Mara?"

"Once, during the first week of January. I couldn't tell you the day."

That lined up with what Mara told them. Amanda got up and walked over to Nick. "Here's my card," she said as she handed it to him. "Stay in town. We might be back with more questions. Understood?"

"Understood." He plucked her card from her fingers.

"And we're very sorry for your loss."

"Thanks." Nick was already back at the bar cart by the time Amanda and Trent hit the entry.

She was part way down the front walk when her phone rang. Rideout's name splashed up on Caller ID, and she answered on speaker. "You have something for us?"

"Oh, yeah. Hailey's murder just became a bigger nightmare."

ELEVEN

Amanda's heart was pounding. Trent parked down the street from Nick's house. "Trent's here too," she told the medical examiner. "He heard what you just said. Talk to us."

"I'll start from the beginning. Lividity was present in her lower back and upper shoulders. In the hours following death, she was on her back, not on her side in the fetal position."

"We figured the killer posed her." A disappointing update, and she failed to see how it deepened the nightmare of the situation. There had to be something else.

"Do you know when or how she was killed yet?" Trent asked.

"I now feel confident in confirming the time of death was between eleven PM last night and five AM this morning. As for how, there was also bruising around her neck congruent with strangulation."

"Do you surmise the scarf was used?" Trent asked.

"It is possible. I will be more confident after I've done further examinations. Now, the external examination revealed signs of abuse no older than three days."

"Just external injuries?" Her body became tight and rigid.

She resisted putting her true question into words. *Are there signs of sexual assault?*

"Yes. But you should know there was some bruising in her pubic region and lower abdomen. This suggests—"

"Yes, I know." Amanda pinched her eyes shut. If only it worked to squeeze out the horrible pictures forming in her mind. This would qualify as a nightmare, but Rideout didn't lead with this. There must be more.

Rideout continued, as if reading her mind. "Now for the worst part..."

How does it get worse? She choked on the question.

"When I undressed her and went to put the tutu into an evidence bag, something in the hem crinkled under my fingers."

What the... Amanda resisted the urge to cut in. Her request would only slow things down.

"I examined further and found a small piece of paper stitched inside. It had a typed message on it."

Chills ran over her neck and down her back. She looked over at Trent.

"What did it say?" Trent rushed out.

She hadn't felt brave enough to ask. The *nightmare* must reference the contents of this note.

Rideout exhaled so deeply that his nose whistled across the line. "It said, 'For Katherine Graves. This girl's your fault. Stop looking or there will be more.'"

"*This* girl? What's that supposed to mean? Are there more?" Trent looked over at her.

Stop looking... Amanda became cold. This could only refer to one thing. "Julie Gilbert," she said in a whisper.

"That young girl who was assaulted, strangled, and murdered in New York twelve years ago? How could Hailey Tanner be linked to a cold case from two hundred and sixty miles away?"

Amanda couldn't bring herself to respond.

After a long stretch of silence, Rideout stated, "I'll leave you two to work on that. I'll call if something else urgent comes up. Otherwise, watch out for my report."

"Thank you," Trent told him, and Rideout clicked off.

Amanda laid a hand over her stomach. "I'm going to be sick." A niggling started the second Donnelly described Hailey as a child star. She just didn't know why. And having been concerned about missing something, she'd focused her attention and suspicions on the wrong people. "There's no way Mara Bennett, Nick Potter, or Susan Butters are behind this. Not knowing what we do now. I can't see any of them assaulting that child. That is pushing it too far."

Trent shook his head. "Me either. We can see if they have a link to NYC for due diligence though. But this person wants Katherine to *stop* investigating the Gilbert case. Is she still doing that?"

Trent knew about the case because when Katherine had been kidnapped about a year and a half ago, they investigated and had discovered a storage locker in her name. It housed Katherine's research on Julie Gilbert, including a suspect board. Trent knew that Katherine had caught the case when she was working with the NYPD, but that's where his knowledge ended. He didn't know that Amanda was helping Katherine, off the books, whenever she had a spare moment. Which was all too infrequent, especially recently. He certainly didn't know why the case was important to Katherine or her personal connection. That never made it to any official record. The only reason Amanda knew was because Katherine had confided in her.

"Amanda, please answer me."

"Yes, she is, and I've been helping her a bit here and there."

"Oh, no. You realize that a huge shitstorm is headed our way?"

She appreciated he included himself in this mess, but it wasn't necessary. "This doesn't involve you."

"It does." His two-word response was definitive, landing like a stake hammered into the ground. "This perv might not know about your involvement, but you and Katherine must be getting close. What recent leads have you been following?"

"That's the thing, I haven't been able to help for months."

"Then Katherine's gotten herself into a corner. And what's to say this psycho won't turn his attention on her? But if she was his target, he would have gone straight after her, don't you think?"

"I don't know about that. This guy seems to have a type."

"Little girls," they said in unison.

"And performers, possibly those who know ballet," Amanda said. "Julie Gilbert performed a piece as her talent for beauty pageants. But where and when did he latch on to Hailey?" As she voiced the question, a fresh chill rolled over her from sheer overwhelm. "The Tanners told us that Hailey wasn't in other performances or competitions. So has this guy been around since before Christmas?"

"Anything is possible."

"It would give him time to plan her abduction. But this would mean he's been in the area for months. Either way, we need to look further into this show and who was there."

"We can see what we can find out, but it was open to the public." Trent sighed.

"Surely, there was some security for the event, names collected or something?" She was grasping. Life experience hadn't taught her to be this optimistic. Though in an ideal world, precautionary measures would have been taken. Especially for a show that paraded young kids across a stage.

"Okay, but if we're right about this, that means this guy has been stalking Hailey since December."

"Uh-huh. Which means we'd need to revisit some aspects of

the Tanner case. The people at the dance school were asked if they saw anything strange on the Friday Hailey was taken. If this guy was around for months, someone could have seen something a while ago that was dismissed."

"We need to start with Katherine, though, and find out what leads she's been following in recent months. If we're lucky, it will lead us straight to this person."

At the mention of Katherine again, Amanda remembered she hadn't seen her at the diner earlier. She might have been in the back. But the scary possibility existed that they were mistaken to assume the guy stuck to little girls. "Get us to the diner. I'm going to try Kat's cell."

TWELVE

Amanda met with voicemail all three times she tried Katherine's number on the way to the diner. "There's no answer," she told Trent.

"We need to let Malone know what's going on. You don't want him to find out from Rideout before he's heard it from you."

"Which would be another shitstorm. And he can never know that I've been helping her."

"I'm with you on that. He's going to be pissed enough that a civilian is investigating a police case. And if Malone or the chief, or even the brass at the NYPD sees her as interfering..."

"I know," she repeated. The consequence would be Katherine behind bars while a killer roamed free, able to torture and kill little girls.

"Then you're going to call Malone?"

"After we talk to Katherine."

"And if we can't reach her?"

"I'll deal with that if and when." She tried the diner this time, and after a few rings, the line was answered. "Is Katherine in?"

"Yeah, just a sec." The call was put on hold, and a broad-caster from a local radio station was soon talking in her ear.

"She's at the diner," she told Trent, breathing easier.

"Good."

"Hello, this is Katherine."

"Kat, it's Amanda." Since Katherine confided in Amanda, they'd become friends. Given how they'd started off it was hard to imagine a close relationship was even possible. When Malone took a brief medical leave, Katherine came in as interim sergeant. Amanda and she had bashed heads.

"Hey, how are you?" Her friendly tone held a leery note. Amanda never called in the middle of the afternoon during the workweek.

"Not good. Trent and I are on our way to talk with you."

"Now you have me worried."

Amanda wished she could assure her it wasn't anything horrible, but that would be a blatant lie. "We'll be there soon."

"Okay." Katherine dragged out the word and ended the call.

"She has no idea what's coming her way," Trent said, keeping his gaze out the windshield.

"How could anyone conjure this?"

They passed the rest of the short drive in silence. Her thoughts were on two little girls victimized by a monster without a conscience. Even if they caught this guy, there would be nothing to truly explain why this happened.

Trent pulled into the lot for Hannah's Diner, and when they stepped through the doors, Katherine was standing right there.

"I'm not waiting a second longer than necessary," she told them.

"Do you have an office where we can talk in private?" Amanda asked, and Katherine took them into the back.

They passed May on their way, and she bunched her fore-head in confusion, then followed them.

"I just need to talk with Amanda and Trent for a few minutes alone." Katherine stared down her aunt until the older woman consented and walked off.

Katherine closed the door behind them and sat at the desk. She pointed at two chairs in the room, where Amanda and Trent sat down.

"You both look pale, like someone ran over your dog. But neither of you have one." Katherine traced her gaze over the two of them. "Talk."

Amanda took a long breath. "There's been a development in the Hailey Tanner investigation."

"I heard her body was found. Customers have been talking about it all afternoon," Katherine said without emotion. It showed the hardened side of her cop shell.

"Unfortunately, she was, but there's far more to it." Amanda wasn't sure whether to dance around it, filling in some details and then landing with the gut punch or whether she should go right for it.

"Just spit it out, Amanda," Katherine said, as if reading Amanda's mind. "What does her murder have to do with me?"

Amanda had to be careful about what she disclosed because it was an open police investigation. Now sitting across from Katherine, she wished she had called Malone first. "A piece of evidence led us to you. A note essentially calling you out."

"I don't understand." She paled and blinked slowly. Two tiny tells that spoke volumes. She was piecing it together. "Is this about...?"

Amanda nodded. "We believe that whoever killed Hailey Tanner also killed Julie Gilbert." She told her the gist of the note.

"Dear God, that girl's death is my fault." Katherine touched her stomach in a fleeting motion, then tucked a strand of hair behind her ear. The latter was a rare trait and alerted Amanda that she was shaken. "Was she...?" Tears beaded in Katherine's eyes, but they were extinguished when her gaze became fire, and her mouth set in a firm line.

Amanda nodded, assuming the question was whether she'd been violated. "Have you been looking into the Gilbert case recently?"

"Not for months. I've just been so busy with the diner."

"When you say *months*? The start of the year? Last year?" Trent asked.

"Late fall, a week or two before Thanksgiving."

Amanda looked at Trent. That gave the killer time to find his way down here and even attend *The Nutcracker*.

"But if I triggered this guy, why not come after me? Why kill another poor, innocent child?" Katherine swallowed roughly.

"This person's clearly a sick individual. Also a coward. A child makes an easier target." Amanda empathized with what her friend must be feeling.

"This sick freak wants to feel powerful," Katherine said.

"It's important that you tell us what you were focused on then," Trent said.

"You know I had five men pegged as suspects?"

"Yes. The men on your suspect board in the storage unit," Trent said.

"That's right. I had three with names, two without. Since then, I've identified both the nameless men and cleared them. Trust me, *completely* cleared. But one identity came to me when I made an appeal on the website I set up."

"*Justice for Julie*," Amanda inserted for Trent.

"I posted his picture and asked if anyone could ID the man. I got a response. Hank Dickson, of Brooklyn. I drove up to his home and had a long talk with him. He's not behind this."

"It's possible our killer ID'd Dickson," Trent pointed out. "How did this person contact you?"

"They filled in the online contact form, leaving the name field blank."

"Tell us more about this picture? Which one was it?" Amanda remembered two.

"The one of a man looking at Julie over his shoulder. It had a creepy feel to it without knowing the context. I found out that pic had been taken at the NYC venue during Julie's last pageant. It was in a cordoned-off area reserved for those with the show who had clearance. Well, Dickson was a janitor there for five years. Looking closer at the shot you can see that he's holding a mop, and a corner of a bucket is visible in front of him. He was called out to clean up a mess made by one of the mothers."

"Where did the photo of him come from in the first place?" Trent asked.

"It was enclosed in a tri-folded white piece of paper inside of an envelope, delivered to the Gilberts' home."

"That's quite a red flag," Trent said.

"Agreed. The Gilbert case was nationwide news, so a lot of people mailed the family letters and photographs of the girl. But with this one not having any postmark or return address, it stood out."

"I assume it was processed for prints?" Trent asked.

"It was, and there weren't any. All this was back when I was officially on the case. I didn't like the angle of the shot either. Most of the shots of Julie were of her performing on stage. This was more intimate, behind the scenes."

"Then you never found out who took the picture?" Amanda said.

"Nope, and after talking with Dickson, that drove me crazy. The photographer must be someone with backstage access."

"Right, so pageant contestants, their mothers, agents...?" Trent rattled off.

"Whoever was an integral part of the entourage. So I also

considered cosmeticians and costume designers," Katherine put in.

"Costume designers..." Amanda said. It might not hurt to disclose one thing about the Tanner case. "The note that Rideout found was stitched into the hem of Hailey's dress. I don't know if it looked professional or not but..."

Trent shook his head at her. She might have crossed the line by disclosing that.

"There were a few male costume designers. I've got their names on my laptop in the storage unit."

"We'll want them," Trent said. "Did you ever question them for Julie's murder?"

"I did. None of them flagged as suspicious. Maybe I made a mistake in assuming that."

Amanda laid her hand over Katherine's, and her friend looked at her. "There's only so much time," Amanda assured her. "You follow the strongest leads you have. Now we know more, it will help us look at things differently."

"Now you have another victim you mean. All because of me."

"The only thing you're responsible for is trying to find justice for a little girl," Amanda said with conviction.

Katherine pulled her hand back and nodded. "So it was after talking with Dickson, part of what I did was reach out to the NYC venue again for employee names. I figured they'd have access backstage."

"And you have those?" Amanda asked.

"I do, and they matched what I already had, which was disheartening. I haven't had a chance to go any further than that."

"The killer is likely someone who knew your interest in those backstage," Amanda said.

"That is a lot of names with no way of narrowing them down."

"Let's say the killer was also Dickson's photographer, what's his end game? Why submit the photo?" Amanda asked.

"We know most killers have egos and God complexes," Katherine said. "It's a game to him. He'd have to know the photo would flag as suspicious. I think it was to steer the investigation away from himself."

"And they go as far as calling in the tip," Trent said.

"He may have thought you'd run into a similar photo of Dickson anyhow. Why not push the limelight off himself?" After she spoke, something else occurred to her. "Katherine, you would have employee names for the venue already, but you never came across Dickson's name before? Pulled a background or seen his picture?" Amanda was trying to understand why Katherine hadn't identified him on her own.

"It's possible I had seen the name, even his picture, but he never flagged for me. And you know how different a person can look in their license photo compared to real life."

No one said anything for a moment.

"What is it about this case, Katherine, that has you holding on?" Trent asked, breaking the silence.

Katherine looked at Amanda.

"I didn't miss that," Trent said. "Is there something I should know?"

The story wasn't Amanda's to tell. She said to Katherine, "Considering where we find ourselves, it might be best to lay it all out."

Katherine rubbed her forehead. "I suppose you're right. I haven't even told Aunt May, so if we can keep this quiet until I've at least had that chance?"

"I don't see why she needs to know," Amanda said, glancing at Trent.

"My lips are sealed."

"Very well. I was raped when I was with the NYPD," Katherine started, her voice like a damp rag. "My rapist was another detective on the force. When I found out I was pregnant, I took time off to have the baby. I put her up for adoption after birth and told no one. Then, six years later, I was called in for the Gilbert investigation." Katherine shared this devoid of emotion as if the subject under discussion was a stranger and not herself. "During that time, I watched a lot of video footage of Julie, and one day it clicked. She felt so familiar, and I'd already felt like I was connected. I'd just dismissed it as being the tragedy of the case, a young girl, and that it hit me for that reason alone. But I did a DNA comparison, off the record, and found out she was my daughter. The one I put up for adoption."

The air in the room became heavy and silent. For the first time since they entered the office, Amanda heard the noises from the diner filtering in.

"Whoa." Trent flopped back in his chair. "That's... I don't even know what to say, except for I'm sorry. I can't imagine how you... what you've been through."

He didn't say it, but Amanda sensed he now understood Katherine's obsession with the Gilbert case.

"I'm not going to lie. It's been hell. I've been haunted by the what ifs. Like what if I'd just kept her? That's the biggest one. But rehashing my personal cost isn't going to help us. It seems like we're in agreement that we need to find the photographer who took Dickson's picture."

"I'd say that's our starting point, no matter how potentially broad," Amanda agreed.

"With focus on anyone with backstage access at the NYC venue," Trent said. "It was where Julie competed in her last pageant, close to where she was killed, and where the photograph was taken of Dickson."

"That still leaves us with a lot of names. As you just said"—Amanda gestured to Katherine—"people travel with the show. So it's hard to track everyone down." Amanda was battling against feeling overwhelmed and losing.

"Only good news is we likely have his name," Trent said, and held up his hands when Amanda and Katherine looked at him. "I know, a needle in a haystack."

"But speaking of names," Amanda started. "Does Mara Bennett, Nick Potter, or Susan Butters mean anything to you?" She was asking for due diligence.

Katherine shook her head. "But people change their names all the time. Criminals assume new identities. You think a woman might be behind this?"

"Or a partnership," Amanda said.

"Which makes more sense to me," Katherine said. "There was sexual assault in Gilbert's case. A moment ago, I got the impression the same applies for the Tanner case?"

"It does, and Butters could have worked with someone," Amanda said, not feeling convinced herself. The woman's self-chastisement for being single rang true.

"Well, do you have pictures of them? I can see if they look familiar. Anything I've seen related to the Gilbert investigation is seared on my brain."

Trent took out his tablet and brought up the photos of Butters, Bennett, and Potter.

Katherine looked at each one. "There's nothing familiar about them at all."

As Trent put his tablet away, Amanda met his eye. This released the three of them from their suspect list. "All right, well, we pare back to what we know," Amanda said.

"This guy came down here because of me and now he's sticking around to see what I'm going to do," Katherine said. "But how can I back off? How can you? He must know we can't do that."

"Which makes me think he's using you as an excuse," Amanda said. "He's not finished, regardless of what you do. But with that said..."

"You think I should back off, leave it alone?" Katherine said.

The immediate image in her mind was that of another dead girl. "I don't see what choice you have. Not with the stakes involved."

"Amanda, you just said a moment ago that what happens next isn't dependent on what I do. Why not let me help? It's not like I'm just anybody off the street. I'm former police."

"Sergeant Malone is likely to take issue with the *former* part," Trent said.

"I get that. I no longer have a badge, but I know more about the Gilbert case than anyone else. I can help."

Amanda looked at Trent. Katherine made a solid point. Her knowledge could prove integral to bringing this creep down. If she worked behind the scenes and kept a low profile, the killer would never find out. "Let's run your helping past Malone."

"Thank you."

It's probably too soon to be thanking me...

THIRTEEN

Amanda watched Katherine's Mercedes following them in the side mirror as Trent drove them back to Central. The plan was they'd set Katherine up in the conference room while they filled Malone in and petitioned for Katherine's collaboration. The conversation wasn't one Amanda looked forward to, but necessary. If there was even a slim chance Katherine's knowledge could help bring this person down, they needed her on the team.

On the way, Amanda called CSI Blair and got a number for CSIs Vanessa Stuart and Ruth Keller, who were assigned to the Tanner residence. She tried Keller first and landed in her voicemail. Next, she punched in Stuart's digits. Another recorded greeting, but she left a message there, exasperated. "Investigator Stuart, this is Detective Steele. Please call me with an update on the Tanner residence." She hung up and turned to Trent, shook her head. "Neither of them is answering."

"They could still be working."

"Taking their sweet time then." She added their names and numbers to her contacts, so she'd identify them when they called back.

"Better thorough than speedy."

"Somewhere in the middle would be ideal."

They went into the station, escorted Katherine to the conference room, and carried on to Malone's office. Amanda knocked on the doorframe, and he looked up from his desk and flipped his readers off his nose.

Amanda sat down. *So here goes...* She laid everything out, the note in the hem, the connection to the Gilbert case and Katherine, stopping short of requesting that Katherine be brought in to help.

Malone's cheeks flamed red. "What the heck is she thinking?"

For him, *heck* was the equivalent of the F-word. "It's clear this person wants someone to blame, Sarge." Amanda stepped up to Katherine's defense. "Whether it was her or another detective poking around, we'd likely be in the same place."

"Except you can't know that. She's a civilian. This is an NYPD case from twelve years ago."

If Malone was looped in on the full picture, he might show more understanding and compassion. Trent looked over at her. "There's something else," she said and admitted they spoke to Katherine before coming here.

"Are you kidding me?"

Amanda shrank in her chair. "She's willing to help."

Malone's face darkened. "Why should that matter? I can't authorize that. Have her hand over the names and step away."

"As Amanda was getting to, boss—" Trent was shut down by a sharp look from Malone.

"Let me guess. Her familiarity with the case could be an asset? But I don't care if she has a lot to offer. She's a *civilian*. How can I possibly justify bringing her in to work on an active investigation in an official capacity? Especially one in which a killer threatened further victims if she keeps poking around."

Amanda questioned the source of his issue. Was it as simple

as he said, or was it influenced by Chief Buchanan's hold over him? But she'd use Malone's "blue" code against him. It was also what he'd said when Katherine was abducted. "What happened to once a cop, always a cop?"

"Don't test me, Steele."

He'd pulled out her surname. It might be time to back off, but she was worked up to defend Katherine as one mother to another. An injustice had been inflicted on her, as it had with Amanda's family. "I'm sure we can assume the threat extends to anyone who tries to stop him. This guy can't be stupid enough to think we'll ignore his crimes and let him get away with them. Katherine can help us, boss. She has contacts and knows this case inside out."

Malone settled back in his chair, dangling his readers between his thumb and index finger of his left hand. "Fine, I'll talk with her, but that's all I can promise."

"All I'm asking. For now." She smiled at him when he drilled her with a serious expression. But she could afford to push things with him a bit. Malone had been a friend of her father's for decades and around her family all her life.

They joined Katherine in the conference room.

"Katherine," Malone said as a way of greeting.

"Sergeant Malone," she responded.

"I'd ask how you're doing, but since I understand you're in the loop, there's no point." Malone sat at the head of the table, putting Katherine on his right.

Amanda and Trent sat next to each other on his left.

"I'm not sure how much you know." Katherine looked at Amanda.

She shook her head, and Katherine put her gaze back on Malone.

"I know you've been investigating an NYPD case since you left there. How you're no longer employed as a cop, yet you insist on acting like you are?"

"I have nothing to say to that," Katherine said at a low volume.

"Amanda and Trent seem to think you can help find Hailey's killer."

"And Julie Gilbert's," Katherine amended.

"Go on." Malone sat back and clasped his hands.

Katherine filled Malone in on what she'd shared with Amanda and Trent. When she finished, Malone leaned forward, his elbows on the table, and his arms crossed.

"Huh. So you're saying we find the photographer, we find the killer?" Malone said.

"That's the running theory. And we think this person ID'd Dickson."

"All right, well, you said he messaged through an online contact form. Digital always leaves a trail."

Katherine inched forward on her chair, matching Malone's posture. "I'm limited in what I can do. I tried emailing the address provided, as the form asks for one, but it bounced back as undeliverable."

"We can take this to Detective Jacob Briggs with Digital Forensics. If anyone can track the sender's location, it's him," Amanda said.

"That's a great idea, Amanda," Katherine piped in.

"It could work," Malone admitted, with far less enthusiasm. "And I think that's our strongest starting point before we invest too much time digging into all the people associated with the pageant and different venues."

"Here's the thing—" Katherine stopped talking when Malone let out a huff.

"Fine, go ahead. Say what you were going to say. I have a feeling I know what it's going to be already."

"I'm not sure if Amanda has spoken to you yet or—"

"Oh, she's spoken to me, and I'm not sure where I stand yet.

She's convinced your familiarity with the Gilbert case will be integral to solving the Tanner murder."

Katherine remained silent, and from Amanda's knowledge of the sergeant that had been a wise choice.

"If, and I mean *if* you're to help us, there can't be any sleuthing around on your own. Any new intel is to be reported immediately, and you will share everything there is about the Gilbert investigation."

"Yes, of course."

"Most of it still in that storage shed?" Malone asked her.

"Between there and my laptop."

"I will be upfront though. I'm not sure how comfortable I am bringing you in on this, Katherine," Malone told her. "I think it's best we stick to legal channels here. We should talk with your former partner. What was his name again?"

"The one who worked the Gilbert case with me is long gone, but my last detective partner was Mickey Fritz," Katherine said.

"Well, he or someone at the NYPD needs to know what's happened here and the link to Julie Gilbert."

"I don't disagree, but Julie's case is taking up space in cold storage," Katherine put out in a level tone. "No one is actively looking for her killer. That's why—"

Amanda shook her head for Katherine to stop. First, she slipped up by referring to the case as *Julie's* not Gilbert's. She might as well have screamed it was personal. Second, alluding to incompetence among the NYPD would never work with Malone. He was true blue to the core and refused to see any wrongdoing in his fellow officers of the law without solid evidence.

"Why what, Katherine? Please continue," Malone prompted, though Amanda saw it as a test.

Katherine straightened her posture. "Someone has to look out for her."

"Yes, well, I'm concerned someone should be looking out for you. I want to get a twenty-four-hour protective detail on you."

"No," Katherine said.

"Excuse me?" Malone pushed back. "He clearly has an issue with you. He came here from New York City because of you. Protection detail isn't an option."

"Fine." The single word left Katherine's lips with exasperation not acceptance. "Does that mean I can help?"

Amanda saw Katherine at the losing end of this conversation and stepped in. "Maybe if you knew why this case is so important to Katherine..." She looked at her friend.

Katherine took a deep breath and let out, "Julie's murder is personal to me," on a labored exhale.

Malone became stock-still. "Which I've gathered. Care to tell me why?"

Katherine laid it all out, then added, "Maybe that can help you understand why I can't stop. Why I *won't* stop."

"I feel for what you've been through. I really do. But are you saying you plan to keep working on this case, regardless of whether we rope you in or not? If so, you do realize I could arrest you for interfering with a police investigation?" Malone strummed his fingers on the table, squinting and huffing a bit.

"We all know how urgent it is we get this guy," Amanda wedged in with some finesse. "We have pressure from the media, the police chief... There's a lot of work here, and we never bank our efforts on one thing. We'd be at a disadvantage without Katherine's knowledge of the Gilbert case. Trent and I would need to read all the files, pull backgrounds, contact everyone. Katherine has relationships with some of these people already."

"I hate to say this, but possibly with the killer," Malone said.

Katherine squared her posture. "Fair enough, but no one knows this case like me."

"Not to mention the workload on me and Amanda just with

the Tanner case," Trent added to the defense. "We'd need to familiarize ourselves with the Gilbert investigation before we could even look for similarities or cross-reference names. And that's assuming this person isn't operating under an alias these days."

"I get it. There's a lot of work," Malone grumbled. After a few beats, he turned to Amanda. "We might not run into his name for a while yet. If we do. We could be looking at a stranger to this family, an intruder in the Tanner home. Do we have an answer on that yet?"

"I had to leave a message with the CSIs," she told him, while trying to bury her frustration that they hadn't yet returned her call.

"They were dispatched there late this morning"—Malone consulted his watch—"and it's after four in the afternoon. What could be taking them so long?"

"No idea," she admitted.

"Well, if you don't hear before five, let me know and I'll make a call," Malone told her.

"Sounds good."

"All right, Katherine, here's the thing," Malone started. "From an official standpoint, I don't want you anywhere near this, *but* if you could be available for consulting—"

"You couldn't stop me."

"As you made quite clear," Malone said. "Amanda and Trent, I want your focus on the Tanner case. On the upside, for this guy to take another victim and call out Katherine, he's emotionally compromised. That means he's bound to have screwed up somewhere along the way. Go over every bit of Hailey's life and see what you can uncover. Then, we'll be in a better position to spot any connections to Gilbert and put a name on this guy."

"You got it, boss," Amanda said. "Do you want me to get Detective Briggs from Digital on tracking the sender of that contact form?"

"Yeah, that's fine. You have a solid working relationship there. As for this list of names you've gathered," Malone started, turning toward Katherine, "I think male costume designers would be the best place to start."

"We still need to confirm if the stitch looked professional or not, though that might not even matter. If I were a professional seam— Seamstress for a woman, but what is it for a guy?" Trent looked around, and Katherine stepped up.

"Just call them costume designers because they do it all," Katherine said. "They come up with the concept and make it happen."

"Well, I doubt judging the sewing job will get us anywhere," Trent said. "A professional could have done a shoddy job to cover his work."

"The only thing I worry about is you spoke to those people back in the fall too, didn't you?" Malone asked Katherine.

"I did, but I could approach things from another angle," she said.

Malone gestured for her to explain.

"Instead of speaking directly with them, I could call their employers from the time. It could give me a read on them without concern I'd be contacting the killer himself."

"And tipping them off," Malone added.

"Exactly."

"Does this mean she's cleared to help?" Amanda asked. "As you just said, you want Trent and I to dig into Hailey's world. That means our time will be quite full just following up leads and talking with people associated with her case."

Malone rubbed his short, groomed beard. The noise of his fingernails scratching his whiskers was the only sound in the room. "I couldn't pay you, Katherine. There is no way that is in the budget."

"I don't need money," she rushed out. "I just want to get this guy and put him behind bars where he belongs."

"I'm not sure if there's an available desk for you to use," Malone said.

"She can use mine whenever I'm not here," Amanda offered.

Malone narrowed his eyes at her before turning back to Katherine. "That's settled, and I'll get you a login for the computer. But before you help in any official capacity, I will need to clear this by the police chief." With that, Malone got up and left the room.

"You're in." Amanda smiled at Katherine.

"I'm not celebrating just yet, and it seems like it would be rather... distasteful if I did. We are talking about a repeat killer who targets young girls." Katherine's eyes blanked over.

"Nothing wrong with being happy you're on the team that's going to bring him down. We're going to find this guy, Kat," Amanda told her friend.

"We better. No ordinary person has the stomach for killing a child, let alone sexually assaulting them. There's no telling what else he's capable of."

FOURTEEN

The meeting with Katherine wrapped up at five o'clock. While she was going to gather her laptop and files from the storage unit to be prepared, Amanda's immediate concern was arranging for someone to take care of Zoe.

"I'm just calling Libby," Amanda told Trent on the way to their desks. "Then we can look at the files from the Tanner case. I'd think that Detective McGee would have sent them over by now." *And speaking of him, he never returned my call...* She'd let it go only because they had dismissed Nick Potter and Mara Bennett.

"I'll go check," Trent said.

Amanda called Libby, and she answered on the second ring. "Amanda? How's it going?"

She asked in a chipper tone, though she must suspect what was coming. "I picked up a new case today."

"Let me guess. It has something to do with Hailey Tanner. I heard about it on the news. What a tragic ending."

And not just with Hailey... It hurt to think she was linked to a twisted killer responsible for at least two murders and threatening more. "It does, and I think you know why I'm calling."

"You need Zoe to stay for dinner or overnight. Either is fine by us. We love having her here."

"Well, Zoe loves it too." Libby was Zoe's godmother, but when the girl's parents were killed, her life circumstances didn't allow her to adopt her. But while taking Zoe in full-time wasn't an option, she and her life partner, Penny, were a constant in the girl's life. Since Libby was a teacher at her school, she brought Zoe home with her until Amanda picked her up.

Trent returned and was shaking his head.

"One second," she said to Libby. "What is it?" she asked Trent.

"The investigation files aren't here yet. I'll follow up with Detective McGee."

"Thanks."

"Amanda?" Libby was prompting from the other end of the line.

"Sorry about that."

"Dinner or overnight?" Libby repeated.

Amanda hesitated to answer. She wanted to see Zoe, but how could she swing that? Though it would take more time waiting on McGee for the files. Amanda could pick them up, and since she'd already be out... "Libby, I'm going to swing past if that's all right and take Zoe out for dinner. But then I'll need to get back to work. If you're good to take her for the night after that?"

"Ah, sure."

"Wonderful. I'll see you in about ten, fifteen minutes." Amanda was smiling when she hung up. A break away from a case in the first twenty-four hours was almost unheard of.

"I overheard. You're running away?" Trent said.

"I am. That's if you're okay to handle things." Maybe she misspoke and assumed incorrectly that he'd be fine on his own. "Or maybe you could pop home and have a bite with Kelsey?"

"Kels won't be home. She just texted a minute ago that she's going out for dinner and drinks with some colleagues."

"Oh." Amanda hadn't intended for that one little word to slip out, and after seeing Trent raise his eyebrows, she wished she could reel it back in.

"Meaning?"

"Nothing."

"No, it's *not* nothing."

"That's a lot of negatives." She grabbed her light jacket and headed for the door.

"Just talk to me."

If there was a way out of this, she'd take it, but he'd stay on her. She stopped walking and turned around. "You know how this job is unpredictable and has us breaking promises to those we love?"

"Yes."

"It's good that you found someone who has fluidity to her life too. Don't take that for granted." Even as she doled out relationship advice, jealousy reared its ugly head.

"It is. Here, let me get the door." He slipped ahead of her and held it open.

"Where are you going?" The question tumbled out of its own accord. It shouldn't matter to her where he was headed.

"I assume I'm allowed to eat too."

"Of course you are. Never mind me." She smiled, but it failed to cut through an awkward undercurrent. In the back of her mind, she was imagining the three of them going out for a meal. That being her, Zoe, and Trent.

"If you and Zoe want company, I could tag along. I'd just hit a drive-thru otherwise."

Now, he's reading my mind... She choked back on the fact that he'd just invited himself along, but why should she make a big deal out of this? Zoe knew Trent was her partner, and she liked him. They all needed to eat... "Sure. Why not? I mean, I'm sure Zoe will be happy to see you."

"Nice." Trent grinned. "She's a good kid."

"That she is."

He stopped walking and looked over the parking lot. "I guess the question becomes your car or mine."

"Let's take your Jeep. I'm good with being chauffeured." The truth was this impromptu *date* had her mind spinning. She was best to focus on the job. "Since we'll be out, we should call McGee again to let him know we can swing by Eastern to pick up the files." She made it sound like the thought just occurred to her. He didn't need to know this was her original justification for stepping out.

Trent unlocked his Wrangler and got behind the wheel while she hefted herself up into the passenger seat.

"I'll call on the way. Just tell me where I'm headed."

She gave him Libby's address, and he got them on the road.

He placed the call to Detective McGee using the vehicle's Bluetooth. When McGee answered, Trent said, "It's Detective Stenson."

"We just spoke. I need more time to get the files together and over there." McGee sounded irritated, and it fueled Amanda's temper.

"That's why I'm calling. No need for you to bring them over or send them with someone. Detective Steele and I can pick them up."

"They're not ready yet."

"We're grabbing a bite to eat. Say in an hour?"

"Yeah, sure. Why not?"

"Thanks." With that Trent hung up and looked over at her. "He sounds thrilled."

"Doesn't he though? I'm not sure how to read the guy. One minute he's indifferent, the next some emotion shows through..."

"Who knows what his story is."

"True enough. Everyone has one." This sentiment daisy-chained to another thought. "I sure hope Katherine gets cleared to help. It would mean a lot to her."

"Me too. She needs this."

Amanda nodded, as her mind tripped down the rabbit hole. She couldn't imagine how Katherine would feel knowing she was inching in on her daughter's killer, but on the ugly flip side of that it had taken another young girl's life to bring it to her attention.

Trent pulled into Libby's driveway, and the front door swung open. Zoe came running out and down the steps.

Amanda's heart lifted, and she couldn't get her seatbelt undone fast enough. Only instead of going to the passenger side, Zoe went straight to Trent.

I'll pretend that doesn't sting... Amanda walked around the front of the Jeep. Zoe didn't pass her a glance.

Trent put his window down and leaned out.

"Hey, Trent." Zoe was grinning up at him, not self-conscious about her missing front teeth. One up, one down. The Tooth Fairy gave her ten dollars each for them, and Amanda encouraged her to save one of those bills. It was tucked into a piggy bank in the girl's room. When its belly was stuffed, Zoe would empty it and take a fourth of the money to buy whatever she wanted and open a savings account with the rest.

"Hey, Zoe," Trent mimicked the girl.

"What are you doing here?"

"Going out for dinner with you and your mom."

Zoe's smile faded, and she faced Amanda but didn't close the distance.

Amanda could see her mind working and feared it might be stuck on the *mom* bit. Trent was looking at Amanda, clearly feeling he'd misspoken, but Amanda shook her head. He didn't need to feel bad for what he'd said.

"Hey, Zoe," Amanda chimed in to take some of the pressure off the girl. Even though she had adopted Zoe almost four years ago, she never expected to be called *Mom*. Amanda appreciated it might be a title reserved for Zoe's late mother, and respected that was Zoe's decision to make.

"Mandy!" Zoe pumped some enthusiasm into seeing her.

Finally... Amanda was close to getting a complex. "So I'm not here to pick you up for the night, but like Trent said, we're taking you out for dinner. Where do you want to go?" With that carte blanche offering, she hoped it wasn't going to be the Waffle House. That girl could eat pancakes for any meal of the day.

"Petey's!"

Amanda could live with that choice. Petey's Patties was a burger joint with checkered floors and vinyl booths. Their menu only consisted of comfort food. "Sounds good to me. Trent?"

"Delicious!"

Zoe laughed.

"Let me just check in with Libby." Amanda hadn't missed that Libby was standing in the doorway still.

Amanda went to her. "Thank you for taking her tonight and letting me pop by like this. I hope it's not too much of an inconvenience."

"Never a problem where you or Zoe are concerned."

Whenever Libby talked about Zoe, Amanda could feel her love for the girl. "Just know you're appreciated."

Libby dipped her head.

"I should have her back within the hour," Amanda said and turned to leave. Summarizing her limited time with Zoe drilled an ache into her chest.

"See you soon." Libby shut the door behind her.

Amanda returned to the Jeep to find that Zoe had climbed

into the front passenger seat. She slipped into the back. "Hey now, what's going on here?"

"Trent said I could ride shoe gun." Zoe giggled.

"*Shot*gun," Trent corrected.

"Yeah, that's it. Close enough." The girl was grinning, her head turned toward Trent. He might be her first crush.

The girl has impeccable taste... The thought fired through Amanda's head at lightning speed. Then she spent the next forty-five minutes telling herself dinner with Trent and her daughter was normal. Platonic. Nothing to it. If only her heart was listening to her head.

They ate cheeseburgers and fries and laughed like a family of three in a corner booth. None of that imagery was helping Amanda stuff her romantic feelings for Trent deeper down. But she wasn't in any position to offer him anything. Kelsey aside. She had her own life to sort out. She was just months out of a long-term relationship. They'd been living together, but when Logan had wanted to take it to another level, Amanda had to face reality. They weren't a great match. Good, but not great. He was a solid father figure for Zoe, but he didn't respect Amanda's work despite his lip service when she cornered him. To him, her being a cop was an inconvenience.

They dropped Zoe back at Libby's, and Zoe waved from the front window as Trent pulled out of the driveway. She was sure most of her daughter's attention was on Trent, not her.

"Zoe's incredible and so sharp for her age," Trent said, waving back.

"Too sharp, sometimes." Amanda smiled. "And stubborn."

Trent grinned. "Makes life more interesting. She seems to be doing good though."

Amanda looked over at Trent, not lost for a second on the meaning. "With Logan gone?"

"Yeah. I know they were close. He ever...?"

She shook her head. "I heard a rumor that he left town. Don't ask me where he went."

"That's too bad."

She studied his profile, unsure whether that was genuine from Zoe's perspective or sarcastic from his own. The tension between the two men wasn't a well-guarded secret. "Zoe was upset at first, but she's doing fine. We had a long talk about him and our decision to split up. She seemed to understand it wasn't about her and said it was like her with Maria. She was one of Zoe's first friends. Zoe said Maria changed, and she doesn't like her anymore."

"Wow. That is smart and rather astute. How old is she now?"

"Nine."

"Wow. That's impressive."

"I swear she's an old soul in a little person." With that said, Amanda's thoughts turned to Hailey Tanner. What had that sweet girl been like? Most of the world lost the chance to know.

Amanda and Trent swung past the Eastern District Station, and after she introduced herself, the officer at the front desk lifted a banker box up from behind the counter. "Here ya go."

"Thanks."

Less than five minutes later, she and Trent were back in the car on their way to Central. Her phone rang, and Malone's name flashed on the screen. She answered on speaker.

"Where are you guys?"

"We just left Eastern with the files for the Tanner case, but we're on our way back now."

"All right. Well, I'm calling to let you know that Chief Buchanan gave Katherine the green light. *But* she's to assist on a consultation basis only."

"Meaning?" Amanda asked.

"She can help us in the background. No field work, but she can help by making necessary phone calls and serving as liaison with the NYPD."

She gave a thumbs-up to Trent. "That's great. I was thinking it might be best if Katherine worked directly with Detective Briggs at Digital Crimes on tracking down the sender of that online form that identified Dickson. She has all the information he'd need to access her site. It makes more sense than sticking myself in the middle."

"Should be fine. I've already reached out to Katherine, and she'll brief us on the Gilbert case first thing tomorrow morning. I think it's best we all get a refresher course on the specifics of the case. We might even learn something new."

"Sounds good. Did you get her a system login?"

"Guy in IT has gone home. I'll get her one in the morning. I still want you and Trent to focus on the Tanner murder though. It might even be best if you treat it as a solo case. That way you won't get distracted by the Gilbert investigation and miss things that may be right in front of you."

"I get that," she said.

"Moving on to forensics... Anything connected to the Tanner case will be assigned priority."

"Speaking of, Sarge, I never heard from the CSIs who worked the Tanner residence." He'd told her to follow up by five if there wasn't any word by then, but she'd been otherwise occupied.

"If you shoot me their numbers, I'll see if I can rouse a response. If not, I'll go above their heads."

"Thanks."

"As you know, Tanner's identity has been released to the media, but the PIO is monitoring the situation and doing their best to make sure the link to the Gilbert case doesn't come out."

The Public Information Office was a branch of the PWCPD that managed what was revealed or held back.

Hinting at a serial offender would create panic. "Sounds like a good call."

"If you need anything more from me tonight, just call my cell phone. I'm headed home." He ended the call as Trent pulled into the parking lot at Central.

It just so happened that he slipped into the spot next to Malone's vehicle.

He was pocketing his phone while Amanda slid hers into her jacket. Trent went into the backseat and pulled out the banker box.

Malone came over, nudging his head at it. "Is that all?"

"Yep," Trent said.

"Doesn't look like a lot."

She'd thought the same, but it carried some heft. And in all fairness, the case only lasted three days for McGee. "I guess we'll find out."

Malone waved at them as he got behind the wheel of his car and drove away.

For the next hour and a half, Amanda and Trent sorted through the contents of the evidence box. It included the list of prestigious people from the Tanners' dinner party. The mayor's face was staring up from the page, but Amanda set it aside. She and Trent read through several interviews Detective McGee had conducted with the Tanners and others in their circle.

Amanda sat back and tapped her fingers on the edge of the table.

"Someone looks deep in thought. And by someone, I mean—"

"Me. I get it." She smiled at him, but he'd cut through her concentration. "I noticed one repeating theme in all the interviews. It was something we briefly discussed before. McGee based his questioning around a more recent timeframe." She met his eye.

"But now we're thinking this person latched on to Hailey back in December."

"Right. So we will need to revisit everyone and ask if anyone new has been hanging around for the last six or seven months. We already touched on going back to the ballet studio. But everyone needs to be asked if there were any relationships or employ—" Her phone rang, cutting her off mid-word. She looked at the screen, and it said *CSI Stuart*. "It's the head investigator from the Tanner residence."

"About time," he said.

"Malone can be persuasive." She hit the accept call button. "Detective Steele."

"This is CSI Stuart. I don't much appreciate your boss pressuring me for results."

Amanda stiffened, and her redhead temper ignited. "With all due respect, you arrived at the Tanner residence this morning, and it's now approaching seven thirty at night. It would be very helpful to know what we're looking at here."

"There's a process, and I don't like being rushed. I don't know how things typically work with other CSIs you've partnered with, but I don't share anything until I feel confident in what I have to say." She paused there, as if using the silence to drill in her point. It felt like Amanda was a scolded child, and Stuart wanted to ensure she received the underlying lesson. Amanda wasn't going to respond.

After a drawn-out silence, CSI Stuart continued. "The lock on the gate blocking the yard wasn't broken, but the trellis in the back appears to have been climbed. It leads right to the girl's window," she added.

"How does it *appear* to have been—"

Stuart cut her off. "There are a few broken pieces of lattice and vertical white scuff marks, which might be rubber from the soles of a running shoe. A swab was taken of one to test its composition. The windowsill was also examined on the outside.

If the intruder took this route, they would have gripped there to hoist themselves up. But nothing turned up."

"But the rubber is proof the room was accessed through the window."

"Not what I said."

This woman's attitude was pissing her off. "What other reason would there be for its existence? And the intruder could have used gloves."

"It's possible, sure, but the window doesn't appear to have been tampered with. No scrape marks."

Amanda took a deep breath. "Do you believe there was a break-in or not?"

"Inconclusive."

"Except for the broken lattice and rubber marks."

"Which is more speculative."

Amanda wasn't sure how this woman got in this line of work if she didn't employ some logic to make deductions. "I assume you'll confirm if that mark was made by a shoe."

"That's the plan, but I'll need to run it past my supervisor. Lab tests take a lot of time and money, Detective. Though I'm sure I don't need to tell you that."

Amanda bit her bottom lip to avoid lashing out at this impossible woman. *Where are CSIs Blair and Donnelly when I need them?*

"I will be running a swab taken from the handle on the girl's closet door. Also from the tote where the slippers were kept. We know those areas were compromised. I'm just not confident if it will lead us to the perpetrator. The DNA may belong to the family."

"We need to explore it, regardless."

"Yes, which is why I just said I'm going to run those tests."

Amanda tightened her grip on her phone. She wasn't often triggered to entertain violence, but this CSI was bringing it out in her. "You mentioned swabs and DNA. Did you test for fingerprints?"

"Absolutely not. The chances of pulling a useful print from a cylindrical handle are near zilch."

"What about the tote, a flat surface?"

"Not sure if you remember, but that tote is weaved with strands of fabric. There's a much better probability of touch DNA being more useful than trying to lift prints. I'm very selective about what I gather and what I test."

That's why it takes all day! "And did you confirm if the brand of the tutu in Hailey's closet was a match for what she was staged in?"

"I will let you know."

"If you tell me what she has in her closet, I can ask." Amanda would have juggled this task earlier if she knew it was going to end up landing on her shoulders.

"I don't have that information at present."

Amanda counted to five in her head. "Please, let me know once the results are in."

"Will do. Next time, please wait for me to call you." With that, the CSI hung up.

Amanda lowered her phone.

"Shit, you look like you're going to explode." Trent scanned her face. "What was all that?"

"Let's sum it up to say I never want to talk with CSI Stuart again. Not when she rides a broom to work." She'd forgive herself this one slip.

"All righty then." Trent raised his hands and sat back. "I don't think I've ever heard you talk about someone like that."

"What can I say? That woman brings it out in me."

"What did she tell you? Signs of a break-in or not?"

"Huh. That's the thing right there. She's not sure." She ran through what the investigator had told her.

"Then we're where we were when we left."

"Yep. Hours later we're not any closer to knowing if it was a welcomed guest or home intruder that took the tutu or the slippers. As for other possible dead ends, let's go talk with the Tanners again."

Trent pinched his fingers together. "A tad more optimism might not hurt."

If he wanted that from her, he'd be waiting a while.

FIFTEEN

Amanda and Trent passed Katherine heading into Central when they were leaving. She confirmed she remembered where Amanda's desk was and kept walking while tossing out, "Good luck," over her shoulder. And they just might need it.

When they showed up at the Tanner residence, three vehicles were in the driveway. None of them belonged to Crime Scene, so at least stuffy Vanessa Stuart had moved on. Amanda wasn't sure she could keep her temper under control if she had to face that woman so soon after speaking with her.

Trent rang the bell, and the chime reached the front step again. The beautiful tune seemed to mock the tragedy that had struck the home's inhabitants.

The door was opened by a woman in her late fifties. The gray around her temples stood out in contrast to her otherwise brown hair.

Amanda flashed her badge, as did Trent. "Detectives Steele, and Stenson. Would Vincent or Jean Tanner be home?"

The woman pinched her lips and backed up to let them inside. Voices in subdued chatter carried from the sitting room to the entry.

"I'm Pamela, Vincent's mother." She pulled her buttoned cardigan tighter around herself.

Hailey's grandmother... Amanda's heart ached for the woman. "I'm sorry for your loss."

"Thank you. Nothing could have ever prepared me for..." Pamela's eyes welled with tears as she spoke, but her words were cut off as she was overtaken by a body-wracking sob. "If you'll..." Pamela shuffled down the hall toward the back of the home, stranding them beneath the entry chandelier.

Amanda and Trent looked at each other, then both ducked through the doorway into the sitting room.

"Detectives?" Vincent got up from the couch and came over to them. "Did you find out who did this? Please, tell us you did." His shoulders sagged when she shook her head.

"Not yet, but trust me when I say we are doing all that we can." As she spoke, it wasn't far from her mind that the sick person who killed Hailey had increased his victim tally to two. *Will there be more? Were there more?* She had to squeeze that invasive thought out. She cleared her throat. "We just have a few more questions for you and your wife." She looked past Vincent's shoulder but didn't spot Jean in the room. She did meet with three curious faces gazing back at her. A woman and two men, all older than Vincent. The couple must be Jean's parents and the remaining person, Pamela's husband. "Is your wife home?"

"She's just lying down. I could get her, but I'd hate to wake her. She took some pills and probably won't be much help anyhow." Vincent then introduced everyone in the room, confirming they were his father and in-laws. "Please sit wherever you'd like."

Amanda wished returning another time was an option, but this conversation would never be an easy one. "We won't be long, but, Mr. Tanner, it might be best if we could speak with you someplace a little more private," she said. "Say, the kitchen or dining room?"

Vincent glanced at his father, then nodded at Amanda. "All right." He took them to the dining table, where he sat on one side, while Amanda and Trent sat across from him.

There wasn't an easy way to bring up what was necessary. She'd get to the point. "Fresh evidence has surfaced, part of which has us suspecting the person who took Hailey latched on to her months ago. Even going back to last fall or winter." Consideration for Vincent's feelings had her going with *who took Hailey* not *who killed her*. It was also why she wasn't going to disclose they suspected a serial killer was behind his daughter's death.

The light dimmed in his eyes. "But you still aren't any closer to finding who did this?"

"We wish we had better news," Trent inserted. "But we're hoping you might help."

"I've told you everything."

"Except that now we're looking at a different timeline," Amanda stressed. "Were there any new friends or acquaintances that surfaced in the fall? New employees at your company? Other people you may have had in your home?"

"We're hiring interns all the time, but they have nothing to do with me. Human resources handle employees. No one from the office is brought into my personal life."

"Yet, it seems Nick Potter was," Amanda pointed out.

"The exception. We were friends before he came to work with me."

"All right, so no employee has dropped off any papers after hours or other such things?" Trent asked. He had his tablet out now and was making notes on it.

"No. When I come home, I shut business off."

"That can't be easy when you're the owner." She had a hard

time separating work from home, and she was a cog in the machine.

"It's not, but it's necessary and only fair that I be present with those I love."

"Any new friends or acquaintances?" She hadn't missed that he hadn't answered this part yet.

He shook his head.

"Fair enough," she said. "Do you know if your wife made any new connections?"

"My wife and I have open communication. If she had, she would have shared that with me."

"And no workmen around the house going back to the fall?" She reiterated her question from a moment ago. They'd asked about maintenance people on their first visit but not with consideration to the revised timeline.

"It's a rather new house, so no."

"What about strangers to the door, offering to do yardwork even? One of them could have gotten into the house." She felt like she was really grasping, but she had to do what she could to get Vincent thinking.

"I work long and unpredictable hours. Jean is busy with her friends and charities, but she never mentioned anyone. Mara might be the best to ask about laborers turning up."

"We will be talking to her again," Amanda said.

"Again? Then you already know that she has nothing to do with what happened to Hailey."

"She's not a suspect at this time. But what about new hobbies you and your wife may have taken up? Any exercise classes or new charity causes?" Thinking the killer was wrapped up in a goodwill organization sliced at her humanity, but evil knew no bounds.

"No." Vincent didn't meet her gaze, and his eyes had this blank quality to them.

He was probably consumed with guilt. Any respectable

husband and father took the role of family protector seriously. But he had failed to keep Hailey safe, and that must sting, even if it wasn't really his fault. "I'd like to ask about your parents—"

"Don't tell me you suspect they're involved somehow?"

She gave him a tight smile. "Not where I was heading with that question, but do they live local?"

"Yes."

"Do they ever come sit with Hailey or invite people into the home?" she asked, getting to the point of her interest in the older couples.

"They come over the odd time to watch Hailey."

"When was the last time?" Trent asked.

"Last summer? Before that? I can't remember. They're usually here when Jean and I are home."

"Okay, thank you, Mr. Tanner," she said. "We'll be in touch if we have any further questions or information to share."

Vincent nodded but remained seated.

Amanda and Trent saw themselves out, and back in the car, Trent turned to Amanda. "Off to speak with Mara Bennett again?"

"Seems like the right next step to me."

SIXTEEN

Katherine found it strange to be back inside the walls of Central. She was no longer a sergeant. No longer a cop. She wasn't even an employee of the PWCPD. No, a darker purpose had brought her back.

When she left to grab her research, she'd stopped by her aunt May's house. The intention was to tell her about Julie Gilbert, but May was getting ready to host her book club. Though more a social event for spreading gossip and consuming wine, cheese, and crackers than discussing literary takeaways, it made her aunt happy. And Katherine didn't want to bring down her mood, so she'd continue to sit with her secret.

Katherine popped another antacid, her fifth since Amanda and Trent showed up at the diner. She doubted it would matter if she swallowed all the chewable tablets in the bottle. The knot in the pit of her stomach was bound to stay there until they caught this guy. But it only added to the ache that had been in her chest from the moment she was called to the Gilbert home eleven-and-a-half years ago. She tried not to think that if Julie were alive today, she'd be thinking about what college to attend and what field to study.

For a reason that she couldn't explain at the onset, this case differed from any previous investigations involving children. She was thrust back to when she gave up her baby for adoption, thinking that was the best thing for them both. After the child had been born, she feared looking at her, afraid that she'd see her rapist's face staring back at her. For six years, she'd pushed the situation and the child out of her mind. Until Julie. Then the trauma resurged with such vengeance, it consumed her. If only she had made a different decision, would that young child still be alive?

Katherine had tried talking to a therapist about her daughter, leaving Julie unnamed. But she resisted their advice on the premise they couldn't relate. From there, her regrets fueled her to find justice for Julie. Even to get revenge, truth be told. But now to think another child had been punished because of her...

She popped the top on the antacids again, but snapped it back down. As she thought before, no point. Same as the killer's request for her to stop.

How could she ever do that? She chastised herself that she'd slipped in the last few months because she'd been busy at the diner. If only she had forged ahead, stayed up later at night, and dedicated every spare minute to finding Julie's killer. Would her efforts have netted their identity and saved the life of another young girl?

There was no way to answer that question. Trying would only drive her mad. No, she had to live with the fact her actions incited this monster to claim another child.

She'd love to write it off as "bad things happen," but it was far more complex than that. God, the universe, the divine, so often got things wrong. No fairness came with the death of a kid. That was why she had to step up, set things right.

Julie was given a different life from what Katherine would have given her. She wouldn't have paraded her around like a circus act, face painted up, and on display for everyone to see, for perverts to gawk at. She only wished she could transfer some guilt onto them. But the Gilberts weren't bad people. In fact, they were quite nice and down to earth. Probably much like the Tanners.

Hailey Tanner was also a little star from what Katherine had gleaned from Amanda and Trent. *A tiny ballerina...*

It angered her that the killer had taken out his issues against her on an innocent little girl. She might have spooked him, but only heaven could help him when she caught up with him.

Katherine set up her laptop on Amanda's desk. Malone said IT would assign her a login and password in the morning. But, in the meantime, she had things to do.

She signed on to her laptop and brought up the file listing the costume designers connected to the pageant circuit that Julie Gilbert had been a part of. She filtered out the ones that were male. As she told Malone, she was going to approach the designers' employers. Most of these were mothers of pageant contestants, and those in that circle were gossips and catty. An unfavorable term, but fitting. They all thought their daughter was special and better than the rest, and all of them would take whatever measures necessary to ensure they won. Whether it took knocking down the competition or sleeping with the judges. It made discerning fact from fiction a challenge. But for the times she'd spoken with the mothers over the years, the conversations were never focused on the costume designers. It would be interesting what they'd say about them.

She sorted her list of male names, each of whom had a column with their employer's name next to it. One was hired by the pageant itself and traveled from show to show, but the remaining seven were employed by the girls' mothers.

Katherine remembered how to use the station's phone system and used the one on Amanda's desk. Her first call rang to voicemail, and she left a vague message. She had better luck in reaching mothers as she moved on, but none had anything to offer the investigation.

She soon found herself down to one. Christi Rowland. As Katherine remembered her, Christi was a trophy wife who played out her own insecurities on her daughter, Kayla.

"Hello," a woman answered on the third ring, just when Katherine thought she was bound for another voicemail box.

"This is Katherine Graves. Is this Christi Rowland?"

"I'm going to need a little more than that."

"I was the lead detective investigating the Julie Gilbert case." The introduction was somewhat deceiving, but Katherine had put it in the past tense. Even before now, Katherine never disclosed she'd advanced rank or even left the NYPD. Any assumptions Christi made were on her.

"Oh? Is there a break in the case? Do you know who killed Julie?"

Besides some creep who's struck again... That thought fired through and had Katherine pinching her eyes shut and taking a few deep breaths.

"Detective?" Christi prompted.

"I'm here. And, no, the case hasn't been solved, but there has been a development." She'd hold back disclosing that *development* was the murder of another child. "I have a question about the man you employed to design and sew Kayla's costumes. Dustin Hawley."

"We parted ways a long time ago. Kayla's not in pageants anymore. She rebelled against it when she hit thirteen despite my argument that she was only hurting herself. I tried to help her see the competitions bring a lot of benefits. Besides confidence in herself, she can make some money, connect with people who can give her life-changing opportunities. But kids blank over when you talk about their futures."

Katherine would take her word on that. Her statement reminded her that Christi's priority had always been to get her daughter admitted to an Ivy League college. She saw the pageants as the path there. "Can you tell me more about Dustin? What was he like?"

"Why? Are you considering he killed that poor girl?"

Julie, just say her name! Katherine screamed in her head, but she composed herself before she spoke. "I'm just dotting more I's and crossing more T's."

"I don't know what else to say that I didn't years ago. The guy was the nicest one I ever met. He'd go above and beyond, even hand stitching sequins until the last hour. He gave up sleep for Kayla, more than once."

"And how was he with her?" Katherine inched forward, disgusted by the need to ask.

"If you're asking if he ever gave me the creeps, the answer is never. He and his boyfriend ended up getting married last fall. He sent me an invitation, but there was no way I was going to drag myself to Florida. Too many old, wrinkled retirees down there. Though, now that Bert and I have separated, maybe it's not a bad idea. I could marry myself a feeble, wealthy widower and be set for life."

From that summation, Dustin Hawley was pushed off the suspect list. "Just one more question. Do you remember seeing anyone backstage at the NYC pageant that stood out to you?"

"The one from just before...?"

"Yes. Julie's last. Anything or anyone at that pageant stand out?" The murder of a young child should be enough to earmark that time in the woman's memory.

"Huh. Now you ask. There was one woman. The rumor was she was sleeping with Mr. Gilbert."

Katherine was scrambling for a notepad and pen. Nothing supported Dawn Gilbert or her husband, Evan, having an affair. Assuming he'd hidden it well, what would have his mistress lurking around backstage at his daughter's pageant? "What was her name?"

"Anne... Let me think. Oh, Harrington."

"Anne Harrington?"

"That's right."

Katherine found paper and a pen and wrote the name down. "Why never mention her before now?"

"Why would I have? You were interested in any creepy men hanging around. The national news said that Julie was... Uh. Assaulted."

"That's true."

"And that's why. But Anne was a real psycho."

"How do you mean?"

"Oh, she went right up to Dawn and played nice, even brought her a coffee. Me and the other moms half expected it to be poisoned. That's why Laura knocked it out of her hand."

The mess Dickson was called to clean up.

"Do you know if Dawn's husband ended the affair?"

"I couldn't say."

Katherine drew a circle around Anne's name and stabbed the tip of her pen to the page a few times for emphasis. "Okay, thank you, Christi."

"Don't mention it. I'm happy to hear the NYPD is still on this case. Julie deserves justice."

Katherine tensed at the assumption but didn't bother correcting her. The woman's wording had also struck close to the name of her website. "Yes, she does."

She ended the call and stared at the name. Anne Harrington.

After all these years, this was the first time she'd come up. But Christi made a good point. Julie had been sexually assaulted. *However...* Katherine trembled. No DNA had been recovered from Julie's body. Had she made a fatal mistake by dismissing that lack of forensic evidence? If so, the FBI had too when they created their profile of the killer.

All she knew was a burning in her gut told her Anne

Harrington warranted further investigation. She looked around the cubicle warren assigned to Homicide. The seats were all empty except for one.

Katherine walked over. "Excuse me."

Natalie Ryan turned to face her. "Sergeant Graves? What are you doing here?"

"Well, not sergeant anymore." Katherine smiled.

"That's right. You retired your badge. I heard you're working with your aunt at her coffee shop."

"I am, but I've been brought in as a consultant for an open investigation."

"Oh, that sounds interesting."

"It's something anyhow." She had no intention of divulging any details to Natalie. "I was hoping you could help me with something."

"Sure, you name it."

Katherine walked into Natalie's office space. "I'm supposed to get my computer credentials in the morning, but I'd like to have a look at a background now. Do you think if I gave you the name, you could look it up and print it out for me?"

"Shouldn't be a problem."

"Wonderful, and I'll let Sergeant Malone know you pulled it for me. The name's Anne Harrington. She'd have had an address in New York City."

Natalie pecked on her keyboard and had the result rather fast. "Forty-eight, still lives in NYC by the look of it. But it looks like she has a few restraining orders to her name."

"I'll need all that information. Please."

"Sure." Natalie gave her a pressed smile. She hit some keys, and the printer in the corner whirred to life. "That will be the background, including the list of restraining orders against her."

"Thank you." Katherine rushed to scoop the paper from the tray and noted all the ROs were filed by men. She was *psycho* according to Christi, and the restraining orders suggested she had a hard time letting go of the men in her life. Could Anne have taken things further with Evan Gilbert? Had she targeted Julie to get his attention, to manipulate his affection? But if a relationship ever existed between her and Evan Gilbert, why wasn't it uncovered? And what could have led Harrington to assault and kill Hailey Tanner? How would she have been threatened by Katherine's sleuthing in the fall? But one step at a time.

SEVENTEEN

It only took Amanda knocking on Kendra Bennett's door one time, before it swung open. Kendra eyed Amanda and Trent with irritation. "If you're here to accuse my sister of anything, she won't talk to you without a lawyer."

"That's not why we're here," Amanda told her. "Can we come in?"

Strobes of colored light danced around the room, and voices came from the television. "Mar," Kendra called.

A light came on, and the TV was turned off.

"Yeah?"

"The detectives are back." Kendra turned to Amanda and Trent and told them they could come inside.

"Thanks." Amanda entered the living room first.

Mara was under a blanket on the couch and struggling to sit up while holding a glass of wine. She set it on the coffee table in front of her next to the bottle and another glass. "If I knew you were coming, I wouldn't be drinking." Mara balled up the blanket and placed it on the middle cushion.

"It's been an unbelievably rough day for her." Kendra poured out the rest of the wine into their glasses, then sat on the couch. "She loved that girl a lot." Kendra buried her nose in her large wineglass.

"We can imagine that it's been a rough few days, starting with Hailey's disappearance on Friday," Amanda said. "But we have a few questions for you."

Kendra pulled her nose out of her wineglass. "You're sure my sister shouldn't have a lawyer present?"

"That's up to her," Trent told her.

Kendra looked at her sister, who shook her head.

"Go ahead, and ask whatever you need to," Mara said.

Amanda dipped her head. "There's evidence that someone got into Hailey's room." She'd hold back the missing tutu and ballet slippers with it being a crucial part of the investigation. The fewer people who knew the better.

"How do you know that?"

"We're not at liberty to say," Amanda told her, while Trent took out his tablet and settled it on his lap.

Mara looked from him to Amanda. "Well, I'm not sure what more you need from me. I told you I had Nick over, but that's all. Did someone break into her room?"

Amanda thought of that miserable CSI with her inability to commit to a verdict. Was it a break-in or not? There wasn't an official ruling, but the unexplained smudges and broken lattice had Amanda leaning toward the former. "It's a possibility, but we need to explore everything. It was initially assumed that someone targeted Hailey very recently, but the investigation has broadened the timeline. Did you let anyone else into the home or around Hailey in the last six months? Say back to November of last year."

"Oh." Mara puffed out a breath, her cheeks ballooning.

"Other boyfriends?" Trent asked.

"Only Nick, who you know about."

"Then you didn't date other men before him? Or even after him?" Amanda wasn't going to limit the timing.

Mara stared into her wineglass and never took a sip.

"If there's something you should tell us, please do," Amanda encouraged.

The former nanny bit her bottom lip. "You asked about anyone who was around Hailey...?"

Amanda nodded.

"Well, I saw one other guy back in February, after things ended with Nick, but it was nothing. We had one date, and the guy ghosted me."

Trent looked up from his tablet. "What was his name?"

"Wilson something. His surname started with an M."

"Do you have any pictures of him?" Amanda asked.

"No, like I said, we had one date. Just a bite and a drink. He tried to get me to go out with him in January, but I told him I was sort of in a relationship."

Was his persistence a red flag, or was Amanda looking too hard? "But he tried again the following month?"

Mara shrugged. "He did."

"What did he look like?" Trent asked.

"Handsome face, cute dimples. Otherwise, just average height and build."

"Hair color? Eye color?" Amanda asked.

"Brown for both."

That vanilla description wasn't going to lead them to an arrest. "Any tattoos or other distinguishing markers?"

"Oh, he has a scar that runs through his top lip. It was obvious but somehow added character."

"Okay, that's good," Amanda said. "Was he ever around Hailey?"

"Once, for sure. I met him at Hailey's school after *The Nutcracker*. He bumped into me and was all apologetic and charming. Hailey was with me, and he made a tremendous fuss over her, telling her she was a wonderful dancer. He thought I was her mother and told me how she must have gotten her looks from me. He asked for my number, and I gave it to him, but then things had started with Nick before I heard from him." Mara stopped her recollection there. Her mouth gaped open, and her eyes widened. "Did I mess up not saying anything? Honestly, I'd put him out of my mind."

Amanda's earlier fears resurfaced. Had this man's pursuit of Mara been a ruse to get closer to Hailey? She tucked that thought away. "You were asked about more recent events. And we can't remember everything all the time."

"I feel so foolish. Was he only flattering me to get closer to Hailey?" Mara said, echoing Amanda's thoughts. She laid a hand over her stomach and sipped some wine. "If I'd kept my wits about me, would Hailey still be...?"

Amanda shook her head. "There's no point going down that road. And you just had that one date back in February?"

"Yeah, just the one."

"It's no wonder you didn't mention the guy. He's no one to you." Kendra placed a reassuring hand on her sister's shoulder.

Mara nodded. "And Detective McGee's questioning was more centered on the last few weeks."

"We work with what we know." It surprised Amanda that she came to McGee's defense. "You wouldn't have this guy's phone number, would you?"

"Actually, I might. I did save him in my contacts."

"We'll take that number if you still have it," Trent stepped in.

Mara reached for her phone from the side table and thumbed through it. Soon after, she was rattling off the digits, and Trent was pecking them into the notes app.

"Just one more thing before we leave. Did the Tanners employ anyone to work around the house? Or did anyone come to the door seeking employment?" They had what Vincent Tanner told them, but as per his admission, Mara would be the best person to ask since she was home most of the time.

"Nothing inside the home."

Amanda perked up at that. Vincent made it sound like no work had been done. "Outside then?" It could still have been a way for Hailey's killer to ingratiate himself with the girl, worm his way into the home.

"They hire a company to do the outdoor Christmas decorations every year, but that's nothing new."

That might be one reason Vincent never thought to mention them. "Do they come into the home? Maybe to use the washroom?"

"No, never. And they'd never have met Hailey. The decorating was done while she was at school, so she could come home to the house all lit up. She loved it." Mara closed her eyes, likely revisiting the memory, and seemed to retreat into it.

"All right. Thank you." Amanda got up, and after tucking his tablet away, Trent followed.

Back in the car, she turned to him. "We need to look further into this Wilson guy. Let's look up his number in the system. See if we get an address."

Trent took out his tablet, brought up his notes, and logged on to the onboard computer. He pecked the digits into the system, and got no hits at all. "Could be a prepaid number," he said as he pulled his phone. "I'm going to try calling." A second later, he was pressing his lips and shaking his head. "Out of service."

"Just like the number used to pose as Jean Tanner. That's probably not a coincidence."

"Even less so if we confirm this number is also attached to Universal Mobile."

"Uh-huh. I'll have Detective Briggs see if he can track who the service provider is for this number." She called Briggs to ask him to look into that and to expect a call from Katherine.

"Where to next?" Trent asked when she'd hung up.

"Well, the dance studio will be long closed, as will Hailey's school. I guess we're at a standstill until morning." She hated this admission, but it always felt like there was something more she could do.

"Not bad. It's only nine thirty. I might actually get some beauty sleep tonight."

She smiled at him. "Enjoy it, because we don't know where tomorrow will take us."

He turned to her and angled his head. "Let's try to stay positive."

"Yeah, it suits you better than me."

EIGHTEEN

Amanda had considered swinging past Libby's and grabbing Zoe on the way home last night, but it had been nine thirty, and Zoe would have been sound asleep. Waking her up just to squeeze her would have been selfish. But at least Amanda had the option to consider, unlike the Gilberts and Tanners. It didn't matter how much they wanted to hold their daughters. It would never happen again.

This morning, Amanda stirred awake before the sun and got an early start on the day. She stopped in at Hannah's Diner on the way to Central and got herself an extra-large coffee. May wasn't in, not that Amanda expected she would be. Since she'd hired more staff, she started after the sun came up.

Amanda reached her cubicle at seven thirty but found her desk occupied. "Katherine?"

"Oh, hi." Katherine pried her gaze from the screen of her laptop.

"You're in early." Amanda stayed in the opening because there was no room for her. Katherine had made herself at home. Papers were spread across every surface, including the floor. If that wasn't enough, the space felt more cramped since Katherine was an Amazon at six feet tall.

"I couldn't sleep." Katherine swiveled toward Amanda. Her eyes were bloodshot, and her cheeks were blotchy. "Any time I shut my eyes... Well, let's just say the images are worse than when they're open. Smart choice in coffee, by the way." She pointed at the Hannah's Diner cup in Amanda's hand.

"It's the *best* choice around here. I would have picked you one up if I'd known you were here."

"How could you have though? Don't worry, I brewed some here, though it's probably tar by now."

"How long have you been here?"

Katherine's gaze diverted for a moment.

"You were here all night," Amanda concluded.

"I'm sure I don't have to explain it to you, Amanda. You're much the same when something nabs your attention. There was no way I'd sleep, and if I'm just sitting around, I might as well be doing something."

Amanda could only imagine how her friend was suffering. "You realize that none of this is on you? This creep hurt and killed two little girls because he is sick."

"I know it here"—Katherine tapped her head, then laid a hand on her chest—"but here isn't buying it. Maybe if I can finally track this bastard down. Assuming we're looking for a man."

Amanda staggered a bit, then leaned against the partition. "Why wouldn't we be? There was evidence of sexual assault in both cases."

"Was there sperm or DNA for Hailey?"

"I'd assume so. I'm still waiting on the full autopsy report." It had to be a man, didn't it? No woman would...

"Well, there wasn't with Julie. There are many things that can explain no DNA, like the use of a condom. But it might be telling us something else."

"Are you suggesting that a woman is the perpetrator?"

"It is possible."

Amanda looked at Katherine's laptop, which was still open on the desk. "Do you have someone in mind?"

Katherine closed the lid and rocked her hand. "Kind of, but I need to dig into her more before I name names."

"Fair enough." The last thing Amanda needed was to be weighed down with another possibility. "Well, I'll share a name. Wilson M-Something. That ring any bells for you?"

"M-Something? Interesting surname." Katherine flashed a smile at her own joke. "No, I can't say that Wilson does. Do you have a photo?"

"Not this time."

"I can't help you then. Oh, look at me. I need to leave. This is your desk." Katherine scrambled to collect all the paperwork and files she'd laid out.

"You know what? Just stay put. Trent's not in yet. I'll just go next door and log on to his computer."

"Are you sure?"

Amanda dipped her head, smiled, and went to Trent's cubicle. The partition fabric must have wicked his woodsy cologne because that's all she could smell.

"Thank you."

"Don't mention it." Amanda logged on to his computer using her credentials. It would pull in her profile and settings. While she waited for it to load, she flipped back the tab on the lid of her coffee cup and savored a long sip.

Katherine was clicking on the other side, her fingertips tapping against the keyboard on her laptop. Amanda was curious about what she was doing but didn't want to subject her friend to an inquisition. If Katherine had something worth sharing, Amanda had faith she would.

Amanda opened her emails and watched two of importance

appear in her inbox. One from Briggs and another from Rideout. She opened Briggs's message first.

> *The number associated with Wilson M will require more digging to track down the location where it was sold. I can request warrant authorization to pursue, but do you have enough to support this? Let me know. I can, however, tell you it was serviced by Universal Mobile like the number used to contact Mara Bennett, posing as Jean Tanner.*

Amanda took another drink of her coffee and sat back satisfied. That both phones linked back to Universal felt too coincidental. Could it be that both tied back to this Wilson M?

She continued reading the rest of Briggs's email.

> *Unfortunately, there is no more I can tell you about the first number that texted Mara Bennett, posing as Jean Tanner. I'm sorry I couldn't have been of more help. Reach out if you need anything else.*
>
> *BTW, I heard from Katherine, and if you want to pass it along that I'm still working on her thing, I'd appreciate that.*

Amanda keyed back a quick response that she'd received his message and would get back to him on justification for a warrant. Then she looked over the partition and passed along Briggs's message for Katherine.

"Thanks. I didn't expect a miracle overnight."

"Then you don't know Briggs, because that man has pulled them off before." She smiled, hoping that the expression would lift her friend's spirits. Katherine put her head back down and was looking at her laptop.

So much for cheering her up... Though, in her place, it would take more for her. Amanda shook off the low-energy vibe and turned to the next email. Not that it helped her mood.

Rideout's autopsy report for Hailey Tanner. Amanda plucked out the highlights, which were more accurately *low*lights for their depravity. She stopped at the first point.

Evidence of sexual assault. No DNA or condom residue.

Could it be that Katherine was on to something with the perp being a woman? In Amanda's opinion, Wilson M deserved more attention. After all, Mara Bennett placed him at *The Nutcracker* making a fuss over Hailey. If only they could establish his identity, they may be on the way to tying him back to Julie Gilbert.

She returned to Rideout's email.

Concluding that cause of death was manual strangulation. The scarf was not used. The bruising provided an estimated handspan that would belong to a full-grown adult—man or woman. However, it's not distinct enough to provide a measurement that could be relied upon.

Time of death, as estimated before, is fixed between 11 PM Sunday to 5 AM Monday.

X-rays showed no broken bones or history of such.

Articles of clothing and scrapings from under the nails were sent to the lab for further processing.

Amanda processed one key takeaway. Nothing confirmed a man had done this.

She closed Rideout's email and saw that a new one had come in from CSI Blair. The subject was *Tanner Evidence*.

Amanda opened it and took in the bullet-point list that the investigator had laid out.

- *Carousel: public playground equipment. DNA and fingerprint evidence too plentiful to be helpful. A*

> *search of the immediate area never turned up*
> *anything of serious note.*
> - *Men's public restroom: garbage bag empty.*
>   *Nothing definitive as evidence connected to the*
>   *perp.*
> - *Hailey's clothing: Tutu and slippers showed no trace*
>   *or DNA other than hers. Female DNA was*
>   *recovered from the chiffon scarf and run against*
>   *elimination samples of Jean Tanner, Mara Bennett,*
>   *and Susan Butters. None were a match. Also no hits*
>   *in the system, period. But there were a few hairs on it*
>   *that came back belonging to a rabbit.*
> - *Tanner residence: Passed along from CSI Stuart*
>   *(seems you made an impression...) DNA swabs from*
>   *the closet door came back a match to Hailey and Jean*
>   *Tanner. Also the ballerina tutu and slippers were a*
>   *match to the ones found on Hailey Tanner in style,*
>   *size, and brand. This makes it likely they came from*
>   *the girl's closet. The scuff mark tested from the trellis*
>   *is a match for rubber used in the soles of commercial*
>   *running shoes.*

Amanda sat back, focused on the one finding associated with the scarf. *Female.*

A woman's DNA was on the scarf. But it could have been purchased by a man after a woman had tried it on and returned it to the rack. Or a man could have stolen it from somewhere as yet unknown.

"Amanda?" Trent was standing next to her. Based on the way he looked at her and the volume he'd used, he'd tried to get her attention already.

"Ah, yeah?"

"You're in my office."

"Nothing's slipping past you."

"Hilarious." When she didn't join in his amusement, he became serious. "What is it?"

"We have the results from Briggs, Rideout, and Blair."

"Sounds like the morning's off to a good start."

"Not entirely. We have another mystery." She ran through the findings with him. By the time she'd finished, he was leaning on the edge of his desk, facing her.

"I'm having a hard time dismissing that Wilson M's phone ties back to Universal Mobile too. But they are a large company." The phone on Trent's desk rang, and he answered. A few seconds later, he was saying, "We'll be right there." When she cocked her head, he filled her in. "That was Malone from the conference room. I guess he's there with Katherine and the police chief already. Time to go get briefed on the Gilbert case."

She got up, thinking she must have sunk into her work. She never noticed Katherine leave her cubicle.

NINETEEN

Katherine watched Amanda and Trent enter the conference room. Amanda's posture became a touch more rigid when she saw the chief, and she gave him a tight smile in response to him dipping his head in greeting.

"If we could get this meeting started, I have another appointment in thirty minutes." Buchanan made a show of looking at his watch by flinging his arm out. His sleeve shimmied up his arm and exposed some fancy timepiece.

"Yes, of course." Malone gestured for Amanda and Trent to sit down.

They sat across from Malone and Buchanan, while Katherine was at the head of the table.

"Considering my familiarity with the Gilbert case, selecting key points was challenging, but I think it's best to establish the basics of the investigation. Julie was found the morning after the Gilberts held a party at their home in NYC. She had been sexually assaulted and strangled. She was only six years old."

"Was the party for any specific reason?" Trent asked.

"Not really. More or less to blow off steam. The pageant had wrapped up that day. Julie didn't win, but the Gilberts wanted to connect with the parents and guardians of the contestants, also the judges."

"A political move," Buchanan said.

"That's right. Somewhere along the lines of keep your enemies close."

"The way you put that, it sounds like the Gilberts didn't get along with others in the competition," Amanda said.

"They got along to get along, but that said, there were no deep animosities between them either. Relatives and friends were investigated with scrutiny."

"Help me understand how the parents lost track of their child?" Buchanan asked.

"There was a lot of drinking and Julie was left to entertain herself," Katherine said.

"Were there other children at this party?" Malone asked.

"Just adults, except for Julie. Later that night, Dawn Gilbert, Julie's mother, told Julie she could sleep in the treehouse in the backyard. After the guests left, the Gilberts stumbled to their bed." After finding out Julie was her biological daughter, it took years for Katherine to forgive the Gilberts for that negligence.

"Not exactly parents of the year," Trent put in. "Unbelievable. You invested time looking into friends and family, but did you question the party guests? I'm just thinking it would make sense considering when Julie was murdered."

"I did my best, but it was a rather open invite extended to everyone with the pageant. Many of the people who we got names for are from other parts of the country. Of course they were pursued as much as possible, but it only led to dead ends."

"I can see how something like this could go cold. Just so many places to look." The chief crossed his arms and leaned back in his chair. His earlier desire to rush out of there must have left.

"Yes, and with an open invite, it was impossible to track

down everyone who was there," Katherine said. "But it's important to focus on what we think triggered this person back into action. The consensus seems that it's related to inquiries I made last fall. I was interested in those with backstage access at the NYC venue for Julie's last pageant, stemming from this photograph." Katherine turned her laptop to face those in the room. It showed a man in his late forties looking over his shoulder at Julie, who was mid-twirl.

"He doesn't look like he's up to any good," Buchanan said.

"Which is what I thought, but that's Hank Dickson."

"Who you cleared?" When she nodded, Buchanan added, "Malone briefed me on that."

Katherine flipped her laptop around and closed the lid. "After the note in the hem of Hailey's tutu, attention shifted to male costume designers."

Buchanan raised a pointed finger. "Did you speak with these people in the fall?"

"I did."

"All right. Go on." Buchanan gestured for her to continue.

"After I was cleared last night, I reached out to the people who employed these male costume designers, viewing this as a workaround. Just in case. It could still give me an idea of what they were like. I had to leave some messages, but I'd like to pull their backgrounds." Katherine looked at Malone.

"I'll make sure you get the IT permissions right after we're finished here," Malone said. "Just tell me if anyone flags."

"Will do," Katherine told him.

Buchanan sat back in his chair, clasped his hands over his stomach. "I must admit that I have mixed opinions about your assisting with this case in any capacity."

Her stomach dropped out. *Is he going to take this away from me now?*

Buchanan continued. "After all, the killer's note makes it quite clear what they will do if you are involved. But with that said, I believe the threat is misleading. This person is wired differently than the rest of us. They've done this at least twice that we know of, and there is very little chance of rehabilitation in this type of individual. That reality is why I consented to your help, but I can't stress enough that you need to watch your back." Buchanan glanced over at Malone. "Did you arrange a protective detail for her when she's not at the station?"

"I have," Malone confirmed.

Katherine shifted on her chair, uncomfortable being discussed as if she wasn't in the room. But that wasn't the only thing making her uneasy. Her next admission was going to rip at her pride. How she might have focused on the wrong avenue for the past twelve years. That was unforgiveable. But she had no choice but to set her ego aside. Not if speaking up meant justice for Julie. No one was speaking, so this was her opportunity. "As I mentioned at the onset, Julie was sexually assaulted, but no DNA was left behind."

"The same is true for Hailey Tanner," Amanda said.

This revelation had Katherine going cold. "Then we could be looking at a woman."

Everyone's head turned to her.

"I think with a crime like this one, it's more likely a man," Buchanan said.

"Well, that's what I'd always thought, but there's nothing pointing to a man directly, just probability. It might be time to open our minds. In that endeavor, I've flagged someone as a person of interest." Now the words were out, she wished she'd held off until she'd gathered more to support her suspicion. But was there any time to waste? "I told you a moment ago that I called the employers of costume designers. Well, one of those mothers ended up letting something slip." She told them about Anne Harrington's alleged affair with Evan Gilbert, how it had been on and off again for years and how Harrington had been present backstage at Julie's last pageant. She stressed again that this was when and where the photo of Dickson was taken. She disclosed the restraining orders against the woman and how she had Detective Ryan pull the background. She concluded with, "I have Detective Fitz with the NYPD stopping by her place, seeing if we can tie her to Woodbridge."

"But surely there must be more than that," Malone put in. "What would make this woman target and hurt children? With that said, you must have established a profile?"

Katherine nodded. "We worked with the FBI's Behavioral Analysis Unit. They put a profile together for us. They figured male, in his early to mid-thirties, likely someone who suffered abuse as a child or was from a broken home with exposure to domestic violence. This person may battle mental health issues and have low self-esteem. They may feel incompetent and harbor shame, and as a result are socially awkward. He will have little going for him in his personal and professional lives, so this reinforces his beliefs of worthlessness. He abuses children to feel a sense of control, as if that can somehow mend his own pain."

"If that's the case, we could be looking at more girls we don't know about," Amanda said, her face pale.

"We could be." Katherine met her friend's gaze. "But going back to Harrington, I'd like to dig into her past more."

Buchanan tapped the edge of the table and got up. "Definitely keep on that, and keep me posted." With that, the chief swept out of the room.

Malone followed soon after with Trent at his heels.

Amanda came over and put her hand on Katherine's shoulder. "We'll find this person. Man or woman."

Katherine wished she felt that confidence, but twelve years of hard work hadn't accomplished that.

TWENTY

Amanda was finding it hard forging ahead after what Katherine disclosed. But on the chance Anne Harrington didn't pan out, she and Trent needed to keep following other leads. That's why she had Trent take them to Tiptoe Studio.

At nine o'clock, they pushed through the door and a bell chimed over their heads. A counter was right inside, backed by a wall with another door. It must have separated the studio from the public eye.

A woman in her twenties came through the door and was smiling broadly until she saw their badges. "Ms. Blackwell said I'm not supposed to talk to the police. I'll go get her."

"Thank you," Amanda told her. Candace Blackwell was the studio owner and who they wanted to talk with anyway.

The twenty-something retreated through the door, and moments later, it opened again. This time a trim woman in her fifties with gray hair emerged. Before she or Trent could say a word, she spoke.

"I have nothing more to say to the police."

"That may be, but we're Detectives Steele, and Stenson and

there are questions we need to ask you about Hailey Tanner," Amanda said.

Candace let out a heaving breath. "You're new to me. Major Crimes or Homicide?"

"Homicide," Trent confirmed.

"I saw the news, but I still can't believe it. Such a horrible shame. I'm not sure what else I can do. I answered all of Detective McGee's questions when Hailey went missing. I never saw anyone suspicious hanging around that day, and neither did any of my staff."

"That's the thing," Amanda began. "Recent evidence has led us to suspect the person who took Hailey may have been stalking her for months. So we're interested in more than just last Friday when she was taken."

Candace gripped the fabric of her shirt over her heart. "My answer doesn't change. No one suspicious stood out to me."

Before Amanda or Trent could say anything else, the front door opened and a woman in her thirties came inside.

Candace smiled at her and held the door. "Emily, please come through."

The woman accepted the invitation, and Candace closed the door behind her. She leveled her gaze at Amanda and Trent. "Now is not a good time."

"It hasn't been a *good* time for Hailey's family either," Amanda said in a level tone, while fighting against anger and the unfairness of what happened to Hailey.

Candace's face softened. "I can give you five minutes, but that's all."

"Thank you." Amanda followed the woman, with Trent behind her, to the second floor. On the way, they passed three dance studios. One door was shut, but an upbeat tempo filtered into the hall.

"Please, sit. Make yourselves comfortable." Candace stood

at the door of a small meeting room and gestured for them to go inside first.

The three of them sat down, and Amanda got started. "So from our understanding, Hailey attended your five o'clock session this past Friday."

"That's right."

"And class ended at what time?" Trent asked, pulling out his tablet.

"It was six. By the time Hailey changed into other clothes to leave, you could add twenty minutes to that. Little girls don't move that fast unless they're going for ice cream." The tiniest of smiles twitched her lips before fading into oblivion.

"I can agree with that," Amanda said. Lindsey and Zoe were the same way. "Did you help Hailey change and lock up her outfit at the end of class on Friday?"

"I did."

Amanda nodded. "So you waited around, locked her locker, and saw her out?"

"Yes, to the first part. She walked downstairs and outside on her own."

She was only six... Amanda kept the thought to herself. "We understand there are no security cameras inside or outside the building?"

"That's correct, but it's a safe neighborhood, a safe building."

"That's why you were comfortable letting Hailey wait for her ride home on the sidewalk? Even though she's six years old?" Amanda couldn't hold back any longer, and the enclosed accusation tumbled out.

"It's not like we just tossed her out the door," Candace rushed to defend herself. "Her nanny always picked her up at six thirty. We could see Hailey through the front window."

"Then you saw who picked her up?" Trent asked.

Candace let out a deep sigh. "No, but Steph, that's the girl who greeted you when you arrived, was working. She should have been posted there."

This news hadn't reached Detective McGee, or in the least hadn't hit the investigation files. And if Steph routinely watched out for Hailey, wouldn't she have seen that someone different had come for her? "All right. We'll want to speak with her when we're finished here."

"That's fine, if she agrees. I'm not going to make her. Tiptoe would never allow harm to come to that girl, but we don't run a daycare either. It's a dance studio."

Amanda could point out that the parents probably saw things differently, how they entrusted their children to Candace's care, but the combative spirit would shut down communication.

"Was Hailey the only one dropped off and picked up for lessons?" Trent asked.

"No, it's what we recommend, so the students aren't distracted. It's never been a problem before. I inherited the studio from my parents, and it's been here for fifty years."

"Congratulations on such a milestone," Amanda said.

"Thank you," Candace responded, ice in her tone.

"Just a few more questions," Amanda began. "Have you had any new hires in the last seven months?"

"No."

"No one? Not even new cleaners?" Amanda figured this one area might be overlooked if someone else was contracted to do the work.

"No."

"Do you handle the cleaning in-house or pay another company?" Amanda asked.

"We all pitch in."

Amanda nodded, satisfied enough to move on. "What about dance competitions and public events Hailey took part in? Anyone new in that crowd, or a person who stands out to you?"

She knew what Jean had told them, but wanted to hear from Candace.

"Most of our students enter competitions, but Hailey never did. That was a shame too. Hailey was an incredible dancer, a true natural."

"Why didn't she?" Trent asked, playing along.

"Her mother wouldn't allow it. Teaching Hailey ballet wasn't about glory or even for her future career. She hoped that dance would challenge and stimulate her from an intellectual standpoint." Candace looked at Amanda. "If you have kids, please be sure to grab a brochure listing all our classes before you leave. I can't recommend dancing lessons enough for young children."

It was distasteful that she'd worked in a sales pitch, but Amanda considered the offer anyhow. Zoe had lit up seeing figure skaters take to the ice near Christmas. She might like ballet. "I'll consider it. I think that's all we have for you, if you could get Stephanie for us?"

"Sure." Candace rose from her chair with the grace of a dancer and left the room.

"I can't believe they just let a six-year-old stand outside alone," Trent said under his breath.

"Me either, even if there were eyes on Hailey. And if there were, I don't understand how she just disappeared."

"That makes two of us. I don't remember seeing Stephanie's name in McGee's reports."

"It wasn't in there."

The woman from the front desk entered the room and took the chair closest to the door.

"Stephanie?" Amanda asked.

"Yes. My last name is Welch."

"Detectives Steele, and Stenson," Amanda said. "We understand you were working last Friday night."

"I was."

"And what is your job at the studio?" Trent asked.

"Reception and clerical. Basically everything administrative."

"Did you see Hailey leave the studio to wait for her ride on Friday?" Amanda just wanted to get to the meat of it.

"I..." Stephanie closed her mouth and flicked her gaze back and forth between Amanda and Trent.

"You can tell us what you saw," Amanda encouraged, sensing her trepidation.

"I never saw anything." She tugged on the cuff of her sleeves and twisted the fabric.

Amanda pointed at her fidgeting. "It seems you did."

"That's the thing. I didn't, but if this gets back to Ms. Blackwell, I'll be in trouble."

"Help us understand," Amanda coached her.

"I'm supposed to be at the desk and watching any girls if they are outside waiting for their ride home."

Amanda had a sour feeling starting in the pit of her gut. "But you didn't last Friday?"

"Yes and no. My personal cell phone rang, and I'm supposed to have it off at work. It was in my purse under my desk, and I bent over to pick it up. I was fast, but by the time I sat back up, Hailey was gone."

Amanda bristled at this revelation. It could have been a deliberate ploy used by Hailey's abductor to distract the clerk's attention. "Who called you?"

Stephanie bit her bottom lip. "This can't get back to Ms. Blackwell. She'd fire me, but I'm looking for a new job. This was always supposed to be a temp thing for me, but with the current job market, it feels like I'm stuck here."

"And this call was...?" Amanda would love it if she just came out with it.

"A call for an interview. It would have been great too, but it didn't work out."

"Where was this?"

"A vet's office in town." She provided the name. "I love animals, and one day I'd love to go to school and become a vet."

"And who was the interview with?" Amanda asked.

"Kim Booker."

"Can I see your phone?" Amanda asked. "I'd like to verify that call."

"Ah, sure." Stephanie pulled it from her pocket.

So much for no personal calls on company time... The fact she had the device on her showed her rebellious streak and her desperation to find another job.

Stephanie unlocked her phone, tapped on the screen, and handed it to Amanda.

It didn't take long to see the call from the veterinary clinic. "Would you mind if I called them?"

Stephanie shook her head, and Amanda pressed the Call button. An eager-sounding employee answered on the second ring. "Could I speak with Kim Booker, please?" When the woman came on the line, Amanda verified Stephanie's story and thanked the woman.

"You really needed to check up on me?" Stephanie asked, her voice a touch shrill.

"This is an open murder investigation. We check up on everything." Amanda handed Stephanie's phone back to her.

"So because of this phone call, you never saw who picked Hailey up?" Trent asked.

"That's right," Stephanie said, working her phone back into her pocket.

"And she was the only one waiting for a ride that night?" One of the other parents or students could have seen something worth following up.

"Hailey was the last one left. I just can't believe that..." A rogue tear splashed Stephanie's cheek, and she swiped it away. "I'll never forgive myself."

Amanda was lost for words. Nothing she could say would offer the young woman solace. Would the person who took Hailey have been identified before they killed her? They'd never know. She just couldn't imagine that McGee had dropped things and never asked Stephanie what they just had. "Did you see anything that stood out to you?"

Stephanie bit her bottom lip and shook her head.

"On another note, did you ever notice anyone lurking around the studio? Not just this past Friday? Anytime in the last several months?" Amanda asked.

"No one that stood out. But why are you interested in that far back?"

"It's possible the person who killed Hailey was stalking her for a while," Amanda said, setting that out gently. Stephanie already held herself to blame for slipping up on Friday night.

"Well, I never saw anyone," Stephanie repeated.

"Thank you, Stephanie." Amanda handed over her card. "Call me if you think of something after we've left."

"Will do."

Amanda and Trent made their way out of the studio, and she was listening to McGee's line ringing before she hit the sidewalk.

"McGee here."

"Detective Steele. Did you speak with Stephanie from Tiptoe Studio about last Friday?"

Trent was watching her as she spoke.

"Of course I did."

"What did she tell you?"

"She said she never saw who picked Hailey up."

"It seems she made it sound to you like she was watching Hailey the entire time she waited for her ride."

"That's how I remember our conversation."

"Well, the truth we just got out of her was she was distracted for a moment or two, and when she next looked

Hailey was gone. So Hailey could have walked off with her would-be killer, even transported in a vehicle that was parked down the street."

"Which is news to me. Hell."

"Why wasn't Stephanie Welch in your report?" Grilling him about not returning her call was pointless, but he wasn't off the hook twice.

"Oh, she's there, but not by name. She's included in the summary that staff at the studio didn't see anyone."

Amanda looked at Trent and shook her head. "You said you checked for security cameras in the area. How far down the street did you check?"

"The neighboring businesses two up and down."

"But not past that?" she asked.

"Not about cameras. The units across the street are apartments. Officers canvassed with no success. They also asked everyone they came across if they saw Hailey that day. Oh, and there's no municipal CCTV in that area."

"Okay, thank you, Detective." Amanda hung up and tapped her phone against her leg as she briefed Trent on the conversation.

"A summary," Trent mumbled.

"That's what he said, but we can likely agree on one thing. The person who took Hailey has their own transportation."

"Which would make sense. How could you abduct a kid or dispose of a body using public transportation? With that said, Hailey must have trusted this person to go along with them. Otherwise, she would have raised a fuss and made a scene, which would have drawn attention."

"Which leads my mind right to Wilson M-Something. She had met him before. If this is Wilson, he could have collected Hailey using a lie that Mara was going to pick her up from his place."

"True. Not that we're closer to his identity. And I'm not seeing how that links to the woman Katherine flagged."

"Who knows if it does? And we still don't know if she is the killer. Did you ever receive the camera footage from the park?" There was the possibility it captured the killer's face. Though it might be a pipe dream to invest hope in netting an ID through facial recognition.

"Not yet, but I expect it should come through sometime today."

"Follow up if you don't have it by noon."

"Sure. But there's something else we might want to consider. Not saying he, or she, doesn't have a vehicle, but do they live nearby?"

Amanda looked at the buildings across the street, the ones that McGee just said contained apartments, but that was a little too close to ground zero. A chill laced down her spine though, and she had the sensation she was being watched. When she looked around, she didn't spot anyone. She glanced up at the apartment windows but couldn't see any shadows behind them either. She dismissed her feelings as her imagination. "The only thing with that theory is we have no way of narrowing that down unless..."

"Oh, I know that face. You have an idea."

"McGee checked on the neighboring businesses to see if they had cameras but hit a dead end. He only went a few doors down on each side though."

"Ah, so you're thinking if he walked with Hailey a bit, then ones farther down the street might prove useful."

"If they have them, yes." While Amanda was hoping for some lead to break this case open, she didn't expect it would be so easy.

TWENTY-ONE

Things turned out just as Amanda expected. They were walking away with no video footage to show for their trouble. It was either broken cameras or none were installed to start with. Most people told them the neighborhood was safe. One person had changed their opinion since Friday, though, and said they'd already contacted a security company to enhance protection, including camera installation. Too little, too late...

Trent pulled into the lot for Hailey's school around noon. The timing should work to catch the principal before they left for lunch, unless they'd slipped out for an early one. She and Trent had grabbed a quick bite to eat before driving over.

They went into the school and were seated in the principal's office within a handful of minutes. Marvin Hatfield was a bit on the stocky side, in his late forties, with a friendly face.

He was seated behind his desk, and Amanda and Trent were in chairs facing him.

"The entire school is in shock," Marvin told them. "It's all so surreal. I worry most about the students. Many of them are struggling with Hailey's murder. We're holding an assembly later this afternoon to let them know the school is here for them, and if they want to talk to someone, the counselor is always available. We'll stress there's no shame in seeking help. In fact, it's a strong thing to do. We'll also cover basic safety measures they can all take to protect themselves. You know, like don't talk to strangers, that type of thing."

"That's an important message," she said, not missing that he'd teed things up for what they needed to discuss. "Speaking of safety measures, does the school have security video outside?"

"It does. On the doors. If you want to watch any of the footage, I can make it available to you. But she wasn't taken from here."

"No, but we've learned Hailey Tanner took part in the school's performance of *The Nutcracker*," Trent said.

"Sure, back in December."

"That event was open to the public, correct?" Trent asked.

"That's right." A tightness edged into his voice.

"Watching any video from that evening could be imperative to the investigation." Though it might be too much to hope they'd be able to pluck Wilson M out of the footage.

"I will get that for you."

"That would be appreciated," Amanda said. "Is there any way of getting a list of names for people who attended the show?"

"No, as your partner said, it was open to the public. Cash only, and no names were collected."

"But the show was performed by young children, Mr. Hatfield. There must have been some concern about their safety." This was the mother in her taking issue with an open house at the school. Anyone could make their way inside, including people with ill intentions.

Marvin stiffened. "We had the standard school security. Bag checks, wands for knives and guns."

"Okay, thank you, Mr. Hatfield," Trent said. "If you could

get that video together and send it to the address on here." He presented the principal with his card, pointing out his email.

"Will do."

Marvin kept his eye on Amanda as she went to leave, which she knew because she was looking at him.

Once they hit the fresh air of the parking lot and got into the car, she turned on Trent. "I feel like I'm on a leash. What was that about?"

"What was what about?" he pushed back.

"You stepped in back there, called an end to the meeting."

"I thought we were finished with him. We asked all we came to ask."

"That's not the point."

"What am I missing? You call an end to most of our interviews, but I never say a thing."

"I'm the senior detective." The words were out, and she wished she could pull them back. He pursed his lips, and his cheeks flashed red. "I shouldn't have said that."

"No, you're right, but I also know you, Amanda."

She couldn't argue with the truth, and they both knew it.

"I could see that you were getting on his bad side. He gets his back up, he's suddenly less cooperative, and we need that video."

"We'd get it even if he didn't like me."

"True. I'm sure we could get a warrant and force him to hand it over, but you're not the only one feeling the loss of that little girl. That man is reeling too. I certainly wouldn't want to trade places with him. Imagine being responsible for Hailey and this happening to her. That's before having it pointed out to him that his school has security loopholes."

"He should already know that. I just hate the idea of strangers wandering off the street into public schools." And like that, this conversation turned personal. Zoe had been kidnapped from her school not long after Amanda had taken her in.

"It wasn't like that, and you know it."

"Do I?"

"Come on, they aren't the first school to hold a public event. They won't be the last."

"Maybe not, but there should be more accountability, more security."

"Sure, but that's a matter for another day."

Before she could respond, her phone rang. She answered without noting the caller's identity because she just wanted a pause from this conversation with Trent.

"It's Katherine. Return to Central. I have something you're going to want to hear."

TWENTY-TWO

Amanda and Trent raced to Central and were directed to the conference room. Katherine and Malone were in there, and both turned their heads to the doorway when they entered. She breathed easier when she noted Buchanan wasn't present. Whether that luck would hold out remained to be seen. "No police chief for this one?" She'd rather be prepared for his arrival if he was expected.

"Not this time," Malone said. "He's in meetings, but I'll be briefing him."

"I'll keep this short and quick." Katherine handed each of them a printout of Anne Harrington's photo. "For all these years the Gilbert investigation was focused on a male perp, as you know."

"The FBI's profile and the sexual assault element," Malone summarized. "But I'm guessing your digging into Harrington paid off?"

"It has. The raw facts are Harrington had no business being backstage that day. She doesn't take rejection well, and the family of her former lover was there. There's no saying how far she would go to retaliate."

"Former?" Amanda asked.

"Yes, I spoke to Evan Gilbert. He admitted to the affair in the years before Julie, and that it was casual on and off after, even at the time of her murder. He said he never mentioned Harrington because he couldn't see her doing this to Julie. When I pushed him on why he'd ended things, he said that he'd had enough of her manipulation tactics. She'd play up feeling abandoned by him when he had to go home to his family."

"Or she *didn't* play it up," Amanda said. "That feeling could have been genuine. She may have been abused or neglected as a child."

"Okay, hell hath no fury like a woman scorned, but don't you think assaulting and killing a child pushes things a bit far?" Malone asked.

"Valid question, and I considered that myself. Short answer, no. Not after speaking with some men who have ROs against Harrington. The three I reached all said the same thing. She was high-maintenance and needy and didn't understand boundaries even before the relationships ended. They said that she would pitch a fit, scream and cry and hurl things across the room, when she felt her control slipping."

"Whoever did this to Julie and Hailey aspires to be in control," Amanda reasoned. "Or at least to feel like they are."

"Exactly."

"Huh," Malone huffed. "I admit the more I hear, the more this Harrington sounds worth investigating further."

"And get this, Harrington used to work at the NYC venue," Katherine started. "Now this was years before Julie's last pageant but..."

"She could have remained in contact with someone who worked there to get backstage," Amanda finished up what she believed was Katherine's thought.

Katherine nodded.

"Which could also be how she found out about your interest in those backstage," Trent put in.

"It's possible. I called my contact there. Leslie Gallagher is the manager and the one I spoke to in the fall. She confirmed she was friends with Harrington for a while, but that they hadn't been in touch for a long time. She told me that Anne had a rough childhood. No father in the picture, and her mother neglected her. Even as a young girl, Anne had to fend for herself."

"Like the FBI profile," Amanda said. "They pegged the killer as coming from a broken home."

"That's right. Now you probably remember my telling you I reached out to Detective Fitz to chat with Harrington. Well, get this. She wasn't home. In fact, the landlord said Harrington rented her place out on short-term lease. The reason? Harrington was going to be visiting family here in Virginia."

"Let me guess. No family?" Malone said.

"Oh, she has family. A grandmother right here in Wood-bridge, and I have her address."

"When did she come here?" Amanda asked. There had to be even more to this find that had netted Katherine's suspicion.

"Detective Fitz said she was here for the start of December."

"In plenty of time to latch on to Hailey Tanner at *The Nutcracker*." Amanda looked at Trent as she got up. "We'll go talk to her right now."

TWENTY-THREE

Amanda banged on the door for a second time. The address of Anne Harrington's grandmother took her and Trent to a small white-sided house. The lot was tiny too, with the front step only about ten feet from the sidewalk. No car was parked in the driveway, but one could have been in the detached garage next to the house.

She was just about to turn around and give up when the door cracked open. An elderly woman with white hair stood there. She was hunched and regarded them with watery eyes.

"Yes?" One word, and the woman's voice sounded stretched, like it took great effort to project that much.

A late-model silver Ford Mustang pulled into the driveway. Anne was behind the wheel. The car came to a jerking stop, and Anne catapulted from it and brushed past Amanda and Trent.

"Grandma, what are you doing up?"

The older woman retreated into the house guided by her granddaughter. Once she was tucked inside, Anne turned on them.

"I don't know what this is about, but my grandmother needs all the rest she can get. She's battling dementia and doesn't need strangers turning up at the door."

"We're not strangers, Ms. Harrington," Amanda said as she pulled her badge. "We're detectives with the Prince William County PD, and we need to have a talk with you."

"With me? Why? I haven't done any— Did Bruce send you here? I called him. That's all. The RO just says I'm not to come within a thousand feet of him."

Amanda glanced at Trent.

"We're going to need to talk with you down at Central Station," he said.

"What? No. There's no way I'm going to leave my grandmother."

"You realize you already had? You just returned," Amanda pointed out.

"I just popped to the store a block down and was gone like five minutes. You can't bully me around. I know my rights." Anne went to shut the door on them, but Trent stepped in front of Amanda.

"So do we, and you're a person of interest in a murder case. It's your choice. You come with us peacefully or we force your cooperation."

Anne's eyes jabbed left and right, and left again. Amanda could call it before the woman set one foot in front of herself. They had a runner. But she didn't head for the front door. Instead, she spun and headed farther into the house. The bottom of her shoes slapped against the old wood flooring, leaving an audible trail to follow. The challenge was navigating the mess of furniture and junk all over the house. Grandma Harrington was a borderline hoarder.

Amanda ran after Anne to the back of the house and through a cluttered kitchen. Dirty dishes and pots were stacked in the sink, on the counters, and on the stovetop. Anne threw a screen door open. It screeched on its hinges and sprung back. Amanda caught it just before it smacked into her and bolted outside.

Anne was taking a sharp left to round the house.

"She's going for her car," she called out to Trent, who spun around and tore back through the house to the front.

Amanda shouted to Anne to stop but no luck. She watched as she slipped behind the wheel of the Mustang. Trent reached the driveway just as Anne was tearing out. The wheels of her car were kicking up plumes of dust from the gravel driveway.

"I'll call it in. You catch us up," she told him.

They were just about to get into the department car when they heard a loud, sickening crunch.

"That can't be good." Trent's words came out in slow motion while they both ran toward the road.

Sure enough, just a few houses down, the silver Mustang was hugging a pole, steam rolling out of the hood.

Amanda pulled her phone to call it in when the driver's door opened, and Anne emerged. She glanced over her shoulder, and upon seeing them, she bolted.

"Here we go again." Amanda tore after her, thankful she kept herself in relatively good shape.

Trent started behind but blew past her.

Ahead, Anne went down a side street and started shrieking for help like she was insane.

"PWCPD! Stop!" Trent yelled, and Amanda picked up speed.

Anne looked over her shoulder just as a van backed out of a driveway a few feet in front of her.

"Stop!" Amanda called out, but it was too late.

Anne turned around only to smash her face smack-dab into the side of the van. She crumpled to the ground.

Amanda caught up to Trent, and he turned to her. "Why do they always run?"

She shrugged. "They think they can get away."

"Then they don't know who they're dealing with." Trent smiled at her, and she grinned back. If Anne Harrington was the monster they were after, she deserved to feel pain.

TWENTY-FOUR

"Tell me what happened. I want to hear everything." Malone only lowered his last request a couple of decibels while he stared down Amanda.

The fact the two of them and Trent were in a hospital emergency room did little to douse his temper. It might have had the opposite effect... "We just knocked on her grandmother's door and—"

"I have a headache." Malone rubbed his brow.

Amanda continued. "Anne returned home and immediately took issue with us being there. As soon as we mentioned a murder investigation, she bolted. She got into her car, took off, and crashed into a pole."

"Then she got out of her car and started running again. This time right into the side of a van," Trent said, wrapping up the recap.

"Sounds about right." Amanda winced. Malone didn't like messy, and this had *messy* written all over it. The owner of the van was threatening a lawsuit against the PWCPD for mental trauma. When Anne had regained consciousness, those were her first words too. Not that either of those threats would carry weight with any judge, in any courtroom.

Malone grumbled. "And now, we're waiting for clearance to question this Harrington lady? But she's going to be all right?"

"I guess we'll find out." Amanda straightened her posture as a doctor in a white coat came over to them.

"Detective Steele?" The man regarded her with curiosity from behind the bluest eyes she'd ever seen.

"That's me. Call me Amanda." She'd almost stammered, and ignored the looks she was getting from Malone and Trent.

"I'm Carter. Well, Dr. Paulsen."

An awkward, silent pause felt much, *much* longer.

He cleared his throat. "I was told that you followed Anne Harrington here and are interested in speaking with her when she's available."

"That's right." Her mouth became dry.

"Is she ready for us now?" Trent asked, stepping in.

Carter pried his gaze from Amanda to look at Trent. "She's suffering from a mild concussion, bruised ribs... Just to make sure I have this right. She was in a car accident and then got out and ran into the side of a van?" He pantomimed the situation, smacking the walking fingers of his left hand into the palm of his right. When he finished speaking, the doctor looked at her again.

"What can I say? It hasn't been her day," she offered.

"I'd say not." Carter smiled at her, and he had such deep-set dimples she could press a fingertip in them.

But just like that, her brain returned. Dimples was one descriptor that Mara Bennett had given them for Wilson M-Something. Though did that even matter anymore? After all, Anne Harrington flagged on paper. Then she ran. Only the guilty ran.

"So the bruised ribs are from the air bags, while the mild

concussion and a fractured nose"—Carter winced when he dispensed that information—"came from colliding with the van."

"Can we talk to her?" Malone asked, his voice laden with irritation.

"You can speak with her, but keep it brief. She's on painkillers awaiting surgery to reset her nose." He locked his eyes with Amanda's until she nodded. "She's in room one twelve. Down the hall, just before the next corridor branches off."

"Thanks," she told him.

"Hard to miss with the PWCPD officer outside her room." Carter flashed her this smile, like the two of them shared a secret, before turning to walk away.

"What the hell was that all about?" Trent asked.

Malone turned to him and popped his eyes. "You need to ask?"

Amanda shook her head. "Let's focus on what's important. Sarge, we need to make sure that Harrington's car gets brought in and processed. Investigators could find a trace of Hailey Tanner."

"I'll make sure that happens," Malone said.

"And a search warrant for the grandmother's house." It was unlikely Anne Harrington had anywhere else to hold Hailey. And with her grandmother going in and out of lucidity, Anne could have made up any story she wanted about the child.

Malone grumbled and walked away. Amanda took that as agreement and led the way to room 112 with Trent at her heels. She and the doctor romantically involved? Such a ridiculous notion. She had better things to occupy her mind than some fantasy over taking up with him. As if she had time for that hot sordid mess. *And he was—* She stubbed the thought out right there. No point entertaining just how handsome he was.

Officer Wyatt was positioned outside the room. He dipped his head in greeting.

Anne Harrington was lying on the bed at a slight incline with her eyes shut. Her face was a tapestry of blues and purples.

"Anne Harrington," she whispered, but the woman's eyes sprung open and jolted into action. "If you're trying to leave..." Amanda pointed at her right wrist cuffed to the frame. "And running didn't work out so well for you the last time."

Anne grumbled, and it sounded like a swear word or two.

Maybe my reminder was a low blow...

"What do you want from me? I can't even..." Anne hissed, and Amanda imagined with the injuries to her face and nose that talking would hurt even pumped full of medication. But Amanda did well to keep in mind that the woman in front of her could be a killer.

"Did you have an affair with Evan Gilbert?" Amanda started with a simple question. Her response would allow her to gauge Anne's honesty.

"Sure. Why would that matter to you?"

"You were sleeping with him, even though he was a married man," she put out.

"I'm not the only mistress in the world."

Amanda didn't care how that painted things despite it being true. "How long were you seeing each other?"

"Have we ever stopped? I know he still loves me." She winced with discomfort, but tried to hide it behind a smile.

Twelve years later? Anne was delusional. "Did you ever stalk him and his family?" Amanda wanted to build a foundation before diving right into Julie and Hailey.

"There's no RO against me."

Evan Gilbert had been dealing with enough after losing his daughter. Reporting Anne would have fallen down the list of importance. "That means nothing."

"It means that he loves me but just can't admit to it."

Her misguided confidence sent chills down Amanda's spine. It revealed a controlling, manipulative personality. A trait that would serve her well in seducing children into trusting her. "Are you still in touch with him?"

"Not in a while, but when I go back home, I'm going to reach out."

"You think he's going to want to see you?" Trent asked.

"It's been a while, but he will. Yes. I'll make him see my side."

Again, Amanda saw that Anne Harrington ticked off most of the FBI profile's boxes, and they were just getting started. "When was the last time you saw him?"

"I saw him at least once a week when I was back in New York. Does he see me? You'd have to ask him."

"Are you admitting to stalking him?" Trent asked.

"I can't help it if he's where I am."

They could get lost in this battle of words all day, but that wouldn't move the investigation along. "Did you know his daughter, Julie?"

Anne's eyes became dark, then lit almost immediately. "She was a beautiful girl. She could have been ours if Evan hadn't been so easily manipulated by his stupid wife. Stupid man."

Witnessing Anne's fluctuation between admiration and disgust was unsettling. Almost like two personalities lived inside her and battled for dominance.

"What do you mean 'easily manipulated'?" Trent asked.

"He could have had a family with me. I could have given him a baby. His own DNA, but he broke things off, telling me he didn't want children."

"But then you found out about Julie." Amanda wagered a guess that would fill in the picture some more.

"Yes." One word and it was cold and mechanical.

"But you do like little girls," Amanda said, tossing in a tight smile despite it churning her stomach. "The way you can dress them up like princesses, how they move and dance on a stage."

"Like little stars," she said, her eyes misting. "Julie was that."

There would be no advantage to cutting right to the question Amanda wanted to ask. *Had she extinguished her light?* She needed Anne to keep talking. "You might have heard about Hailey Tanner in the news."

"She was a beautiful girl too. A performer like Julie? She was in a ballerina costume."

Amanda's breath froze in her lungs. How Hailey Tanner was found was withheld from the public. "How do you know that?"

"There was a picture in the paper, provided by her family when she went missing."

Could Amanda trust that's all it was? Anne lived in a fantasy world where every man adored her. "But you know Hailey has since been found?"

"No. That's good though. Right?"

It was hard to tell if Anne was putting on a performance or being genuine. "She's dead. Discovered in a local park."

"Her too? Monsters."

But her reaction fell flat, like she was saying the words she deemed appropriate but didn't feel. "Why are you in Woodbridge?"

"To visit with my grandmother, and I need to get her set up in a nursing facility. Oh, Grandma." She shifted again, as if she were going to get up, and tugged on the handcuff.

"Yeah, you're not going anywhere, but I'll make sure that someone goes by to check on her." Amanda turned to Trent, who nodded and stepped into the hallway. Being a good cop didn't follow a strict guidebook. The primary rule was protecting and taking care of people, and the grandmother shouldn't suffer the consequences of their interest in Anne.

"How long have you been in town?" She needed to verify what Katherine had found out.

"Since the start of December."

With that, the timing was confirmed. She was here before *The Nutcracker*. "Then it seems like you've had a long time to set something up."

"Not really. Homes have long waiting lists. But you don't believe me. Why should I be surprised? Why are you interested in me anyhow?"

"You seem to enjoy watching people, even when they don't know they're being watched."

"So?"

"It must make you feel untouchable, powerful. Do you like watching little girls like Julie Gilbert?" Amanda asked.

"I saw her with Evan and that bitch of a mother, but what are you implying?" Her voice turned menacing.

"And you saw Julie backstage in NYC for her last pageant?"

"I did."

Amanda was shocked that she admitted as much. "That must have been thrilling to mingle with Evan's wife, all the while knowing what it was like to have sex with her husband."

"Not going to lie."

"Then, tell me, were you at the party the Gilberts held afterward?"

"I wasn't exactly on the guest list."

Not that there was one... Amanda stiffened. "That wasn't my question."

"Yes, I was there."

Trent returned to the room. "An officer is going over to be with your grandmother," he told her.

Anne didn't acknowledge he'd spoken and kept her gaze locked on Amanda. "You were at the Gilberts' party," Amanda repeated for Trent's benefit. "Julie was killed that night."

"I heard."

Spoken devoid of emotion, and chills ran through Amanda. "Where were you last Friday night?" Amanda asked her.

"Home with Grandma. I'd tell you to ask her, but you know... Her mind." She circled her left index finger next to her head.

"Then you're sure you didn't pick up Hailey Tanner from her dance lesson?" Amanda asked.

"I did no such thing."

"Did you take her home, hide her from your grandmother, hold her for three days, assault then kill her?" Amanda asked.

"No."

"You saw the little girl you wanted in Julie. Maybe that urge never left, and when you saw Hailey, you just had to have her." The words were pouring out of Amanda like a torrent. Trent touched her briefly on her shoulder, but she kept her gaze fixed on Anne.

"That's not true. Oh my God, you think I touched Julie and this Hailey girl? And killed them too?"

"Did you?" Amanda tossed back. "Little girls would be easier to control than men."

"I would never! I'm not a monster!"

"I'm not so sure I believe you."

"Lawyer." She dragged out the word and hit the button to call the nurse.

"We were leaving anyhow," Amanda said, "but you won't be going anywhere. Even if you figure a way out of the cuffs, there's a uniformed officer outside your room."

A nurse came into the room and halted her steps at the sight of Amanda and Trent. "Is everything all right here, Ms. Harrington?"

"Get them out of here." She jabbed her eyes at Amanda and Trent.

Amanda swept past the nurse. Before talking to Anne, she

had her reservations about her guilt. But after speaking with her, they were melting away. Anne's shifting moods made her unpredictable, borderline unhinged. She could be the killer they were after.

Amanda turned to Officer Wyatt in the hallway. "Don't leave for one minute and call us the second her lawyer gets here."

Wyatt bobbed his head. "I can do that."

"Thanks." She and Trent almost made it to the doors when footsteps rushed toward them. She turned around and came face to face with Dr. Paulsen.

"Amanda? Ah, Detective Steele," he corrected.

Hearing him say her given name caused more sensations in her body than she cared to admit.

"I'm glad I caught you," he said, breathing easily despite hustling to get to her.

Healthy heart... check. She stiffened and cleared her throat. "Why's that?"

"Anne Harrington is scheduled for reconstructive surgery on her nose at ten PM. I thought you'd like to know when she comes out of surgery. If I could get your number, I'll make sure that you're contacted as soon as she's ready to have visitors again."

"Ah, sure." She handed over her card.

"Great. I'll call you then."

"Thank you."

He smiled and dipped his head before walking away. Trent was shaking his head and started moving again. She was flattered by the doctor's interest. He had confidence but was unassuming, and she found that refreshing.

She joined Trent outside.

"You know that line he gave you was entire BS? He wanted your number for himself."

"I'm hoping he does." She smiled at Trent, but he wasn't

smiling. "And if he does... Why should that bother you?" She hated how her walls came up, but he had Kelsey. Didn't she deserve someone too? When she dared to look at him again, his lips were in a straight line, his brow was set, and a slight hue colored his cheeks. He said nothing.

TWENTY-FIVE

After briefing Malone, she and Trent clocked out. A search warrant was being executed on Harrington's car and her grandmother's house, but neither required them on scene. With their prime suspect unavailable for questioning until sometime the next day, it presented a natural cut-off point. She picked up Zoe from Libby's a bit before six, and they were on their way home.

"So what do you say to pizza for dinner? I already picked up a fresh ball of dough." Amanda bobbed her eyebrows at Zoe in the rearview.

"Yeah!" Zoe giggled, but quickly covered her mouth as if she was self-conscious.

"What was that about?" Amanda imitated what she'd done with her hand, and Zoe became serious. "Come on, tell Mandy." She talked about herself in the third person in a playful tone, hoping it would lure the girl to confide in her.

"It's just some kids at school."

"What about them?" she asked, though she had an idea where this was going.

"They're teasing me. Calling me a toothless old lady." Zoe

scowled and crossed her arms. Such a serious expression on her beautiful little face seemed out of place.

"Everyone loses their baby teeth at some point. It's part of growing up, maturing." She added a bit of zest to that word, knowing how Zoe liked to point out she was getting too old for certain things she used to enjoy. Thankfully, she'd outgrown the need to watch *Frozen* on endless repetition, but that was good for more than one reason. It had been a movie she watched with her late mother. Letting *that* go told Amanda that Zoe was healing.

"I know. And I guess once one of *them* loses two front teeth at once..." Zoe grinned unabashed.

"No, you won't. You know how it feels to be teased. Being mean to others isn't the type of person you are."

"I want to be like you." She imitated a gun with her hands and said, "Bang, bang."

Amanda would laugh if it wasn't serious. "You know I rarely fire my gun. My job is to protect people." As she said this, taking in Zoe's delicate features, Amanda felt an ache in her chest. She'd failed to do that for Hailey. But like her father reminded her before, the past couldn't be undone, the victims' fates rewritten. The only sane choice she had was to look ahead and prevent further crime, further pain.

"Yes, but you carry one." Her eyes twinkled, making Amanda nervous.

"Being a cop is about so much more than carrying a gun. You know that?"

"Yes. It's selfish."

The word halted Amanda for a second until she realized what her daughter had meant. "You mean selfless."

"Yeah. Aunt Libby told me you're the most self... *less* person she knows." Zoe seemed to struggle with the pronunciation.

"That was nice of her."

"She's a nice person."

"She is." Amanda pressed the button on her rearview mirror to open the garage door, as she turned down their street. For the longest time, the bay was stuffed with boxes full of mementos from her previous life. A while back she'd whittled down the keepsakes to a single box, which she now stored in the basement.

She pulled into the garage and lowered the door. Now that she was using her garage for its intended purpose, she couldn't imagine ever doing without it. As she was juggling to get her house key out, her phone rang. "Here." She passed off the key to Zoe, while she answered her phone formally.

"Detective? Still in business mode, I see." It was Becky Tulson, Amanda's best friend since kindergarten.

"When am I not?"

Zoe put the key into the lock and was twisting the handle but without success. It didn't help that her backpack was bigger than her torso. She looked like a turtle in danger of flipping back on her shell.

"Just a sec," she told Becky and stepped in to help Zoe.

They went into the house. The door for the garage opened into a small mudroom that bled into the kitchen. Zoe shrugged out of her shoes, bag, and coat in seconds. Amanda was reminded of what the dance teacher had told them about kids getting ready. It applied more to the putting on of clothes than shedding them.

All Zoe's items lay discarded on the floor until Amanda made eye contact with the girl.

"Fine." Zoe set about picking them up and putting them on hooks at her height. Kevin, Amanda's late husband, had put them in for their daughter, Lindsey.

"Mandy?"

It took a few seconds for Amanda to clue in to where the voice was coming from. *Oh, Becky!* She lifted her phone back to her ear. "Sorry about that."

"From the sounds of it, you're home. It's just after six."

"I know, eh? Mark the calendar."

"Do you have any plans? I could come over."

Amanda heard the television come on and hung her jacket and slipped out of her shoes. She wasn't worried about what Zoe would watch as she had her own profile for each of the streaming services that limited the programs to ones suitable for children. "Pizza Tuesday, but other than that... not really." They broke the norms for Tuesdays whenever Amanda was home from work for dinner. Pizza, never tacos.

"Oh, pizza. I love it. Can I come over? That sounds amazing."

"Why not?"

"Awesome. I'll be there in ten, fifteen minutes."

With that, Becky ended the call, and Amanda told Zoe they were having company.

"I love Becky."

"I know, baby." She mussed Zoe's blond hair on the way into her bedroom to change into something more comfortable. Her typical detective attire was slacks and a nice shirt, sometimes paired with a blazer.

By the time Amanda had changed into yoga pants and a T-shirt, someone knocked on the door. Becky was serious when she said ten or fifteen minutes. Only she didn't find Becky standing there.

Zoe came up behind Amanda. "Trent? Yay! You never told me he was coming too." She hugged Trent's legs.

"Hey, Zoe," he said to her while looking at Amanda.

"Baby, why don't you go back to your show? Trent and I need to talk."

"Okay." Zoe left and sat cross-legged on the floor in front of the TV.

Amanda stepped outside. The evening air was a little chilly, and she shivered.

"I'll be fast. You shouldn't be standing out here without a jacket tonight."

When they'd parted ways at Central, things between them had been a little messy. She wasn't going to prod into the reason. If Trent and Kelsey were having problems, that was none of her business. And if he wanted to have another talk about how they couldn't explore their feelings for each other, she might explode.

"I just wanted to apologize face to face if I was being strange about Dr. Handsome and..."

If... She'd let that go. "So you noticed, eh? The handsome part?" She winked at him, not wanting to dig into this... whatever *this* was, any further.

"Yes, I noticed. I am a detective, after all." He smiled, but the expression was quick to fade. "But you're right. It's not my place to think anything of it."

A car horn was honked a few times. Becky was grinning as she pulled in behind Trent's Jeep, parked, got out, and started up the walk. "Trent Stenson, as I live and breathe. It's been a long time." She gave him an enthusiastic slap on the back.

Becky and Trent used to work together at the Dumfries PD. While he'd advanced rank and transferred to the PWCPD, Becky was content remaining at the smaller station as a uniformed officer.

"Yeah, you too," Trent told her. "But I was just heading out, so I'll need you to move your..."

"Of course." Becky smiled at Amanda and pulled her in for a quick hug before heading back to her car.

Amanda ducked inside and watched them from the window in the door. They talked in the driveway for a few minutes, and Amanda wished she was better at lip-reading. Soon, both were pulling out, and Becky was driving back in. Her horn honked as she locked the doors with her key fob.

Amanda opened the door, and Becky stepped inside holding a bottle of red wine.

"Hey, Becky!" Zoe smiled at her and hugged her.

Becky squeezed back. "Oh, thank you for that. That air has a bite tonight. But this should warm us up." She handed the wine over to Amanda.

Any other Tuesday, Amanda would protest the offering as being made on a *school night*. But after that strange visit from Trent, a little wine wouldn't be the end of the world. "Sounds good." She headed to the kitchen with her friend and Zoe trailing her.

"When are we going to eat? I'm starving." Zoe slumped, bending at the knees and letting her arms dangle.

"I'll get you some apple fries to tide you over. That sound good?"

"Okay."

"Oh, what's that?" Becky pointed at Zoe's mouth. "Open wide."

Zoe did, with pride, and pointed at the holes left from her latest baby teeth falling out.

"Look who's a big girl now." Becky hugged Zoe.

"Yes, yes, that's me." Zoe rolled her eyes and collected the sliced apple that Amanda prepared for her.

"Eat it in the living room, and I'll call you once the dough's rolled out," Amanda told her.

Zoe sauntered back to her perch in front of the TV and resumed the playback of her program.

Becky was reaching into the cupboard for wineglasses, and Amanda pulled out the dough and a rolling pin.

"So what's up with you?" she asked Becky as her friend moved on to unscrewing the lid on the wine.

Amanda nudged her head toward the bottle. "I see we're living it up tonight. Twist top?"

"You don't drink for years and now you're a wine snob?

Well, I'll have you know, don't let the twist top fool you. And in answer to your question. I just thought I'd call, see what was up." Becky poured some red into two glasses and handed one to Amanda. "To spontaneity. Because I swear without it these days, we'd never see each other."

Amanda echoed the toast and clicked her glass to Becky's.

"Now, what's this I hear about some doctor?"

Amanda choked on her mouthful of wine. She started coughing.

"Oh, it's more serious than I thought." Becky's eyes were twinkling with amusement.

Once Amanda could breathe without a catch in her throat, she spoke. "There's no doctor. And there's nothing serious."

Becky pointed toward the front door. "That's not what Trent said."

"Really?"

"Yeah, I hear he's some hottie who couldn't take his baby blues off you."

So, he caught that... "Let's not do this." Amanda spread some flour on the counter and unwrapped the ball of dough.

"Do what? Mandy, you and Logan broke up six months ago. It's time to move on. You're too young to close up shop."

Amanda paused on the analogy, took a sip of wine, then picked up the rolling pin.

"You must be lonely."

"I have Zoe." Amanda couldn't even look at her friend right now. If she did, she might succumb and admit that some male companionship would be nice. The catch was the man she was primarily interested in wasn't available. She pressed the pin firmly against the dough and rolled.

"You know what I mean. Are you scared? You don't have to be. It's like riding a bike. You just have to get back on."

At least she didn't say horse... "It's not that easy, Beck." Amanda stopped rolling. "I have Zoe to consider."

"So take things casual. Keep it from Zoe."

"I don't keep things from her."

Becky angled her head and pierced Amanda's eyes, calling her bluff.

"Fine, there are some things. Only for her own good."

"Like Mr. Hot Doctor?"

"Shh." Amanda feared Becky said that a little too loudly.

"Sorry. I'm just worried about you. You have so much love to give, and you deserve it too."

"Thank you."

"You're welcome." Becky pushed off the counter she'd been leaning against. "Now tell me what I can do to help."

"Ah, not so quick. You're here doling out relationship advice, but when are you and Brandon going to make things more official?" Becky had been dating Brandon Fisher, an FBI agent with the Behavioral Analysis Unit, for several years. Their relationship hadn't progressed past a commitment to keep things exclusive.

"Dear God. No."

"No, what?"

"We were talking about you."

"We *were*. Now it's your turn."

Becky drained an unhealthy amount from her wineglass. "Brandon was married before. You know that. Well, he's in no rush to do it again, and I'm fine with the way things are. So..." She shrugged and lifted her glass but lowered it again without taking a sip.

"Uh-huh. Well, I worry about you. You have so much love to give, and you deserve it too."

"Oh, shut up." Becky roared with laughter and flicked some flour at Amanda.

"Food fight!" Zoe ran into the room, and Amanda had little time to wonder how much she'd overheard. She was hit in the face with a small chunk of dough, thrown from her own daughter's hand.

"Why you little..." Amanda snatched some dough and made like she was going to hurl it at Zoe.

The girl squealed, running around the kitchen island with her arms waving in the air. She knocked over the bag of flour, and it spilled onto the floor.

"I'm going to get you," Zoe threatened Amanda as she bent over to grab a handful of flour.

"Oh, no, you're—" Amanda received a tongue full of flour and spat trying to get it out of her mouth.

Becky doubled over in laughter.

"I got you!" Zoe did a victory dance, and Amanda used her distraction to her advantage.

She grabbed some flour. "Hey, Zoe," she called for her attention. The girl no sooner turned to look at her than Amanda threw flour at her face.

"Mom!" Zoe yelled, and all fell silent after the word left her mouth.

Becky stopped laughing. So did Amanda. Time stood still. Swelled. Just like her heart.

Amanda went to Zoe and got on her knees, holding her arms. "I would love for you to call me *Mom*, but only if you're comfortable with that." She wanted to give her daughter a way to back out, undo what she'd said. She could appreciate the deep bond a girl had with her mother. Zoe's birth mother was gone, and Amanda never wanted to be seen by the girl as trying to take her place.

Zoe wiped some flour off her face and away from her eyes and nodded.

Amanda hugged her and didn't want to let go. Ever.

TWENTY-SIX

Amanda woke up the next morning with joy in her heart. She felt more alive than she had in years. *Mom.* She replayed Zoe's little voice saying that a thousand times. Something about it made her and Zoe even more official. Though their instant connection and natural chemistry said they belonged together from their first meeting. While Amanda always thought Zoe had saved her, she could see now that she had repaid the favor. She'd given Zoe shelter from the storm, provided her a sanctuary to heal and grow.

For the first few hours lying in bed last night, she questioned whether she'd dreamed it, but the recollections were clear. Zoe had called her *Mom.* And not just once, but twice. The second time came after Becky had gone home, and Amanda had helped Zoe with her bath and tucked her into bed. She turned out the light in her room, and Zoe had said, "Night, Mom."

And then this morning when she dropped Zoe off at school, she called her *Mom* for a fourth time.

There was no sweeter sound, and Amanda would be playing

it on repeat all day. It would be what carried her through, what gave her the added strength to take down the serial killer who targeted young girls. Anne Harrington was going to pay. Amanda would do it for Julie Gilbert, Hailey Tanner, other victims they might not know about, and to prevent others from coming to harm. *Might not know about...* And just like that her light mood swerved into the darkness. What if there were other young victims claimed by this monster?

Her phone rang over her car's system, and the hospital showed on caller ID. She answered formally, though she expected to hear Dr. Paulsen's voice. She was met with a woman's voice instead, who identified herself as Lorraine, a nurse, from the hospital.

"I'm calling about a patient by the name of Anne Harrington. She's in recovery from surgery and doing well. You can come and talk to her whenever you wish. Just check in at the nurses' station."

"Thank you."

"Uh-huh." The nurse ended the call, and Amanda was curious why the doctor hadn't called himself. Maybe she and Trent had made a bigger deal out of his wanting her number than it warranted. And maybe that was a good thing.

She was about to call Trent when her phone rang again, and *Unknown* splashed on the screen. That wouldn't stop her from answering since she gave her card out to a lot of people with the job. "Detective Steele."

"It's Officer Brandt. I'm here outside Anne Harrington's hospital room. Wyatt said you wanted to know when her lawyer turned up. Well, he's with her now, and she's good to speak with you if you wanted to come over."

"Thank you, Leo." Amanda ended the call and selected Trent's number.

"Good morning," he answered.

"You have no idea how good it is." She was thinking about Zoe calling her *Mom*.

"Oh?"

"Mind out of the gutter."

"Okay, what is it?"

"Anne Harrington's lawyer is with her, and she's good to talk to us." She'd stick to business.

"These people are up and at it early, but that news was hardly worth the buildup."

She debated whether to share the latest between her and Zoe, but decided not to for now. At the start of her partnership with Trent, she was much better at adhering to the line between personal and professional. Somewhere over the years, that line had blurred, curved, and faded into obscurity. "Early is right, but I'm already on my way to Central."

"I'll be here waiting."

"Wait's over. I'm pulling into the lot now. Meet me outside." She ended the call, walked to the lot with the department cars, and Trent came out a few minutes later tossing a key fob in the air and catching it.

"You know if you break that it's going to be a couple hundred bucks to replace," she told him.

"I won't break it then." He smirked at her as he got into the driver's seat.

He got them on the road and looked over at her. "We okay?"

"Of course we are." She smiled. The expression, a little too eager, had her pleasant mood oozing from her despite her intention to dial it down.

"Hmm. You seem uncharacteristically chipper this morning. Want to tell me why?"

"It's a sunny day. We're going to close this case and get justice for two girls today."

"Even if we do, I sense there's more than that."

She wriggled a pointed finger at him. "Just focus your detective skills on the case."

"You say everything's okay between us, but you're acting weird. I meant what I said last night. I kind of got cut off with Becky turning up, but I was going to add, who you date or even if you do, isn't any of my business."

"Zoe called me *Mom*," she blurted out. Anything to end the agony of Trent's rambling.

"Wow, that's a big deal. That's the first time, isn't it?"

"Yeah." Amanda's large grin was making her cheeks ache. She probably looked like a moron, not that she cared.

"That's incredible. Congrats? I don't know what to say." Trent was smiling too.

"Thanks, Trent. Honestly, I'm speechless about it."

"Well, you're so good with her. It was bound to happen eventually."

His genuine words hit her heart and sank in her gut. His opinion mattered to her. Possibly more than it should. "Thanks. And as for Dr. Paulsen, we all read him wrong."

"*Pfft.* I don't think so. That guy was drooling over you."

She scrunched up her face. "Do people even say that anymore?"

He shrugged. "I just did."

She loved his easygoing nature, and while he had a strong moral code and values she shared, he wasn't about conforming to please other people. Another thing she respected about him.

"And how do you figure we read him wrong?" Trent asked as he turned into the hospital parking lot.

"He didn't call. A nurse did. He wanted my number for business reasons."

"Hmm. I'm not sure about that. Ask me and there's more to it."

They got out of the car and headed to the nurses' station and announced who they were and who they were there to see.

"Yes, you're interested in Anne Harrington," the nurse said with confidence.

"That's right," Amanda told her.

"I'm Lorraine, the nurse who called you. Dr. Paulsen apologizes he didn't do it himself." Amanda's confusion must have been easy to read. "Oh, let me back up here. Dr. Paulsen finished out a twenty-hour shift at two AM, called me at six after speaking to the attending to check on Harrington's recovery. He sounded drunk exhausted and asked if I'd call you. Guess he was supposed to."

Trent nudged the toe of his shoe into the side of her foot. Amanda stiffened.

"Thanks," she said.

"Don't mention it. She's back in room one-twelve. Do you need me to take you there?"

"No, we'll be fine." Amanda set off, taking the lead.

Trent caught up and whispered to her. "Guess we didn't misread anything."

But did that really change things? She had Zoe. They had it good together. Her phone rang, yanking her out of her spiraling thoughts.

She stopped walking to answer. Trent stood next to her as she pulled out her phone. "It's Malone," she told Trent before picking up.

"Where are you two?"

"At the—"

"You know what? It doesn't matter. Another girl is missing."

The world around Amanda became still for a second, then chirps from machines and soles slapping and squeaking against the linoleum flooring came into focus. Nurses and patients walked past them.

"Just hold on one sec." She looked for a private place to put the call on hands-free so Trent could hear. The only space within eyesight was a restroom. She ducked inside and pulled

Trent's shirt to drag him in with her. She checked on the stalls, and once she confirmed they were alone, she closed the door behind them and hit Speaker on her phone. "Go ahead." Her heart was pounding. Not just because she had Trent's woodsy cologne lodged up her nose and on her palms.

"Eloise Maynard, seven years old, was discovered missing when her mother went to wake her up this morning. Detective McGee from Missing Persons shot this one right over to us."

"Are we sure it's connected to Gilbert and Tanner?" Trent asked. "Though what are the chances it isn't?"

"Slim to none," Malone amended. "But they're connected all right."

The skin tightened on the back of Amanda's neck. "You know this for certain."

"There was a printed note on her bed addressed to Katherine."

"Shit." The expletive slipped out. "Does Katherine know?"

"She does. And you should know that I've sent her home. The chief's orders."

Amanda stiffened. "None of this is her fault."

"That's not the point. You know the chief's primary concern."

Optics, but she left it unsaid. That was a battle for another day. Poor Katherine. She must be spinning out. "Tell us where you want us to go."

"The family home." Malone gave them the address. "Detective McGee is already there, being the first to receive the report. Obviously, he's there with first responding officers too."

"All right. We'll head right over."

"Harrington has officially been released of suspicion. Clearly, we went down the wrong path there. The search on her home and car got us nowhere either."

"Okay, thank you," she told him.

Malone clicked off, and Amanda and Trent were left looking at each other.

"I can't believe this is happening again," he said. "And so soon."

"Me either." Her stomach tossed. "And poor Katherine. I should call her."

Trent nodded and headed for the restroom door. "I'll make sure the officer on duty uncuffs Harrington."

She nodded, with her phone to an ear. Katherine's phone rang once before pushing Amanda to voicemail. *Rejected...* "It's Amanda. I promise you I'm going to find this guy. *We're* going to. I'm here if you need to talk." She ended the call, not knowing what else she could say. Was there anything she could say that would comfort Katherine? Amanda doubted it. To think how this day started off on such a high note, and in a matter of a few hours had crashed and burned.

TWENTY-SEVEN

Katherine's head was spinning as she drove away from Central. Another little girl was paying the price because of her. All because she just couldn't leave things alone and let Julie go.

Not just a little girl. Say her name, coward...

"Eloise Maynard." Katherine spoke out loud and caught herself in the rearview mirror. Her eyes filled with tears, and a few fell. She swiped them away. Indignant and angry at the undeserved display of emotion. As the cause of Eloise's abduction, she had no right to fall apart. None. Just as she had no right to be involved in Julie's case. She'd given that right away the second she resigned from the NYPD. And before that when she gave her beautiful baby girl up for adoption. But how was she supposed to turn her back on her own flesh and blood?

A car horn blasted her from her thoughts. She found herself in the oncoming lane with a pickup barreling straight for her. Cranking the wheel of her Mercedes, she overcorrected, and by some miracle didn't spill over the curb onto the sidewalk.

That was close!

Her heart pounded as she heaved for breath.

If she went home to her empty house and stared at the

walls, she'd go crazy. But if she didn't get off the roads, she might kill herself or someone else. And she already had enough deaths on her conscience. She pulled over to the side of the road. She'd give it a few minutes before she decided what to do next and where to go.

If only she'd had the courage to keep Julie all those years ago, but she just couldn't swing it then. She couldn't even face her rapist day in and out at the NYPD, and had slunk away for a few months to have her baby. It was her shame, and she even kept it from her mother. A tough feat because she loved that woman and still did. The veil of death wasn't strong enough to shatter love. If so, there would be far less suffering in the world.

For years, Katherine had buried her secret so deeply inside, she could convince herself it was someone else's story. Then came Julie Gilbert. Once Katherine pieced together that Julie was her biological daughter, the wound reopened. She transformed into a mother bear wanting to protect her daughter, but since she was too late for that, she was intent on catching her killer. But that intention escalated to obsession.

When she was overlooked for a promotion within the NYPD, she saw it as the chance for a fresh start somewhere else. But that wasn't the only reason she considered a move. After her mother was murdered, she needed a change. It was around this time she saw the position for interim Homicide sergeant with the PWCPD come up, and the posting seemed meant to be. The location made it possible to connect with her mother's estranged sister, May Byrd, and build a relationship with her. But she discovered that geography did nothing to sever her bond to the Gilbert case. It might even have made it stronger. She rented a storage unit and dedicated that space to finding the person who killed Julie, her *Amy*. That's what she would have named her if she'd kept her.

Aunt May... Her name swept through. She was just one

more person who knew nothing about the baby girl she'd given up for adoption. It might be time to confide in her.

Katherine got back on the road and drove to the diner. The lot was packed, making it a challenge to find an available spot. To think when she came to the county, she believed it would also give her the chance to simplify and slow down the pace of her life. The plan was working until she handed in her badge and started full time at her aunt's cafe. Then Katherine took it on as a personal mission to expand the business. She taught herself social media advertising through online courses, and it turned out she was quite good at putting what she'd learned into practice. The diner's business boomed.

But at what cost?

Katherine swallowed a lump of regret as she pulled into a newly vacated spot. The energy she'd directed toward Hannah's Diner had taken her focus away from Julie's case. Her daughter's case. If only she had scaled back some on marketing, Katherine would have had time to pursue the angle she'd started last fall.

It's my fault that Hailey is dead, and Eloise was snatched from her bed... If not for me, both girls would be alive and safe with their families...

The thought made her want to take further action, not retreat. But what was she supposed to do? She could endanger yet another child or be sent to jail for interfering with a police investigation. She didn't have a badge anymore, and the police chief had made his position clear when he'd had Malone toss her out the door. The sad part was she could even appreciate it from their viewpoint.

Her phone rang over the car's speakers, and Amanda's name came up on the display. She didn't have the bandwidth for a conversation with her right now. She just had to push forward. She rejected the call, shut her car off, and headed into the diner.

Regulars smiled at her. Her aunt was cashing out an order and looked at her with eyebrows raised in surprise at seeing her. Katherine had told her she was taking a few days off and Aunt May hadn't pressed her further. Since they'd been separated for years, they had started from strangers a short time ago and some boundaries still existed.

But upon seeing her aunt, Katherine realized this was where she needed to be. Another project, another focus, something to distract her from her culpability.

Her eyes burned with a fresh batch of tears, but she took a deep breath and headed behind the counter. She pressed on a smile for her aunt. There was no way she could tell her right now.

"What are you doing here? I thought you said you were taking some time off?"

"If anyone needs that, it's you." Katherine admired her aunt's work ethic and how, even well into her sixties, she was still tireless and dedicated to her diner.

May batted her hand. "Ridiculous." Then she turned to the next customer. "What can I get for ya today?"

"Let me take care of this, May. Go rest your feet for a few minutes."

May narrowed her eyes but relented.

Katherine looked at the man across the counter and smiled at the regular. "Let me guess, a large half caf, half decaf with one sugar and a splash of milk?"

The man smiled. "You remembered?"

"Just be a second." Katherine made up his coffee, appreciating that this task was mundane and took little thought. But because of that, her mind had free space to chastise her.

Julie, Hailey, and now Eloise... They are all my fault.

She jumped and cried out when a splash of hot coffee hit the back of her hand. Cussing under her breath, she popped the lid on the to-go cup and handed over the coffee to the waiting customer. After collecting his money, she sent him off with, "Have a good day."

He lifted his cup to her as if in a toasting gesture. "Oh, I plan on it."

The next person in line stepped up to place their order, but Katherine couldn't stay here. She'd been mistaken to think she could just shut everything off. Maybe if she told her aunt, she'd get some peace.

Katherine turned to another server as they walked behind her. Hattie Knox, a woman in her fifties, was one of the first employees at the diner when business started taking off. It looked like she was just returning from break. "Could you...?" she asked her, the implication being that she take over her line.

"Of course." Hattie wasted no time helping the next customer.

Katherine headed to the back of the diner in search of Aunt May. This might not be the optimal time and place, but she deserved to know the truth. And if Katherine didn't tell her now, she feared her secret would burrow between them and suck her soul dry.

TWENTY-EIGHT

Amanda sat back in the passenger seat as Trent drove them to the Maynards' house. Her mind was chastising her for bringing in Katherine and advocating for her help. She got carried away, swept up by emotion. "How did this person know Katherine was still investigating?"

"I don't think it's even necessary they did. That's what we've been saying all along."

She wished she believed that, but now another girl had been taken, she was left second-guessing. "This person is getting more brazen, taking a second girl within days of killing the last one."

"Agree with you there."

Trent pulled up in front of the Maynard residence and parked on the street behind a PWCPD cruiser. Three vehicles in the driveway. Two belonged to civilians while the third had a plate attached to the department.

The house was a two-story with a public sidewalk along the right side of the property that cut through to an adjacent street. The Maynards' property was surrounded by a four-foot-tall chain-link fence, offering no security or privacy.

Trent rang the doorbell, and the door swung open a moment later.

Detective McGee was standing there, a solemn expression on his face. "Nothing personal against you, but I could have handled not meeting again under similar circumstances."

Amanda and Trent stepped into the entry with him.

"Nothing personal," Amanda parroted, "but back at ya. So tell me what we should know."

"I've mostly been a sounding board thus far, not probing them with a lot of questions. They're still trying to process this. I'm going to be upfront and say there's nothing that indicates Eloise was murdered or even injured. I'm not sure how much you know about the situation." McGee stopped there, hands on hips, looking at them.

"Seven years old, an envelope addressed to Katherine was found on the girl's bed," Trent recapped.

"Okay. Yeah, well, that's a whole thing right there. The mother discovered it, and she's an absolute mess."

Amanda stiffened. "What does it say?"

McGee produced the note from his pocket, sealed in a clear evidence bag.

Amanda held it so Trent could read it as well.

I knew you wouldn't take my warning seriously. Now this girl's fate is on you, Katherine Graves.

Amanda balled her hands into fists, feeling nothing but white-hot rage. Katherine wasn't going to recover from this blow. She blamed herself already and had let this freak into her head. Now this bastard was coming right out and assigning her blame a second time. But this letter also contained a taunt. The implication being the girl's life could be saved if they accepted this invitation to play his game. *Assuming it's a man.* Just because Anne Harrington didn't pan out, that didn't exclude all

women. Amanda looked at Trent to confirm he'd finished reading. He nodded, and Amanda handed the note back to McGee.

"I'll give you a heads up," McGee started. "The girl's
parents want to know who Katherine Graves is. So far, I've
skirted the question, but that won't hold out forever."

Amanda studied McGee. "You know?"

"That Graves was a former PWCPD sergeant and that
there was a note to her found with Hailey Tanner? Yeah, I
know. I don't know what the killer was referring to when he told
her to stop."

Amanda didn't want to get into all the details. "How do you
know about that note?"

"You might think I'm cold or question my competency, but I
care. Too much, to be honest. I had Rideout copy me in on his
autopsy findings. He mentioned finding the note in the tutu's
hem."

Amanda's cheeks became hot with shame. She'd judged the
man from snippets without considering the full picture. With
what he said, she got the feeling he had a case hit close to home
that was his unresolved White Whale. It might have happened
after he'd landed in Missing Persons, or it might be why he
worked there. "I didn't realize..."

"How could you? We don't know each other."

"Well, smart call on not telling them more about Katherine.
That could place her in danger," Amanda said. The Maynards
could make things personal with Katherine and go after her.
Even kind people were capable of drastic measures under these
circumstances. Logic fled.

"Which I understand, and it doesn't shed a favorable light
on the PWCPD either. Anyway, I just wanted to prepare you
for what you're headed into. They will press you on it. Moving
on, Crime Scene has been called in to process the girl's room. I
took a quick look around the house and couldn't see any obvious
signs of forced entry."

If it made a difference, Amanda would cross her fingers that CSIs Blair and Donnelly were assigned. She didn't have enough self-control for another round with CSI Stuart.

"There wasn't anything conclusive to indicate that at the Tanner home at first either," Trent said. "Is there a connection between the families?"

"Hard to say. The Maynards only recognized the Tanner name from the news. And my bringing it up wasn't received well. I'll leave the matter for you two to investigate further."

Amanda couldn't imagine the comparison drawn from a murdered girl to their Eloise would be easy to handle. They'd also want an explanation for why the PWCPD hadn't taken this person off the streets yet. "All right, could you intro—?"

A knock on the door had Amanda turning. Two figures were visible through the sidelight, and at the sight of collection kits, she opened the door.

CSIs Blair and Donnelly were there, and Amanda let out a breath of relief. She stepped back to let them inside.

Detective McGee handed the sealed note over to Blair. "This is for you. I'll take you up to the girl's room and explain."

CSI Blair tapped Amanda's shoulder on her way past.

Amanda turned to Trent. "Guess we'll introduce ourselves."

They went deeper into the home, following the sound of sobbing. It drew them all the way to the back where a living room was off the kitchen. A man and woman were huddled together on the couch, and they looked up at her and Trent.

"Mr. and Mrs. Maynard, we're Detectives Steele, and Stenson," she told them.

"Damon and Krista," the man said. "Please, sit wherever you'd like." He gestured to the other chairs in the room, and Amanda and Trent each selected one and sat down.

"We can only imagine what you're going through," she began. "I assure you that Detective Stenson and I will do all we can to find your daughter safe and sound." She'd do whatever she could to make good on that intention.

"Eloise. Please, just say her name. She's special to us." Krista hiccupped a sob, and when she raised her hand, Amanda noticed a photograph in her hand.

"Yes, of course. I apologize. *Eloise.* Is that a picture of her?" She pointed to what Krista was holding, and the woman nodded. "Could I see it?"

Krista nodded, and Amanda got up and took the photo from her.

"It was taken yesterday at her birthday party," Krista told her.

Eloise was bright-eyed with blond hair and green eyes. She was a sweet, innocent child. Anger swirled in Amanda's chest as she tightened her grip on the photo paper. The image appeared to have been printed from a home computer. A quick look around the room showed the couple favored abstract paintings on the walls instead of framed photographs. There were no shelves or units that displayed any either.

"We don't like clutter," Damon offered, as if realizing that's what Amanda had observed.

She nodded, accepting that only because the home had a rather clinical feel. "She's beautiful," Amanda said, holding the picture for Trent to see before handing it back to Krista.

The mother said nothing but palmed her cheeks and stared at the image.

"When did you last see Eloise?" she asked, as Trent pulled out his tablet.

"It was last night," Damon said. "Krista puts her to bed."

"What time was this?" Trent asked.

"Eight o'clock. I read to her for about ten minutes and then it's lights out." Krista sniffled, and her husband gripped her closer to him.

Amanda could only imagine the living nightmare this

couple was experiencing. They put their daughter to sleep, likely feeling that security as she had with Zoe last night, only to wake up and have her gone. "Is there any security system on the home?"

The Maynards shook their heads in unison.

"You can bet when we get her back, that's the first thing I'll have installed," Damon said.

Amanda was impressed by his positive mindset. While it wouldn't have a direct bearing on the outcome, it would keep him going. "A doorbell cam?"

"No," Damon said.

It could have shown the perp. "What time did you notice Eloise was missing?"

"It was at seven when I went to wake her up to get ready for school." Krista's voice was robotic as she spoke. Her gaze never left her daughter's face.

"Krista screamed, and I went running down the hall," Damon picked up. "By the time I got there, she was holding a note in her hand. Ah, the other detective has it. He bagged it for forensics."

"Yes, we saw it. Detective McGee handed it over to the CSIs to be processed for prints and DNA, to see if that gets us any closer to who took her. Do either of you have any enemies or people in mind who might have done this? Any new people in your lives?" It was unlikely their killer had stalked both Hailey and Eloise for a length of time. Though if his intention was always a third victim, it was possible.

Damon looked at his wife, and they both shook their heads.

"Who is this Katherine person?" Damon asked. "The other detective wouldn't tell us anything about her."

"Our baby was taken because of her, whoever she is," Krista spat before Amanda or Trent could respond to Damon. "Do you think the same person who killed that Tanner girl took our Ellie?" The woman's face was bright red, and angry tears fell.

Damon handed his wife the tissue box from the table next to him. "Please excuse my—"

"If you're going to apologize for me, I'd stop and think that through." Krista drilled her husband with a fiery gaze.

He held up his hands in surrender.

"All we can say with confidence is the investigation into your daughter's disappearance is just beginning," Amanda said.

"You're covering something up." Krista crossed her arms and thrust out her chin.

"I can appreciate you want answers, that you want your daughter back." Amanda was quick to amend her statement. "And we will do all we can to bring her home to you."

"And if you can't? This Katherine lady needs to pay." Krista smacked her mouth shut when her husband rubbed her arm.

Amanda appreciated that grief and anger looked for an outlet, someone to blame, a way to find relief, but Katherine was the wrong person for them to focus their energy on. "The only person responsible for your daughter's welfare right now is the person who took her. Do either of you know the Tanner family?"

"No," Damon said. "We told Detective McGee that."

Speaking of the man, he is taking his sweet time returning...

"What do you do for work, Mr. Maynard?" Trent asked Damon.

"I'm an electrician for LiveWire. They're a local company."

Amanda nodded, having heard of it. A job in the trades was a far different world to the Tanners' one in investments. Their paths were unlikely to have crossed. Had the killer targeted Eloise at random? There didn't seem to have been time for them to stalk the girl for any length of time. "What did Eloise do yesterday?"

"She went to school," Krista said.

"Which one does she attend?"

Krista told her the name of a different school than the one Hailey had attended. Detective McGee returned and sat down.

"You mentioned it was Eloise's birthday," Trent said. "Did you do anything special for her after school?"

"We had a small party at the Scoop. It's an ice cream parlor," Krista told them.

Amanda had taken Zoe there, and Lindsey before her. The place had been in business for a long time. "Sounds like that would have been fun for her." Amanda was endeavoring to relax the mother some.

"It was."

"We're going to need the names of all the kids there, any parents that tagged along," Trent said.

"I can get that for you," Krista said.

"Does Eloise love the spotlight? Maybe she has dance lessons or performs in competitions, pageants?" Amanda asked.

"Oh, she loves being the center of attention, but nothing like what you mentioned. She is obsessed with princesses, though, and insisted on wearing her pink gown and tiara to her party."

Amanda said nothing to the Maynards, but she slipped a subtle side-glance at Trent. Again, it would seem, their killer had a type. And given what they'd just heard, it sounded like little Eloise was targeted on the spur of the moment. The killer was getting careless.

TWENTY-NINE

Amanda was grappling with frustration at how she went from waking up that morning with a prime suspect in custody to no one. At least no one tangible. The closest they had for a lead was Wilson M-Something, the nanny's onetime date, but that might be a stretch at this point. There was more digging left for the Tanner case, but the clock was ticking on this new one. And they had a chance to save Eloise.

"Did you notice anyone lingering around, watching the party?" Trent asked, beating Amanda to a similar question.

Krista shook her head. "I was paying attention to Ellie, making sure my baby was happy."

Damon took his arm from around his wife and took her hand into his instead. "Krista's a good mom."

"No one is saying otherwise," Amanda assured him. "We just need to ask these questions. Do you remember any other customers who dined inside?"

"A few, but their faces..." She flung her hand. "They're all a blur."

"Men and women?" Amanda asked.

"Both."

"And the server who tended to the party?" Trent looked up from his tablet, where he'd been tapping a moment prior.

"There were two. Well, a woman at first, then a man helped too."

Amanda perked up at that, even though there could be an innocent explanation. She still resonated more with a man behind the murders and Eloise's kidnapping. "Do you know why?"

Krista shook her head. "I just assumed the woman needed help to serve our party."

Goosebumps trailed down Amanda's arms. What better place for a sexual deviant to gain employment than an ice cream shop? They'd have their pick of children. But acknowledging this grim truth, thinking like these deviants, made her sick. Though, if Eloise was the victim of circumstance, and he was working, how could he have followed the family home? "Do you remember their names?"

"No." Krista squeezed her husband's hand. "I don't think they had name tags on their aprons."

Amanda nodded. They'd visit the Scoop and find out who served the party, get some names, question them. "Did you notice if anyone followed you home?"

"No, but it's not the type of thing I look for."

"That's understandable." For the average person, it wouldn't be something they'd need to consider. "Can you describe the servers?"

"You think one of them took Ellie?" Damon asked.

"We're just trying to get some details," Trent stepped in and assured the man. He gestured toward Krista to answer Amanda's question.

"The woman was blond, in her twenties, pretty, I guess. The man had dark hair, brown eyes, an almond-shaped face, lean, late thirties. He had a cut or a scar on his top lip."

Damon searched his wife's profile with his lips pursed and

his brow pressed. He was curious about the amount of detail his wife recalled about the man. It struck Amanda too as Krista just confessed to not paying much attention to people around them. But Amanda was reeling for another reason. *The scar on the top lip...* She might be grasping. Most of the attributes were vague, but the package sounded a lot like the nanny's Wilson M. After all, how many people had an obvious scar on their lip? "You ever see either of them before?"

"The servers?" Krista asked, and when Amanda nodded, she said, "The woman, yes, but I think the man was new."

Amanda glanced at Trent, who met her gaze. "Going back to last night, did either of you hear anything?"

"Nothing," Damon said. "Making all this even more shocking. But there was the matter of the front door." He glanced at Krista.

Amanda angled her head. "What about it?"

"It was unlocked."

"But you lock it at night?" Amanda's own parents didn't always lock theirs despite her father being the former police chief. It was a soft spot in rural and small-town living. Some people were too trusting. Some had a shotgun at the ready.

"Always."

Yet no sign of forced entry. Picking a lock could still leave marks, unless they were skilled. But it's possible the killer accessed the home another way, such as a window, and walked out the front door with Eloise. How brazen, though. Even if they took Eloise during the witching hours when everyone in the neighborhood was asleep, doorbell cameras didn't sleep. They'd need to check with the neighbors across the street. They might get lucky. "What was Eloise wearing?"

"Her pink and teal unicorn pajamas," Krista told them.

It would be rather cool at night for that alone. "Any other articles of her clothing missing? Toys?"

"Her stuffed unicorn," Damon said.

"It was her favorite," Krista added.

"Any coats? Shoes? Was she wearing socks?" Amanda asked the probing questions, hungry for more information.

"No socks when she went to bed. I never checked on the other." Krista left the couch and padded down the hall. A few moments later, she called out. "Her coat and shoes are here." She returned and nestled back on the couch and into her husband's side. He wrapped his arm around her again.

Eloise was out there with only PJs to keep her warm. "Does Eloise have any medical conditions?"

"No, thankfully," Damon said.

"You've done very well," Amanda told the Maynards. In fact, she was very impressed by their overall composure during the interview. Hope was doing its job and holding them together. "Detective Stenson and I have enough to start our search for Eloise, but before we leave, we're just going to pop upstairs and look at her room, if that's all right?"

"Yes, of course," Damon told them.

"Please just send the list of people who attended the birthday party to the email noted on my card." She gave one to Damon, who passed it along to Krista.

Amanda left the room with Trent, and McGee returned. She overheard him asking the Maynards if he could call anyone to come be with them, as she started up the stairs.

The sound of CSIs Blair and Donnelly moving around helped direct Amanda where to go.

She found Donnelly bent over a section of floor with a sheet of mylar laid down. Amanda had seen this process before and knew that she'd be electro-charging it with a special apparatus to lift shoeprints unseen to the naked eye. Amanda wondered if CSI Stuart, for all her supposed thoroughness, had done this. If she had, she hadn't said anything about it.

Blair stepped over to the doorway, a camera strapped around her neck. "Two in a matter of days. What's going on?"

"We're trying to find out," Amanda replied, turning to Trent. "Whoever is behind this is escalating. They acted impulsively by taking Eloise. So much so their MO has changed. He's breaking into homes now. CSI Stuart wouldn't commit to that being the case at the Tanner home."

"CSI Stuart doesn't commit to much. She's very black and white. Too much so, if you ask me," Blair said.

"A person has to know their mind and stand their ground." Amanda took in the room. The bed was slept in. The sheets were disturbed, and the blanket was on the floor.

"Emma?" Donnelly called for CSI Blair's attention. "There's something under the bed here. Hand me a marker, and photograph it, please."

Blair grabbed a yellow evidence marker from a kit and walked around to where Donnelly was pointing.

Hairs were standing up on Amanda's arms, as she walked to where the CSIs were bunched together. "What is it?"

"Could be socks, a bunched-up shirt... Fabric anyhow." Donnelly's voice was strained and then petered out as Blair took a few pictures, the flash widening out.

Then Blair reached under the bed and pulled out Donnelly's find.

"Way to steal a woman's thunder," Donnelly mumbled.

"You'll get over it," Blair said drily and came out holding a microfiber cloth in her hand.

"Dropped there by someone who was cleaning?" Trent said.

Blair's response was to sniff it. "Chloroform."

Donnelly came to her with an evidence bag, and Blair dropped the cloth in and sealed it up.

"I guess we know how he got the girl to stay quiet." Though Amanda's mind tried to fill in the rest of the blanks. Had he taken her limp body out the front door in his arms?

"You said *he* for a second time." Trent squinted, peering at her face.

"Because I think we're after a male here. Not going at this with a closed mind or anything, but I'm reverting to statistics and a gut feeling. We also can't ignore the mystery man we have with the Tanner case we haven't yet tracked down."

"There's always one." Donnelly smiled at Amanda.

At least the investigator found it amusing. "Job hazard, but a look at our track record also tells us they don't stay a mystery for long."

"That's right." Blair smiled. "Now, I will tell you we processed the note and found one print. We ran it through a new mobile device we have."

"New tech? I guess we're moving up in the world," Trent said.

"Yeah, yeah," Blair said.

Amanda just wanted to get on with the result. "And what did you find out?"

"No hits in the system. But I understand we think this abduction and Tanner's murder are both connected to Julie Gilbert. I know about Tanner, but any prints on Gilbert?"

Amanda shook her head. "Whoever we're after has covered their tracks well. Or did." There could be light in that latter point.

"Not that the print is getting us anywhere. He doesn't have a record," Blair said.

"Anything else before we go?" Amanda asked.

"All we've got for now," Blair confirmed.

"Trent and I are going to speak with some neighbors across the street, see if we can find anyone home," Amanda said.

Trent turned to her. "We are?"

"Yes. It seems like this guy may have taken Eloise right out the front door. I'd like to see if any of the houses across the street have doorbell cams. If they do, one of them might have picked up movement at the Maynards' house and caught this guy."

"Well, good luck to you," Blair told them.

"Actually, we still don't know how this guy got in," Amanda began. "If you and Isabelle could do a quick look around all ingress points to see if there's any sign of forced entry, that would be great."

"Was part of the plan," Donnelly chimed in.

"Just let me know what you find out," Amanda said on the way out of the room with Trent. They told McGee and the Maynards they were leaving and headed across the street.

"Doorbell cams may pan out," Trent told her. "It also reminded me to tell you we have other videos to watch. One from the park and the one from Hailey's school came in."

"Good to know. But since we're here, we'll stick to the immediate plan."

The house across the street didn't have a doorbell cam. Neither did a few others. They walked farther along and found one three houses down did.

Its recording light switched on when she pressed the button. A standard *ding dong* sounded but otherwise nothing.

"I don't think anyone's home," Trent said.

"We'll need to look up who lives here and call them."

They headed to the car, and Trent did a search, found a number associated with the homeowner and had to leave a message. "Okay, well, there's that. Even if it caught something, there's nothing to say that it will be what we're after. The Maynards' house is there." He pointed at it as if to make his point. It would mean the perp walked down the sidewalk for a bit with Eloise in his arms. This reminded her of another earlier thought she'd had.

"Actually..." She turned away from the car, shutting the passenger door again, and walked toward the pass-through next to the Maynards' house. "He might have parked in the subdivision backing this street and slipped with Eloise down here." She looked up as she walked along the path. "Only one light post along this stretch. It would be shadowed, more discreet than walking along the street."

"Though as you pointed out before, if he took her during the witching hours most people are sleeping."

"We should have officers canvassing anyhow, seeing if anyone saw a stranger or an unknown vehicle lurking in the neighborhood earlier in the day. I'm going to get that going." She pulled her phone and placed a call to the on-duty sergeant of the uniformed officers. A moment later she was hanging up. "It's in the works. More officers should be out soon."

Trent pointed at the Maynards' fenced backyard. "He could have accessed the home through an entry point in the rear, but going out with Eloise through the front makes sense. There isn't any gate in the fence."

"Right. Which I figured would be the case." She still had her phone out and keyed a quick text to Blair, then filled Trent in. "I just asked CSI Blair to put focus on the entry points at the back of the house. We've got to find this girl alive and well, Trent."

"We're going to do our best."

"Let's hope that's enough."

THIRTY

Amanda and Trent scoured the houses on the rear street, but no one had a doorbell cam or any other video setup. By the time they left the Maynards' neighborhood for Central, uniformed officers were canvassing the street and the rear subdivision. CSI Blair confirmed scrape marks had been found on a basement window where someone might have worked the edge with a pry bar. When she spoke to the Maynards they confirmed they never got around to replacing the screen in that window after it got a tear in it last summer. Unfortunately, the frame and latch didn't offer up any prints or touch DNA.

"So what? This guy wore gloves to enter the home but didn't when he handled the note?" Trent said.

Amanda considered it for a moment. "Or wore them the entire time except for when he loaded the paper into the printer."

"So it just so happens the page used for the note was the top or bottom sheet?"

"Stranger things..."

"True."

Trent parked in the lot at Central, and they headed to his

desk to watch the video from the park. The ultimate hope was that they'd catch the man's face and be able to identify him. Though short of that, even his face would be a breakthrough. They might even glimpse his vehicle.

At the sight of her empty cubicle, Amanda thought of Katherine. She hadn't returned her call yet.

Trent didn't waste any time loading up the video. He forwarded in slow motion. The lights on the parking lot caught the eyes of an animal, which showed up as two red orbs in the dark.

"Huh." Trent paused the feed and leaned back.

"What are you doing? Play it. We need to get to Eloise."

"Just one thing first. Rabbit eyes show red when light hits them."

"And there was rabbit hair on the scarf around Hailey's neck. Doesn't mean we're looking for someone with a rabbit."

"No, it would just take one or two coming over to inspect Hailey's body."

"So how long was she left out there?" Amanda strained to see past the circle of light, but there was no way to see the carousel.

"Unless we catch it on camera, only best guess."

"Here's the thing, though..." Amanda paced a few steps within his cubicle, circled back. "He takes her to a park, so she's found, but what's to say this guy didn't hang around to wait until she was?"

"The woman who found Hailey didn't see anyone."

"He could have stayed well hidden. Human eyes don't reflect though, do they?"

"No. We don't have the night-vision that animals do. The light reflection is associated with that."

"Too bad. We could keep watch for two other colored dots." She returned to her post standing at Trent's side, and he resumed playback.

Raccoons were scurrying across the parking lot, but no humans.

"This doesn't make any sense. He wouldn't have walked a long distance with her dead body. Someone could have seen him. He had to come in a vehicle."

As if responding on cue, headlights cut across the lot. The time stamp read 3:35 AM.

Amanda waited for the nose of the vehicle to inch forward. All she'd need was a sliver of the hood, and she or her brother Kyle could identify the make and model. He was a mechanic, and lived and breathed cars. But no such luck. "This is probably our guy with Hailey Tanner."

"If he knew about the camera, he would have done everything to avoid it."

They continued to watch as the car's lights cut out. No one was within sight for a few moments. Then a fresh beam of light flashed, but the source was out of the camera's range. This light was also weaker than the ones in the lot, pinpointed, and moving.

"A headlamp," she said. "That bastard is right there, and we can't do anything about it."

They continued to watch the light grow dimmer as the man put distance between himself and the security camera. It almost faded to nothing when he would have been around the area of the carousel. About ten minutes later, it moved again.

"He's headed toward the restroom."

"Did he wait it out in there?" She felt a spark of hope light her chest. If he stayed in there until daylight, they'd have him on camera when he headed out.

The headlamp disappeared, as he must have gone into the restroom. Amanda remembered that an outside lock on the building had been broken, but hadn't offered up any forensic evidence.

Trent forwarded the video until just before sunrise. In the

growing light, they could see the carousel. They watched as Susan Butters went over and found Hailey's body.

The door to the restroom cracked open. A sliver of light from inside gave them a silhouette.

"It *is* a man," Trent said.

"Yep, and that bastard is right there. Watching everything." She gripped her head as they continued to watch. "Officer Wyatt told us there were two doors. One in the front, and another in back. He could have left through there."

"Would make sense. But you're telling me that Susan Butters never saw him?" Trent continued to play the video, but the man must have taken a different path back to his vehicle. He didn't show up on screen.

"He knew about the camera, all right. And I'm with you. I don't understand how Susan Butters could have missed this altogether. She told us she didn't see anyone in the park. I realize the scarf around Hailey's neck didn't tie back to Susan, but we need to talk with her immediately."

They returned to the car, and Trent got Susan's address from the onboard computer. They were banging on her apartment door ten minutes later.

"Don't tell me she's not—" The door opened, interrupting Trent.

"Detectives?" Susan opened the door wider. "What are you doing here?"

The woman's eyes were red-rimmed, and she had an angry-looking cold sore on her bottom lip. She was wearing a ratty bathrobe at one in the afternoon.

"We have some questions, if we can come in." Amanda made the slightest move toward the apartment, and Susan stepped back to let them inside and took them to her living room.

The place smelled like burned garlic bread.

Amanda and Trent sat on the couch, while Susan dropped

into a chair. A vacant dog bed, toys, and chews remained as a shrine to her late furry companion.

"Susan, we need you to think back to Monday morning," Amanda started.

Her eyes filled with tears. "It's all I think about. And it was Hailey Tanner. That's what they said in the paper. Her poor parents. That poor girl." She sobbed, and tears flooded her cheeks.

"I can imagine the last few days have been extremely rough," Amanda empathized. "Have you reached out to Victim Services?"

Susan nodded. "Speaking with them is the only thing keeping me from losing it altogether."

"I'm sure it will get better over time, but I need you to try and remember. Was any vehicle in the parking lot when you arrived?" Amanda asked her.

"Yes? No? I don't know. I'm sorry, but I came by foot through another section of the park."

"You never saw one then?" Amanda reiterated.

"No."

"And you never heard anything?" Amanda was pressing harder now. The man was flesh and blood, not a poltergeist.

Susan opened her mouth, closed it. "Actually. I think maybe there was something..."

Amanda inched forward on the couch. Her entire body was rigid, her chest frozen. "Talk to us." She did her best to sound encouraging while tamping down her roused suspicion.

Susan's eyes were glazed over as she stared at the floor.

"Susan," Amanda prompted.

"Oh my God, I can't believe I forgot about this, but it was right when I found..."

"It's okay, Susan. Please continue," Amanda appealed in a soft tone.

"I was fumbling to get my phone out and call nine-one-one,

but I vaguely recall the sound of a car starting up and the crunching of gravel." Susan's brow furrowed. Conjuring the memory appeared to take effort.

"Did you see the vehicle?" Amanda thought she'd ask again.

"Actually, yes. It was a car. Gray. I still can't believe I forgot to mention this. It's just... I was so... I messed everything up, didn't I? I'm such a self-absorbed loser."

It hurt Amanda's heart to hear this woman talking about herself in such an unkind way. "Please don't beat yourself up over this. You were going through a lot in your own life, and finding Hailey would have been traumatic enough on its own. As for you not remembering, that's understandable. The mind releases things, memories, at its own rate when dealing with a highly stressful situation." She offered these words of encouragement while battling frustration. Eloise's abduction may have never happened if they had this information sooner.

"You said it was a car, though," Trent put in. "Do you remember the make and model?"

"No, I'm sorry."

"It's fine. Did you see who was behind the wheel? A man or a woman?" The size of the silhouetted figure suggested a man, but that didn't mean a woman wasn't in the driver's seat. That was Amanda covering all the bases, but she didn't want to influence Susan's response.

"I just saw a bit of the trunk."

"Okay, thank you. If more comes back to you, call me. Please." Amanda got up, and she and Trent left Susan Butters with just one more tiny piece of the puzzle.

THIRTY-ONE

Amanda did up her seatbelt and sank into the passenger seat, rolling over their one new clue. A gray car. Why couldn't it have been neon green or orange? And was it new or older? Sedan or two-door?

"So do you want to go back and watch the footage from Hailey's school or head over to the Scoop and talk to them there?" Trent was looking over at Amanda from the driver's seat.

"Option two seems the stronger choice to me. We might get a more concrete lead there. With the school video, we don't even know who we're looking for and we're just hoping that we see something that flags for us."

"I get it. The ice cream shop it is. Though the Scoop sounds more like it should be a newspaper."

"Agreed."

Trent got them to the Scoop, and the front door chimed when they entered the business. The smell of waffle cones and sugar had Amanda's stomach grumbling for food, but she pushed it aside.

At two in the afternoon on a Wednesday, they had the place to themselves, which worked better for their purpose.

A balding man in his fifties wearing a bright blue apron came to the counter from the back. "What can I get you fine folks?" he asked, tagging on a smile.

Amanda swept her jacket back exposing the badge clipped to her waist.

His lips fell into a straight line. "What can I do for you, Officers?"

"Detectives Steele, and Stenson," she said. "We have some questions about a birthday party you held here yesterday."

"Why would the police care about that?"

His response seemed rather defensive, but she let it go. "We'll get to that. First, if we could get your name, sir...?"

"Greg Loudon, and I own the place." He walked toward the counter, and she and Trent followed.

"The party was for Eloise Maynard," she supplied. "That sound right to you?"

"Yes. I booked it myself. Is she okay?"

The fact he'd asked about Eloise wasn't suspicious on its own. For one, the police were asking about her. Two, Hailey Tanner's disappearance and subsequent murder had shaken the town. It would be on most people's minds. "We're trying to find that out. We'd like to speak with the servers responsible for that party."

"It was only a group of twelve. Six kids, six women. Tammy was the primary server, and Alec was to back her up. He cut out early though."

"Why was that?" Amanda had her own theory.

"Wasn't feeling well."

"Were you here?" Trent asked.

"Not last night."

Amanda nodded. "We'd like to talk with Alec for a few moments."

"Can't help you there. He called in sick this morning. Must have one of those twenty-four-hour bugs."

It didn't feel like a coincidence that Eloise was taken last night, and this guy left early. But how did that line up with him calling in? If Alec was their killer, would he have bothered? "Is Alec a new hire?"

"Nah, he's been here for a couple of years."

"What does he look like?" Trent asked.

"Alec's a ginger, round face, can't seem to hold a razor. Scruffy all the time. What's this about?"

That wasn't close to the description Krista had provided. "Eloise Maynard was taken from her home overnight. We're trying to track her last movements, see if we can find the person who took her."

"Wow. Okay." Greg rubbed his jaw. "But there's no way Alec's involved with any of this."

"We were told that the party had a male and female server," she said.

"I don't know who it was then. As I said, Alec went home."

"This man was described as having brown eyes and hair, of average build and height, with a scar through his top lip. Do any of your staff fit that description?" she asked.

"Not at all. Did this person say if the man was wearing one of these aprons?" Greg pointed at his own. The Scoop logo of a rainbow landing in a sundae was embroidered front and center.

"She didn't say," Amanda said. It wasn't something she thought to ask Eloise's mother. The man must have looked like he belonged.

"Well, all employees do. Though Alec has lost several of them. I ended up telling him to keep his at the store unless he needed to launder it."

"Is his apron here?" Trent asked.

"It should be. Let me look." Greg disappeared into the back and returned with the apron. "This is it."

"We'd like to take that with us," Amanda told him.

"Ah, sure, if you'll return it when you're finished with it."

"We will." A few things with this scenario didn't gel for Amanda. She'd begin with the foremost one. "Did Tammy comment about anyone else helping her?"

"No."

"We'll need Tammy's number and home address." They needed to have a chat with her.

"Sure."

"Do you have security cameras in here?" Trent asked.

"No. Now I'm wishing we did."

"We'll take Tammy's information now." Amanda wanted to get moving. While they were chasing leads, little Eloise was out there.

THIRTY-TWO

On the way to speak to the Scoop employee, Amanda kept replaying the name they were provided with in her head. Tammy Welland. Would she give them something to break this case open? "This guy is bold. Putting himself in plain sight. And serving a table of twelve."

"I wonder if he wants to get caught. It wouldn't be the first time some sick freak wanted intervention."

"I don't know if I'd go quite that far, but I don't see him stopping unless someone makes him." And she planned on being that person.

"All of this is so unsettling. He could have chosen Eloise from a distance, but he didn't. He served the girl and her mother."

"Definitely a game for him. It also goes back to what Katherine said on Monday. This is about power and control. By besting us so far, he's showing us he has the reins. He has the power, and we can't stop him."

"Only we will. We'll save Eloise too."

Amanda nodded, squeezing out thoughts about what Eloise

might be enduring right now. Her focus needed to stay on saving the girl.

They reached Tammy's apartment building and went up to her floor. She answered after they knocked once.

Amanda held up her badge, as did Trent beside her. "Are you Tammy Welland?" she asked.

"Yeah."

Amanda tucked her badge away and introduced herself and Trent. "Do you have a minute? We have some questions for you."

"Why not? Come in." Tammy was in her twenties, and her energy was laid-back and casual. Her house smelled of sage, and she had a figurine of a beagle posed in meditation on the entry floor.

"That's Rex," Tammy offered, when she must have noticed Amanda looking at it. "I have a habit of naming everything. So what is it?"

The conversation should be brief, so Amanda didn't request a place to sit. "You worked a birthday party yesterday at the Scoop. Is that right?"

"Uh-huh. Good bunch of kids too, but hyper. Though when are they not when they're consuming sugar?" She shrugged and smiled. "What about the party?"

"You worked it with Alec?" Amanda asked.

"No. He went home not feeling well just before, but he sent a friend to help."

The back of Amanda's neck tightened. "A friend?"

"Yeah, that's what he told me anyhow."

"Alec told you this?" Trent asked.

"His friend did. He had an apron, and I assumed Alec gave it to him."

Probably the one sitting in an evidence bag in the trunk. "What was this friend's name?"

"He didn't offer. I didn't ask. I thought about calling Greg to check it was okay, but I didn't want to land Alec in trouble and I needed the help. The place was busy. It was just nice to have an extra set of hands, though he bailed after the party was over. I couldn't find him anywhere."

Amanda resisted the urge to look at Trent. Whoever had worn that apron was the guy they were after. "Is there anything else you can tell us about him? Does he speak with an accent? Did he share anything personal about himself with you?"

"Nothing I noticed, and he wasn't the talkative type. I was just wanting to get my shift over with so I could curl up on the couch and read a book."

"Did you notice if he paid close attention to the girls at the party?" Trent asked.

"Ick. Do you mean it the way I think you do?"

Trent nodded. "Specifically the birthday girl."

Tammy curled her lips in disgust. "I didn't pick up on that, but he had a dark aura. That I picked up on."

"Okay. Thank you for your time." Amanda gave her a business card and said that if she remembered anything distinctive about him to call, whether it was day or night.

"No problem. Would you be able to tell me what all this is about?"

"The birthday girl was taken from her bedroom last night," Trent told her.

"Oh."

"You wouldn't have a number for Alec, would you?" Amanda asked.

"I'll do you one better. He lives down the hall. Apartment three-oh-seven. The second he feels better I'm going to lay into him about how his friend bailed on me too. Though..." She studied their faces. "You don't think that guy was his friend, do you?"

Amanda shook her head and left Tammy's. Trent knocked on the door for 307.

After a few more tries, the door was opened, and a man in his twenties was standing there. His hair was sticking up in the front. "Who are— Police? Is everyone all right?"

"Not exactly," Amanda told him. "We need to talk to you about your friend who stepped in for you last night after you went home sick." She ran with the story as they were told it.

"Huh?"

"He helped Tammy at the ice cream parlor," she elaborated.

"Listen, I don't know what you're talking about."

"Then you never sent a friend to help Tammy at the Scoop last night?"

"No."

"Okay. Thanks. That's all." She bobbed her head at him as if to say he could return to his life. It took a few seconds for it to penetrate.

"Okay," he dragged out and closed his door.

Amanda and Trent regrouped in the car.

"So our killer impersonates a server, when he could have just as easily posed as a customer," Trent said.

"He wanted to get as close as possible, and like we talked about, this is a game to him. He must have seen Eloise celebrating with her friends, ducked inside, and seized an opportunity to get close. We need to revisit Mara Bennett and press her more on this Wilson M. So far, he's our strongest lead."

"Only I got the feeling she told us all she knew."

"Are you willing to take the chance she missed something? Because I'm not."

"All right."

Trent got them headed to the apartment being shared by the sisters, and Amanda pulled out her phone. She debated whether she should call Katherine again and decided in favor of. She answered after the second ring. "There she is," Amanda said. "It's me."

"I see that. It's a fancy new technology called Caller ID."

At least she was holding on to her sense of humor. "Not so *new*, but that aside, how are you doing?"

"Please don't even ask that. There are no words."

If Amanda could reverse time, she wouldn't have asked. "I know Malone sent you home."

"And the chief. But I'm not alone. I've got twenty-four-hour security detail in case this guy comes for me."

"I don't think you should take any chances. Let's just say nothing would surprise me at this point."

"What do you mean?"

"He's getting brazen, making himself more visible, almost like he's taunting us, challenging us to find and stop him."

"I just hope you find that little girl alive. Though..."

Amanda's mind slipped where Katherine's might have gone. Even if they saved Eloise's life, they might be too late to preserve her innocence. "I know what you're thinking, but we can't go down that road. We do what we can."

"If I hadn't wasted your time with Harrington, then maybe..."

"There's no benefit to thinking that way. Everyone understood what you saw there."

"Well, you're more forgiving of me than I am."

"We're always harder on ourselves."

"But hold up, you said *he*. Do you know that for sure now?"

Amanda thought back to the size of the silhouette in the park's restroom. "We do."

"Well, I left the lists of names behind. I put them in the top drawer of your desk. The ones connected with the pageant and the NYC venue. They are clearly marked."

"Okay, thanks. Did you hear any more from Briggs about the sender of the online form?"

"He was able to track it back to New York, but that's it."

"Which doesn't come as a surprise."

"Nope, but I just can't seem to get anything to click. I'm out of touch or too close. Maybe in too deep."

Amanda sympathized with her friend, and she didn't say as much but stepping back might be the best thing. "Just take care of you."

"Thanks. Talk soon, and please let me know when you find Eloise."

"Will do."

During her conversation with Katherine, Trent had already parked in the lot at the apartment building. It was midafternoon, so there was a chance that Kendra wasn't around to hover and play protector of her sister.

Mara Bennett answered the door and let them in. "Kendra's at work. It's just us, but I've said everything I can think of. I don't know who took Hailey."

"There's another little girl who has been taken," Amanda said, laying it right out there.

Mara lowered onto the couch. Amanda and Trent sat in other chairs in the living room.

"I never heard about that on the news."

"It probably hasn't hit yet. She was taken from her home last night," Trent said.

"That's horrible, but I don't know what I'm supposed to do about it."

"To start, does the name Eloise Maynard sound familiar to you?" Amanda asked.

"No. Is that the girl's name?"

"It is. As I'm sure you can appreciate, we are doing everything possible to save her. You said that you had a single date with a man you met at Hailey's school, the night of the *Nutcracker* performance."

"Just the one. I told you everything I know." Her voice trembled.

"I don't mean to upset you, Mara, and even if this man is

behind all of this, none of it's on you. You understand that, right?"

Mara nodded.

"Good. Now, you said his name was Wilson and his last name started with M. Do you remember what that is now?"

"No. I'm sorry."

"That's fine. Would you know the date when you went out with him?" Trent asked.

"Actually, yes. I keep everything in my Google calendar." She picked up her phone from the side table and worked her finger across the screen. "It was sometime near the end of February. One second..." Mara tapped away on her phone. "Here it is. February twenty-second. Right, I should have remembered. He said that's a lucky number. Two, two, two. I thought it was strange, but I know some people are into numerology. I wrote it off as him being quirky and charming."

Having this snapshot of the dating world, Amanda wasn't in any hurry to go back in. So many people were into playing games, and she had enough drama with the job. "Where did you go on this date?"

"Out for dinner at Flanigan's. It's an Irish pub with traditional Irish fare."

Trent had his tablet out and was working on it.

"And did he share anything at all about his life with you?" Amanda was certain that he would have lied about most things, but some gem of truth could have made its way in there.

"Hmm. Come to think of it, he flipped any question I asked back on me. He also doled out a lot of flattery."

"Who paid for the meal?" Trent asked, likely considering tracking a credit card, if he'd used one.

"I did. He acted all embarrassed saying he forgot his wallet. No cards in his phone case or stored on his phone either, he said. Which was weird, because who relies on an actual wallet these days? But he said he'd cover the check next time. I made a joke of that in a text he never replied to."

Amanda agreed that relying solely on a wallet was increasingly unusual. But Wilson clearly had a ready excuse, and Mara had said he was charming. "Did he pick you up for your date?"

"Uh-huh. He was driving a gray Kia K5. It was a few years old."

It was an unlikely coincidence that Susan Butters saw a gray car near the park. "Is there anything else you can remember?"

Mara shook her head and stopped. "We went for a walk after dinner and passed by a house in the throes of a party. He grabbed my hand and said it looked like fun, and we should crash it. But that's not who I am. He tried to convince me to go, saying he'd done it a million times and that it was fun to pretend to be someone else sometimes. I didn't think much of it. Maybe I should have." Tears fell, and she pressed her palms to her cheeks.

Grief messed with a person's mind, but what Mara had just said clung like a burr. *It's fun to pretend...* If this was the man they were after, he'd pretended to be a server at the Scoop, but what other roles had he played? Mara had described him as quirky yet charming, which didn't align with their killer's profile of someone who was socially awkward. He must be able to put on an act. But all this sparked a theory, and she needed to talk it out with Trent. She stood. "Detective Stenson, we should go." She was at the door when she called back a "Thank you" to Mara.

She started talking while she and Trent headed for the parking lot. "There was something that Mara said in there that got me thinking. We know the killer is someone who can be charming and manipulative. Learning that he likes to play different roles or put on personas isn't much of a stretch."

"Okay, I'm following so far."

"Well, Mara said this guy wanted to crash a party. The Gilberts held a party the night that Julie was assaulted and killed."

"Right, but Katherine reached out to everyone she knew attended and cleared them."

"Everyone she knew about. It was an open-invite kind of deal, though."

"Shit, so you're thinking the killer wasn't a guest, but an outlier, a party crasher?"

"That's exactly what I'm thinking."

"All right, but even if that's the case, how would we go about finding him?"

"I don't have all the answers, but maybe if we revisited the people we know about, someone will remember this guy."

"A man with brown hair, brown eyes, dimples, and a scar on his lip? Even that seems a stretch."

Her enthusiasm dampened. "You're right. It's not reasonable, but this might be a new angle that Katherine hasn't considered."

"Though it's possible, there won't be a trail for us to follow."

"I disagree. The only reason he's resurfaced, even calling Katherine out, is he must have been aware she was poking around in the fall. Either directly or he's still in touch with someone who was backstage. We reach out to those people again and see if they remember a person of his description."

"If we don't talk directly to him. On another note, I'm pretty sure this guy's real name isn't Wilson."

They got into the car, and Trent keyed into the onboard computer. A few seconds later, he confirmed. "No gray Kia K5s registered to any Wilsons."

"Not much of a surprise. I'm calling Katherine."

"I thought Malone wants her off this now."

Amanda shook her head. "He said he told her to go home. I doubt he stated explicitly she's not to touch this anymore."

"I feel that was the implication."

"Fine, I'll run this past Malone." Amanda got into the car and shared what had transpired in their conversation with Mara Bennett.

"Let me get this straight. You think the killer crashed the Gilberts' party twelve years ago?" Malone asked when she'd finished looping him in.

"That's right. We need Katherine to reach out to everyone there that night that she knows about."

"Including the potential of talking to the killer himself again."

"But that's the thing... I'm starting to think this person was on the periphery, which means Katherine's calls since she's been helping us didn't trigger this guy to take Eloise," Amanda explained.

"Yet, you've hinged everything on this guy getting spooked in the fall. He's in touch with someone. And you do realize that Katherine was sent home? We can't take the chance this guy will take another child," Malone said.

"We need to focus on saving Eloise. Having Katherine helping us again can make that happen faster. And when time is..."

"Of the essence, I know." Malone's side of the line fell silent for a bit. "Fine. Rope Katherine in again. I'll speak to the chief and let him know the latest development."

"Thanks, Sarge."

"You might be getting ahead of yourself." With that, he was gone.

Next, Amanda called Katherine on hands-free. After explaining the situation, Katherine said, "And you cleared this past the chief?"

"Past Malone. He's handling Buchanan."

"Well, that's just one aspect of the nightmare. How do you expect me to track an invisible man who turned up at a party twelve years ago? It would be easier to pull a rabbit from my hat."

"And you can do that, Kat." She didn't say it, but thought, *For Julie, Hailey, and Eloise...* "We're likely looking for someone linked to a guest, who also had backstage access at the NYC venue for Julie's last pageant."

"Based on me spooking this guy in the fall."

"Correct. He's got brown eyes, brown hair, dimples, and a scar through his top lip. This person..." Amanda was going to say *outgoing*, but had another thought.

"Amanda?" Katherine prompted her.

"The profile noted the killer is likely socially awkward, likely quiet and reserved. I was thinking how he might want to play at being someone else. Say, the life of the party. Now I'm rethinking that. If he was there with people who knew him, he wouldn't have been that way. He would have been a wallflower who disappeared."

"Making my life harder. It's hard to find someone who is invisible."

"A little girl's life is on the line. We need to ID this guy and find him fast."

"I'll do what I can. You know I will."

"Good luck."

"I'll need it."

Katherine clicked off, and Amanda turned to Trent. "Let's get the apron to the lab, then head to Flanigan's. Let's see if we can get this guy's face from security cameras."

"You got it."

As he drove, Amanda hoped they were on the right track with this. If they weren't, she didn't even want to think about all the lost time and what that might mean for Eloise.

THIRTY-THREE

The last time Amanda had been to an Irish pub was with Kevin when they were first married. Before Lindsey came along, they made a point of trying out different restaurants. Once they were parents, they stuck to their favorites on their rare nights away.

Malone called on their way to the pub with news of his own. Though for a few seconds, Amanda feared he was calling to say the chief vetoed his approval for Katherine to help again. Instead, he informed her that an officer canvassing the subdivision behind the Maynards' house had an eyewitness who saw a gray Kia K5 pull away. A man was behind the wheel. This was the third mention of a gray car, and the second time for this make and model. It was hard to ignore the connection to Wilson. They had to figure out this guy's real identity.

A young woman at the host stand smiled at Amanda and Trent when they entered the pub. "Bar or dining room?"

Amanda showed her badge. "A manager," she said with a smile.

The woman nodded and looked over her shoulder. A man in his forties was watching and came walking over.

"Can I help you?" While the wording of the question could

be taken as friendly and cooperative, his tone was all business. He wanted them *dealt with* so he could get back to things.

"We're hoping so," Amanda said and stepped to the side when a few more people entered the pub.

"How about we talk in my office?" the man suggested.

Amanda nodded, and she and Trent followed him, still not knowing his name.

The *office* was the size of a janitorial closet with a desk and chair squeezed in there.

"Thank you for agreeing to talk with us," Amanda began and introduced herself and Trent. "You are the manager?" It seemed rather straightforward that he was, but she wanted to confirm it.

"Yeah. Roman Crawford."

"If we wanted to see security video, would that be something you could help us with?" She'd noted the cameras over the bar as they'd walked past it to get back here, but that didn't mean they were working.

"I'd have to ask what this is about." Roman narrowed his eyes. "Police business obviously, but...?" He was fishing for details she wasn't willing to divulge.

"I can't provide specifics as it's pertaining to an open investigation," she said, "but your help could mean the difference between life and death."

"Life and death?" Roman didn't seem to buy it, and Amanda could appreciate it sounded dramatic, but it was the truth.

"I assure you that's what's at stake," she said firmly.

Roman held her gaze, then nodded. "All right. I'll do whatever I can to help, and we have security cameras."

"And they are working?" She was reserving her enthusiasm.

"They work, and it's all stored on site. Just tell me what time and date you'd like to see."

Amanda told him and watched his eyes shadow when she said February 22.

Roman winced. "Yeah, I might have gotten carried away. That's three months ago, and we only store the last sixty days. Otherwise, our computer would get bogged down."

And that is why I rarely get excited in advance...

"I could check the old shift schedules," Roman went on, "see who was working that day? Show them a photo of whoever it is you're looking for?"

"We're working on a description only for now. But we can revisit that in future if needed."

"Sure thing."

"Okay, well, thank you for being willing to help," Amanda said, making a move to leave.

"Sorry I couldn't," Roman said to her retreating back.

Amanda and Trent were at the exit when Trent's phone rang.

He took out his phone and checked the screen. "Unknown number," he said then answered. "Ah, yes, thank you for returning my call. That would be great. We'll be right there. Thank you." He pocketed his phone. "What's that saying? One door closes, and another...?"

Opens, or God opens a window... She'd heard it both ways. "Just tell me there's reason to hope."

"There is," he reiterated. "That was Tessa Keirns."

"Which you say like it should mean something to me."

"It's the homeowner from the Maynards' neighborhood with the doorbell cam."

"Get us there." And just like that, any caution to reserve enthusiasm was cast aside. With a little girl depending on them, they had to grasp any lead that came their way.

THIRTY-FOUR

Amanda listened to the doorbell melody finish and was about to ring it again when a petite woman wearing a T-shirt and yoga pants opened the door. She was enveloped in a cloud of strong rose-scented perfume. She looked past Amanda to Trent.

"Detective Stenson?" she asked.

"I am, and this is Detective Steele. Tessa Keirns?"

"Yes." Tessa stepped back to let them inside. "You said you were interested in watching footage from my doorbell cam?" Tessa said, and for the first time showed a bit of hesitation.

"That's right," Trent told her. "Does your device just record around the time the doorbell is rung or is it triggered by a motion sensor?"

"The latter, and it's too sensitive if you ask me."

That ever-crippling hope was making further inroads. "What is its reach? Would it catch movement across the street, for example?"

"It does. Hence too sensitive. I want to know if someone's on my porch, not if a neighbor's walking by with their dog, you know?"

"I get that," Amanda said. "But that sensitivity could be

important here. Could we see whatever footage you have for the wee hours of this morning?"

"Sure. I have the app on my tablet, through here." Tessa led them to the living room and grabbed it from an end table. She opened the cover, tapped on the screen, and wriggled her finger around. A few seconds later, she handed the tablet over to Trent.

He held it so that Amanda could see the screen.

"You just have to hit the play button there," Tessa said to them, leaning across Trent's arm to point out where to click.

"Thanks." Trent pushed the button.

At two AM, a dark-clad figure walked partway through the lane next to the Maynards' house. It was too dark to make out much of anything else. Digital techs might make more of it by zooming in and cleaning up the pixels.

The figure hopped the chain-link fence and went into the Maynards' backyard.

"Did that guy just...?" Tessa had creeped in behind them and must have caught sight of the screen.

Trent pulled the tablet to himself. A matter of too little, too late, though.

"Are you guys investigating a break-in? Should I be worried about my safety? I noticed the cops down the street." Tessa was breathing heavier, and her cheeks paled. "I live here alone."

"We don't believe there's any reason for you to be concerned," Amanda assured her.

"Okay? I don't understand. But usually when one robbery happens in a neighborhood, more follow."

Trent glanced at Amanda, and she nodded.

"Do you know the family who lives in that house?" he asked Tessa, pointing at the Maynards' place on the screen.

"No. That might make me sound like a bad person. It's just life is so busy."

Amanda smiled at her. "It's understandable, and you're not the only person who doesn't know their neighbors."

"I know the ones on each side of me. Well, just on a first-name basis and to say hi when we see each other."

"You're doing better than most people," Trent told her. "But that house is home to a family of three, including a seven-year-old girl, Eloise. She was taken from her bed last night."

Tessa gasped. "That poor girl. Is she okay?"

"We're not sure. That's why we need to get to her as soon as possible," Amanda said, urgency in her voice.

"Yeah, of course. And that's why you want to look at my video. Is it helping? Is that the man who took her?" Tessa pointed toward her tablet nested in Trent's hands.

"We believe so. Now, we need to look at some more footage. I assume the camera was triggered a bit after this?" Amanda said, looking at Tessa.

"Let me see." She put her hands out for the tablet, and Trent passed it over. She fussed with it for a moment. "A few more times after that from the looks of it."

They watched a racoon race across the street and a piece of trash blowing down the sidewalk. But they struck gold on the third video. The time stamp was 2:27 AM.

It showed the dark-clad figure again, but this time he was carrying a limp Eloise in his arms.

"Is she—?" Tessa clamped a hand over her mouth.

"Ma'am, it might be best if you leave this to me and Detective Stenson," Amanda said, drilling her with her eyes.

"Ah, sure." Tessa backed up to the couch and sat down.

Trent, who had paused the video at Tessa's interruption, resumed the playback. On screen, the dark-clad figure hustled down the sidewalk toward the pass-through. He ducked down there and disappeared out of sight.

Once the video cut out, Trent looked at Amanda. They'd caught him in the act, and that revelation packed an emotional punch. This strange man had just helped himself to the Maynards' sweet daughter. As a mother, Amanda was triggered. She would sacrifice everything to see this through and stop this guy. They needed a digital copy of this video to take with them and to forward on to Digital Crimes, but one other thing stood out to her. "Tessa," Amanda said, turning to face the woman on the couch. "Could we get a copy of all the videos shot in the last twenty-four hours?"

Tessa pushed off the couch and came over to them. "I'm sure I can figure out a way to share all the files."

"Thank you," Amanda said.

"If I could?" Tessa held out a hand for the tablet, and Trent passed it over to her. She studied the screen, her brow bunching down in focus. "Ah, here it is. Where should I send it?"

Amanda rattled off her email address.

Tessa pecked at the screen as Amanda spoke, and soon after said, "Done. Did you receive it?"

Amanda pulled out her phone and checked her email app. One filtered in from Tessa. She opened it and counted the attachments. "Twenty videos?"

"Yeah, but they're short. Only ninety seconds each."

That didn't sound as overwhelming as it could be. "This is wonderful, Ms. Keirns. Thank you."

"Don't mention it. I hope you find the girl."

"We're going to do all we can," Amanda said, and she and Trent left Tessa with a card and a request that she keep all that footage backed up somewhere, despite Amanda now having a copy.

Trent slid behind the wheel. "He knew what he was doing. There was no hesitation about jumping the fence."

"I noticed that too. He had in mind where he was going to enter the home."

"So he must have scoped things out before he came to take Eloise," Trent put in.

She nodded and smiled at him. "Exactly."

"That's why you asked for that extra footage from earlier?"

"Yep. If there's video of him when the sun was still up, we just might get a clear shot of his face."

"We can hope."

"Yes, we can." She was making peace with hope.

"Back to Central?" Trent asked, looking over at her.

"Yes. We're going to watch all these videos and get anything we need over to Digital Crimes."

"Sounds like a plan. We also have the school video to watch."

Malone called her phone, just as Trent was pulling away from the curb, and she answered on hands-free.

"Where are you guys right now?" he asked, getting right to the point.

"Heading back to Central."

"Good. Time to talk. Chief Buchanan's called a meeting."

That statement felt like a looming thundercloud. "Trent and I just got a huge lead. We'll be there in under ten." She ended the call and looked at Trent with pressed lips.

"Wonder what he wants."

"I don't know what his agenda is, but at least we're going in with something to offer him." She hoped it would make him happy because she didn't have the bandwidth to defend herself and Trent to the police chief.

THIRTY-FIVE

Amanda and Trent walked through the side door at Central and headed straight to the conference room. They found Malone, the chief, and Katherine waiting on them. Seeing her was an unexpected, but welcome surprise.

Amanda sat beside her friend, and Trent next to Amanda. Malone was across the table from the three of them, and the chief was at the head of the table.

"After speaking with Sergeant Malone again, I've brought Katherine back in to help." Buchanan looked at Amanda. "While I am still concerned with her safety and the department's reputation, she is in a unique position to aid this investigation." Buchanan turned to Katherine. "Have you made any progress linking our killer to the Gilbert party?"

"I've made some calls, but haven't unearthed anything yet," Katherine said.

The chief nodded. "Stay on it. Now I called this meeting to let you know the PWCPD is preparing to go public with Eloise Maynard's abduction. As part of this, we are going to make an appeal encouraging anyone to come forward who has any information on Eloise or Hailey Tanner."

"I'm not sure such a public appeal is wise," Amanda said. "It might spook this person into taking rash action." *And Eloise will pay the price...*

"Detective, the PWCPD is charged with keeping order and protecting its citizens. We need to show we're proactive, not just sitting back while some deviant wreaks havoc in Prince William County. Enough is enough."

It was hard not to take offense at his implication. "I assure you that Detective Stenson and I have been tirelessly working this case from the moment we were called in. We've followed every lead, and we believe the perp targeted Eloise Maynard at her birthday party. It was held at the Scoop, an ice cream parlor, the night before her abduction. We also believe that same man ingratiated himself to the Tanners' nanny, Mara Bennett, to get close to Hailey."

"All right. Good, good," the chief said. "Some of which I've heard from Sergeant Malone."

"Well, here's something that's new," Amanda began. "Detective Stenson and I just came into possession of some video footage that could give us his face."

"You have his face?" Katherine muttered.

Amanda turned to her. "We could have. Trent and I were coming back here to watch the video footage."

"So you haven't seen it yet?" Buchanan asked.

"Not all of it, but enough to see a dark-clad figure enter the Maynards' backyard and hustle down the sidewalk about thirty minutes later with Eloise in his arms," she told everyone.

The energy in the room intensified.

"I want to see this video. Now," Buchanan demanded.

"There are twenty videos, for a total of thirty minutes." Amanda didn't think the chief would have that sort of time to dispense.

"Play them, Detective."

"Ah, sure." Amanda looked at Trent, who was a bit more tech savvy.

"Here, hand me your phone," he said. "You turn the TV on."

It was possible to project her phone to the large flatscreen mounted to the wall, but she couldn't always remember how to do it.

A moment later, they were watching the first video. This was the one that showed the perp jumping the Maynards' fence.

"Guy's lithe," Buchanan commented.

"He's strong and in shape," Amanda agreed. "At two twenty-seven AM, you'll see him carrying Eloise down the sidewalk."

"And yet no one calls it in." Buchanan was shaking his head.

"At that time of day most people are sleeping," Malone pointed out.

"I suppose so. It's just a shame, that's all," Buchanan lamented.

They watched the other video that she and Trent had watched at Keirns's house, and then they went on to the new footage. They struck gold with a video from the night before at seven PM. A blue van drove past, followed soon by a gray Kia.

"That's him," Malone said.

Due to the angle, no plate was visible. But the car slowed down as it approached the Maynards' house. The van pulled into the garage.

"He followed them home from the birthday party," Trent said, looking at Amanda.

They moved on to another video taken at seven thirty. It showed a man walking down the sidewalk in blue jeans, running shoes, and a black jacket.

Amanda leaned in. "Trent, can you go back to the one of him carrying Eloise?"

Trent did as she asked, and when it started playing Amanda rushed to the TV and pointed at the screen.

"It's the same guy at seven thirty. Both are wearing blue jeans, but what stands out to me are the bright white running shoes."

"Huh," Trent muttered.

"What is it?" She turned to him, reading off her partner that something had hit him.

"Running shoes don't stay bright white for long, but new rubber soles might be more likely to rub off than ones that are worn down." He met her gaze.

"Which brings me to where I was headed. The scuff marks left on the lattice outside of Hailey Tanner's bedroom," she said.

"Uh-huh."

"All right, back to Eloise," Buchanan inserted. "If it's the same guy, we have him scoping out the Maynards' place. Bring up that video from seven thirty again, Stenson."

Trent resumed the playback, and the man in jeans walked down the pass-through. He was creeping along and looking into the Maynards' backyard.

"He's deciding on an entry point," Trent said.

"The basement window, which we now know," Amanda put in.

"Well, we've got a clear shot of his shoes, but no face yet. Tell you what, I'm going to leave, but you get that, send me his picture." Buchanan stood and headed for the door.

All righty then...

Trent was reversing the video and zoomed in.

"Do you see something?" Amanda asked him, and it stalled Buchanan's steps. All she saw was a rather vague character despite the sun being out, given the angle of the doorbell cam in relation to the sidewalk. Even when he reversed course and walked back to the street from the pass-through, he kept his head down. Had he been considering security cameras, or was he just trying to hide his face in general?

"Unfortunately not," Trent said.

Buchanan left, and Amanda looked at Katherine. She was flushed. Amanda touched her arm. After all these years hunting the man who killed Julie Gilbert, seeing him on the TV must have been surreal.

"Did you need help calling anyone?" Amanda asked her.

"No, that's why I'm here. There are other things you could do," Katherine said. "If we split our efforts, we might track this guy down. Could you forward the videos to me, Trent? I'd like to look at them more. If I find the guy's face, I can forward it along to the chief too."

A tiny tell in Katherine's tone and flicker in her eye had Amanda suspecting she had seen something. "What aren't you saying?"

"There is something familiar about him, but I can't put my finger on why."

Malone perked up at that, as did Amanda and Trent.

"Please, don't get too excited just yet," Katherine said. "If it comes together, I promise I'll share."

"See that you do." Malone hastened out of the room, leaving Amanda with Trent and Katherine.

Trent turned the TV off and handed Amanda her phone back. She forwarded the email with the videos to Katherine.

"On another matter, you ever hear more from Briggs about the sender of the online form?" Amanda asked.

"Just what you already know. The sender tracks back to NYC." Katherine opened the lid on her laptop, getting comfortable right there in the conference room.

"You can use my office, if you want," Amanda offered.

"I'm fine right here."

"Suit yourself." Amanda led the way from the room with

Trent. She glanced over her shoulder at Katherine and found her friend staring at the screen of her laptop. Whatever was familiar about that man, Amanda hoped it would come back to Katherine before too much time passed.

THIRTY-SIX

Watching the videos was like a car crash, and Katherine couldn't turn away. She watched the one of the man carrying Eloise in the dead of the night. Why she was torturing herself God only knew. Her poor daughter would have known those arms. *Only she stopped being my daughter when I gave her away...*

What burned now was despite spending the better part of the last twelve years searching for this man, he got to Katherine first. But if he assumed she was the timid sort to back off from a challenge, he had no clue who he was dealing with. He'd made a mistake by taunting her, and soon he'd realize that. She also didn't stand on her own. She had a team to support her, to back her up. Because of their work, he was on her screen. But why was he familiar? And something had been said about a scar through his top lip... She'd spiral into insanity if she tried to force it.

She had reached out to the Gilberts. Evan by phone and Dawn by email, which was how she preferred to be contacted. This suited Katherine, who feared if she called the woman, her voice would give her away. Dawn would detect Julie's killer had claimed other victims. As the woman who took Julie in as a baby, she didn't deserve to feel any more grief or guilt. Katherine knew that she had struggled with what had happened to Julie, how it had scared her sober and that she hadn't touched a drop of liquor since.

"If I hadn't been so drunk..."

Dawn's statement had regurgitated through Katherine's mind many times over the years to the point of obsession. While one mother battled with guilt, so did another. Only Katherine had done so in secret.

The conversation she'd had with Evan about the party wasn't helpful. She turned to her email hoping her luck would change. She found a reply from Dawn and clicked on it.

Hi Katherine,

It is always good to hear from you. At least I know my daughter is still remembered after all these years and that someone else cares. I miss her every day with an ache in my chest that won't go away. I'm learning to live with it, while I'm also adjusting to being single. Evan and I separated a couple of years ago, as you know. The divorce finalized last week. I know people are holding divorce parties these days, but it didn't seem appropriate. I grieve the death of our relationship too. But losing a child in such a horrific way... Nothing can prepare you.

As much as I want justice for Julie, and the man responsible behind bars, at some point I need to release this part of my life and move forward.

Katherine stopped reading there, finding her heart was pounding. She wished to reach through the ether and shake the woman. How could she ever expect to move forward? As healthy as it sounded, was it feasible? Katherine hadn't even changed one of Julie's diapers, and she was in love enough to sacrifice every moment to getting the man responsible. Though, could she claim that when she'd slacked off the last few months?

Katherine returned to Dawn's email.

You might not understand my need to do this, but I've been working with a new therapist. Peace of mind is of the utmost importance and living in the past is no way to find it.

Again, thank you for your dedication over the years, to searching for the man who did this and holding them responsible, but I kindly ask that you leave me out of this loop in the future. That is unless you find this man. Then I want to know, and I will be there in court.

You asked about the people at that party... I still only remember glimpses of it. None of them are clear. A lot of strangers were there, people I didn't know. People from the pageant circuit and the NYC venue. I was so busy bragging to anyone that would listen that I had the most amazing daughter.

Now I must go. Take care of yourself and don't lose yourself in the past either.

Katherine's cheeks were wet, and she swiped them, not realizing tears had fallen as she read. The email was a lot to digest, and she didn't know why but the tidbit about people being there from the NYC venue stuck. Was it plural to cover those from the circuit or did more than one person from the actual venue go to the party? Katherine knew of one person from there who had attended.

She brought up the number for Leslie Gallagher from the venue. Leslie had worked there for fifteen years, making a career out of overseeing the place. Katherine had talked to her about the party years ago, but now there was one fresh point worth bringing up.

Leslie answered on the second ring. "Katherine? Two calls

in one week." Leslie's tone was brisk, but she must have seen her name and answered anyhow.

"I won't take long, as I sense you're busy."

"I'm always busy, but I'm not sure what else I can do for you. I've given you everything you asked for."

"You were at the party that night, the one when Julie Gilbert was killed," Katherine said, cutting right to the point. "Was anyone else from the venue there?"

"I don't remem— No, wait, now that I think about it, Marshall popped by."

"And who is Marshall?" Katherine brought up the venue's employee list. "There isn't one on the list you gave me in the fall."

"Then Marshall screwed up."

"Marshall compiled the list?"

"I don't have time for something so trivial. I can't believe he was so incompetent as to forget his name. That's a new level. I don't know how I put up with him for as long as I did."

The skin tightened on the back of Katherine's neck. No one could be so sloppy as to exclude their own name by accident. "*Did?* So you've fired him?"

"Yes, back around Thanksgiving. Near the time you asked for the list again, actually. I'd had enough of his screwups."

Nice. "And you never reviewed the list before sending it over?"

"As I said, I don't have the time. My assistant's to take care of the tedious stuff."

"How long was he with you?"

"Fourteen years."

"Did he gather the names twelve years ago too?"

"He would have."

His name never made the list the first time around either. "What's his last name?"

"Wilcox. But you can't seriously consider Marshall is involved. Trust me, he isn't who you're looking for here."

Katherine wasn't so sure about that. She'd never heard his name before. He must have left his name off the employee list on purpose. *Twice.* Was Marshall the man they were after? When she contacted the venue in the fall, it must have spooked him. "Does he have a scar through his upper lip?" She went with the one distinguishing attribute. After all, hair color could change and a lot of people had dimples.

"Ah, yeah."

Katherine's entire body was shaking. "And you're sure Marshall was at the Gilbert party that night?"

"Well for a minute or two. Someone bumped into me and got red wine all over my white dress. I had him bring me over a change of clothes."

"That party went late into the night."

"Oh, Marshall would drop everything and do anything I asked. No life outside of work. In fact, *that's* why I put up with him for so long. He was my lap dog from the moment he walked into the interview room and saw me."

This guy was ticking off the boxes on the profile. *No social life, an entry-level job for more than a decade...* "Is he timid? Awkward?"

"Both. He was rather quiet around me from the start. I remember hearing him talking loudly in the hall with the intern that showed him to the interview room. When he saw me, he zipped right up."

His behavior could be nerves at seeing his potential new boss, or there might be more to it. "Was he reserved with everyone, or just those in management positions like yourself?"

"I couldn't say."

Without a solid answer, anything Katherine reasoned would be conjecture. But did Marshall battle with low self-esteem and fear those in authority? Did he funnel his frustration from feeling insignificant into targeting little girls? To feel some self-worth and assume control over one aspect of his life? "How long did he stick around at the party?"

"I don't know."

Katherine wondered if she even would have noticed. Her comments so far made it clear she considered Marshall beneath her. But Katherine had heard enough. Marshall Wilcox was the killer they needed to stop.

THIRTY-SEVEN

Amanda adjusted her posture in her chair. She had hers rolled up next to Trent's, and they were watching the video from Hailey's school from the day of the *Nutcracker* performance. People were going in and out of the school. Some of them were stepping off to the side of the walkway, lighting up cigarettes. Some were alone, others were in small clusters. Without a distinctive image from the doorbell cam footage, pinpointing one person in the crowd was near impossible.

It wasn't until they reached the footage showing people leaving after the show that Amanda sat up straighter. "That's Hailey Tanner with Mara Bennett." They were walking out together hand in hand. "But look there." She pointed at the corner of the screen, where a man was leaning against the side of the school. He was watching Hailey and her nanny.

"Is that...?" Trent paused the video and zoomed in. "He's wearing bright white running shoes, and he's the right size for the man who took Eloise."

"Look how fixated he is on Hailey."

"I'd say." Trent advanced the video in slow motion, and

they watched as the man followed Hailey and Mara until all three were out of the camera's sight line.

"He'd have no reason to follow them from the school," Amanda said.

"Agreed. I'm thinking he spoke to Mara and got her number earlier."

"He couldn't be confident she'd lead him to the Tanners' house. This way he could have tailed them and figured out his best approach."

"There is that. Well, we have his face. Let's try facial rec—"

"No need for facial recognition." Katherine's breathless voice caught Amanda by surprise. When Amanda turned to her, Katherine was staring at the screen.

"Do you know him? You said the man from the doorbell cam felt familiar," Amanda said.

"I think I might. Bring up a background on Marshall Wilcox."

"Okay." Trent did this, and a few moments later they were looking at his license photo.

Katherine gasped. "Half caf, half decaf."

"Kat?" Amanda looked from her friend to Trent and back again. "What is it?"

"That's his regular order. I thought a scar in the lip sounded familiar, but I couldn't place it. But that's him. He comes to the diner. Just this morning, I told him to have a good day, and he said he planned on it. I'm going to be sick." She put her hand over her stomach.

"You were at the diner?" Trent asked.

Amanda shook her head. *Not the point...*

"After I got the boot, I was trying to figure out what to do with myself, so I went there."

"But that would have been just hours after he took Eloise," Trent began. "So what does that mean for the girl?"

They all remained silent for a few beats.

"I guess I'll just come out and say it." Goosebumps laced down Amanda's arms. "Either he's holding Eloise somewhere he can leave her without risk of her being found or she's already dead."

THIRTY-EIGHT

Amanda paced outside Trent's cubicle. Marshall Wilcox lacked imagination, choosing an alias so close to his own. Wilson M-Something. *Please.*

Katherine filled them in on her conversation with Leslie Gallagher. "I can't believe after all this time we have the guy."

"Having his name is one thing. Tracking the asshole down is another," Trent pointed out.

"Is he always like that?" Katherine jacked a thumb toward Trent.

Amanda shook her head. "Usually the opposite, but he's right. Wilcox isn't going to make it easy for us to find him."

"You sound like you're defeated."

"Then you don't know me as well as I thought," Amanda pushed back.

Katherine lifted her hands. "I apologize. It's just after all this time the guy was right there, and I had no idea. He slipped right through."

"Does this guy have a vehicle registered to him? A local address?" Amanda asked Trent.

"He just shows an NYC address. No vehicles tied to him,"

he told her. "Current place of employment listed as the NYC venue."

"Which is clearly out of date," Katherine said. "I just told you that Wilcox was fired last fall. Another thing that stuck out to me was the boss described him as quiet around her. But he wasn't quiet with interns."

"So he is comfortable around people he sees as his equal," Trent said. "He could have a problem with authority."

"I thought the same, but his boss couldn't say one way or the other."

"We unravel that mystery, we might gain some insight into why this monster targets little girls," Amanda said. "Do you know why he was fired?"

"All I was told was his incompetence got to be too much," Katherine said. "But in response to the other thing you said... about why he targets girls. Statistically, the answer to that would go back to his childhood. Who hurt him? What did he suffer so that he thinks what he does is justifiable?"

Amanda looked at her friend. She'd had years to process Julie's loss and consider the type of person who killed her. And while Katherine's words suggested empathy, they had rolled off her tongue with a bitter malice.

"Well, if his termination was the proverbial straw," Trent inserted, "I see how losing his job, combined with Katherine circling back to the venue, could have gotten his attention."

"Thing is, though, he supposedly only popped by the party," Katherine said.

"You can't be doubting his guilt now. That's what his former boss told you. She probably didn't even pay him any attention," Amanda said. "Same may apply to everyone else based on what I've heard. It sounds like this guy lives rather under the radar."

"Which might be why he gets a thrill from crashing parties and pretending to be someone he isn't," Trent said.

"And he might have been fueled to do this more after he got

away with doing so at the Gilberts' party. After..." Amanda left the rest of that unsaid out of mercy for Katherine.

"He got a thrill from hurting Julie," Katherine said, going right there.

"All right, priority one is finding this guy. Figuring out any properties he has connected to him and getting out there." Amanda refused to give up. She wouldn't fail Eloise like she had Hailey.

"As I said, only one address in NYC," Trent said. "It looks like it's an apartment."

"Probably is," Katherine said. "The Big Apple isn't a cheap place to live, and someone who worked as an assistant wouldn't have much money."

"He must have low self-esteem to stick around that long in an entry-level job," Trent said.

"And putting up with Leslie Gallagher. She strikes me as a real bully," Katherine said.

Amanda was squirreling away all this information as it provided a glimpse into Marshall Wilcox. But she was hungry for more. "We need to find out as much as possible about Wilcox. His background, his upbringing, anything that might give us insight into why he'd victimize children. We also need to get someone out to his apartment and see what they can find out from his neighbors or friends. For all we know Wilcox is commuting back and forth, but I think he must be holding the girls somewhere nearby. Someone might be able to point us in the right direction." It niggled that they didn't have the scene of Hailey Tanner's murder, but Amanda would guess once they tracked Wilcox, they'd have that. It was the waiting game that was painful.

"I'll call Detective Fitz." Katherine already had her phone in her hand. "He can handle everything you just mentioned in New York, Amanda. Hopefully, we'll find something we can use." Within seconds, she was talking into her phone. At least there wouldn't be a delay caused from waiting for a call back.

Amanda turned to Trent. "While Detective Fitz is busy with that..."

"We'll look into car rentals and Wilcox's credit history," he finished.

"Yes, but waiting on the financials to look for charges from a rental company will take time."

"Which we don't have. We could call around to some rental companies," Trent suggested. "Though for this to benefit us, he would have needed to use his real name."

"At least we know he likes to use Wilson as an alias." She wasn't going to consider he might have a few to pull from. After all, Hailey's nanny told them he enjoyed pretending to be someone else. Another indicator he wasn't happy in his personal life. Not that this was surprising considering what he did to feel powerful.

Katherine ended her call with Fitz. "He's going to Wilcox's address right now, and he'll let us know what he finds out ASAP."

"Good news," Amanda said. "We need to rope in Sergeant Malone and the police chief on our discovery and get some other things moving."

The three of them set off to Malone's office. They found his door shut but saw through the window in the door that Chief Buchanan was inside.

Amanda rapped her knuckles on the glass. Both men looked her way. Malone was flushed when he waved them in. She'd guess their arrival was a blessing for him.

"We have an ID on our killer," she said, getting right to the point. "Marshall Wilcox. He's from New York City." Amanda filled the sergeant and chief in on Detective Fitz and the suggestion she'd made to Trent.

"There won't be an issue with getting the warrant for his

financials," Malone said. "I'll get on that myself. You said you wanted to call vehicle rental companies in the area. That will keep you busy for a while."

"Thanks, Sarge," Amanda told him.

"Okay, go. Track this bastard down." Buchanan nudged his head toward the door.

Guess we're excused... Amanda was the first out of the office.

"I'm going to make some calls," Katherine told her and Trent, stopping their strides.

"To?" Amanda asked.

"To Wilcox's coworkers from the NYC venue to see if any of them have anything that might help us track him down."

"That's a terrific idea," Amanda told her, and Katherine returned to the conference room. She turned to Trent. "You ready to start on the rental companies?"

"I'm already on with the first one." He smiled at his hyperbole, but she appreciated his eagerness to get going.

"I'm right behind you, but I have a feeling I better arrange some care for Zoe tonight."

They returned to their cubicles, and Amanda called Libby first and explained the situation.

"Please don't worry yourself about it at all. I'd love to keep her overnight..."

The way the sentence dangled, Amanda got the sense a *but* was coming. "If tonight doesn't work, I can arrange for someone else to come get her." The last thing she wanted to do was take advantage of the woman's kindness and love for Zoe.

A few seconds then, "If you could. It's just that Penny and I had planned to spend some time together tonight."

"A date night on a Wednesday, at that. Way to keep the passion alive." Amanda was smiling, happy for the couple.

"Yeah, well, you can wish me luck too."

"Luck for— Oh." Amanda pieced it together. While Libby

and her girlfriend had been living together long enough and were like a married couple, the law wouldn't recognize their union. Amanda suspected Libby wanted to make it legal. "Are you going to ask—?"

"I am."

"Well, you don't need luck for that. She loves you. And don't worry about Zoe. I'll get someone over to pick her up right away."

"Thank you."

Amanda hung up from Libby and called Kristen. Her sister answered in the middle of the second ring. She ran through the situation and struck out again. She had three other sisters and a brother, but she opted to call her mother.

"Mandy? Is everything okay?"

Such a loaded question... "I need someone to take Zoe overnight, or even stay with her at the house. Could you?"

"I'd love to."

"Wonderful. She's at Libby's if you could pick her up. As soon as possible," Amanda added slowly.

"Yes, I will drop everything because it's Zoe." Her mother had a dry sense of humor sometimes.

"Thanks, Mom."

"Hey, it gives me some time with my granddaughter."

"Just don't keep her up too late. She has school in the morning. And are you going to my house or...?"

"Yes, I would think that would be easiest." Her mother's smile traveled the line.

"Wonderful." Amanda ended the call feeling some sense of satisfaction. Zoe would be well taken care of, so Amanda could devote her entire focus to finding Eloise.

Trent was on the phone in his cubicle, already calling vehicle rental companies. He hung up. "No luck there."

"Who's left?"

"Five others in the area."

"All right. No time like the present. Give me a couple, and I'll get started."

Trent handed her some names, and she called them. The first wasn't willing to part with the information even though the police were asking. The second had no record of a Marshall Wilcox or a Wilson M-Something or even renting out a Kia K5.

Trent hung up his phone and looked over the cubicle wall at her, just his eyes and the top of his head showing. "No luck here, though I had to leave a message for the manager at one. I'm not holding my breath."

"Guys." Katherine came hurrying toward them, panting. "I've got something, and you're not going to believe it."

THIRTY-NINE

Amanda found it hard to believe the creep they were after ever had a girlfriend. She rang the bell, and footsteps pounded toward the door. It swung open.

"What are you doing here?" Anne Harrington stood there, her nose bandaged and her face black and blue.

"We need to talk to you for a moment," Amanda told her. "So if we could come inside?"

"The last time you wanted to talk to me I ended up with a concussion and a broken nose." She lifted her hand but stopped short of touching it.

Her injury was technically on her for running away, but Amanda was about picking her battles. She needed Anne in a cooperative mood not an argumentative one. "We shouldn't take much of your time."

Anne narrowed her eyes but stepped back. "Keep it down though. Grandma's having her after-dinner tea and watching the news."

Amanda could hear the TV from the door. "It might be best we talk outside."

"Sure, out back. I don't want all the neighbors gawking.

They're already gossiping about me enough." Anne hustled through the house and out the back like the last time. Amanda was prepared to catch the screen door.

They stepped on the deck into the warm early-evening air.

Anne leaned against the railing and crossed her arms. "What do you want? I just took another dose of pain pills, and I'm about to nod off."

"Does the name Marshall Wilcox mean anything to you?" It was a throwaway question to set up the conversation. They were here because one of Katherine's phone calls had paid off.

"So what if it does?"

"We've learned that you dated Marshall back when you were working in NYC at the venue where they hosted pageants," Trent said. "Is that correct?"

"Yes."

"What happened to that relationship?" Amanda asked.

"*Relationship* is a little much. And for the record, I dumped him. I had to ghost him for months before he got the message I wasn't interested."

"You're sure it wasn't the other way around?" Before coming, Amanda reviewed the names on the restraining orders filed against Anne, and Wilcox wasn't among them.

"Yeah, I'm sure. The guy's a loon."

"Why do you say he's a loon?" Trent chimed in.

Anne rubbed her arms. "It was just an energy he gave off, and he was never really with me when he was with me. Ya know? And he was very aggressive and domineering in the bedroom. A little I'm okay with, but not to where he took things."

Amanda had no interest in probing this any further, but she had little choice. "And where was that?"

Anne's cheeks flushed. "He liked me to dress up in a baby-doll dress and put my hair in pigtails. He'd spank me and say, 'You've been a very bad girl.'"

Amanda was sorry that she'd asked. Now she felt like throwing up. They were certain that Wilcox was the man they were after and knew what he did to little girls. Hearing this made the picture too vivid. "When was the last time you talked to him or saw him?"

"It's been years."

Amanda believed her. "When you were seeing each other, did he ever talk about his childhood?"

"No."

"Did he mention friends or family?"

"No, and I'd be surprised if he had any friends. The guy was a loner. I took pity on him and look where that got me."

"Okay. Thank you." Amanda headed for the stairs off the deck, deciding to walk around the house to the car.

"Wait." Anne pushed off the railing. "Is that all? Why are you asking about— Oh? You think that he, that he did what you thought I did?" She put a hand over her stomach. "Huh. Yeah, I can see that he'd do something like..." Anne turned and vomited over the railing.

That was Amanda's cue to get out of there. She pivoted and hurried to the car. Being so close to emptying her stomach, catching one whiff would do her in.

After doing up her seatbelt, she turned to Trent. "What made Marshall into a monster?"

"Well, you remember the profile. Sexual abuse as a child is likely."

"There is that. Now Katherine told us he was uncomfortable around his boss, but what if it wasn't so much that she was in charge, but that *she* was a *woman*?"

"He may have suffered at his mother's hand, and now he takes it out on innocent girls."

"Just might be the case. Yet he was domineering with Anne."

"In the bedroom, with her already in a vulnerable state. And them both playing a role."

"True."

Her phone rang, and he pulled away from the curb and got them on the way back to Central.

"It's Katherine," she told him before answering on speaker.

"I heard from Fitz," Katherine said.

The fast response lined up with the detective that Amanda had dealt with when Katherine was taken. He never wasted time getting things done. "What did he find out?"

"Marshall's illegally subletting his place to someone. Has been since December."

"Since he found out about your renewed interest in venue employees," Trent interjected. "And after he was fired. That can't be a coincidence."

"Unlikely," Katherine said. "I guess Wilcox flapped his jaw and told these people that he was going away for a few months. For, as he put it, 'peace and quiet in the country.' He didn't tell them where he was heading or how long he'd be gone."

Woodbridge would count as *country* next to New York City. Though many places could be seen that way. "Where do they send the rent?" It felt like too much to hope they mailed a check these days, but it might be a transfer to an account at a local bank.

"They paid cash upfront for six months."

Couldn't be that *easy...* But six months, including December, would put them through May. This month. "And if he was staying away longer?"

"He told them, he'd reach out. And before you ask, they haven't heard from him."

"But they have a phone number for him?" If so, they could track the phone.

"Nope. He just has theirs, and he's never called."

"We can't say the guy's a complete idiot," Trent said. "And

that rent money could be how Wilcox is funding this little venture. How much are we talking about?"

"Twenty-one thousand dollars."

Trent whistled. "Tidy sum."

"I told you. Rent in NYC isn't cheap, but he's probably making a healthy profit. Housing is scarce."

Amanda was disheartened by one fact. "Cash doesn't leave a trail for us to follow."

"Well, Malone's requesting his financials. Wilcox could have slipped up. But I don't see him updating his address with any institution when his move was temporary," Amanda said. "NYPD should watch his place."

"All arranged. Fitz went to his sergeant, and there will be a uniform posted at Wilcox's apartment until we apprehend him. Fitz spoke to the building manager and found out the guy provided references, but they all turned out to be bogus. So no luck tracking down any of Wilcox's friends. The next of kin on file is his mother, but she's been deceased for years."

"Well, we just finished speaking with Anne Harrington, and she provided us with some valuable insights." Amanda shared what they'd learned.

"He had her dress up like a...? Sick freak," Katherine muttered across the line, and Amanda was impressed she went with the PG-version.

"I think he's a victim of childhood sexual assault. Possibly at the hands of his own mother." Since there was a chance of her theory being right, Amanda felt no remorse at casting a stone at a dead woman. "And I say this because he wanted to assume a dominant sexual role with Harrington. Then, there was the whole 'you've been a bad girl' thing."

Katherine's end of the line went silent.

"You still there?" Amanda prompted.

"Oh, I'm here, and I don't think you're far off the mark. When I was talking to Wilcox's former boss, she said that he fell quiet upon seeing her in the interview room. Before that he was chatting away loudly with an intern. I don't know the intern's gender, but as you know, the boss's name is Leslie. A unisex name."

"Maybe he was expecting to be interviewed by a man, not a woman," Trent said.

"Holy shit. I think we're on to something here. And sexual abuse at his mother's hand could explain his dysfunctional relationships with women," Katherine said. "His boss and Harrington, just two that we know of."

"And his only way of coping with his feelings of inadequacy is to take it out on little girls," Trent said.

"We've got to save Eloise." Katherine's voice sliced across the line. "I'll make some more calls, see if I can get anywhere else."

"And press Briggs about that online form too," Amanda said. "It's still feasible that Wilcox identified that janitor to keep the spotlight off himself. And, yes, I realize this is before you started pushing more about venue employees, but this guy is anxious, in my opinion. He's likely been keeping tabs on the investigation and you from day one."

"Nothing creepy about that thought," Katherine said.

"Well... it makes sense he'd be watching you and your website," Amanda said.

"He'd want to know if you were getting close to finding him," Trent added.

"Even if that's the case, we're getting close to stopping this guy now. I must believe that."

"I think we all do," Amanda put in.

With that, the call ended, and Trent was pulling into the parking lot of Petey's Patties.

"I think you took a wrong turn." She pointed from the restaurant to the road.

"Nope. I'm starving, and there might not be another time to

eat. And before you say, how can I eat at a time like this, let me tell you. I'm with Katherine. I feel it in my gut that we're narrowing in on this guy. We're going to save Eloise, and to do that I need my strength. So you can eat or not. That's up to you, but I am." Trent parked, turned the car off, and got out.

She followed a few seconds later, and he was waiting by the car. "I'm with you. Just don't tell Zoe we ate here without her."

Trent smiled. "I promise."

Amanda's phone rang with Malone's name on the screen. She answered.

"Just calling to let you know the appeal to the public has been issued and calls are already coming in."

"Any panning out?" She had little respect for the media, nor did she agree with Buchanan's decision about posting Wilcox's face out there. For the off chance someone would recognize him, she felt the risk was too high. All they'd learned so far painted the picture of a man who didn't like the spotlight.

"Nothing yet, but I'll keep you posted if that changes. I take it you and Trent struck out with vehicle rentals?"

"So far. Trent's waiting for a call back from one company in the area."

They ended the call a moment later, and she updated Trent and added, "I still have this horrible feeling the public appeal is going to spook Wilcox and make him do something rash." Though even as she said that she recognized the irony. His recent actions showed he was already there.

"It could, but it also might help us find the guy."

"Yeah, well, I'm thinking we should contact the rental companies near Wilcox's apartment in NYC. Even if there are several, it's better than sitting on our hands."

"Okay, I get you want to do something proactive."

"You bet I do." She was quaking with frustration and worry over Eloise. "And maybe it makes more sense he'd rent a car in NYC. Otherwise, how did he get to Woodbridge?"

"Train, bus... He could have even hitchhiked. The possibilities are endless. And let's face it, he would have watched his steps and kept a low profile. Those options would provide that more than renting a vehicle, which requires a credit card."

"But we've seen cases where that's been waived by a rental company before. Not that it matters since we don't have his financials. But the cash he collected from subletting his apartment would have made it easier for him to stay off the grid."

"One light in that tunnel is he's been messing up since he got here. The notes to Katherine, snatching a second girl. He's getting sloppy."

"Which is good for us." Not that this made her feel better.

"Amanda, I know you want to save Eloise. So do I, but just doing things for the sake of doing something isn't productive either."

"It feels better than waiting around."

Someone came out of the burger joint, and she and Trent stepped out of the way. The smell of the barbecued patties had her stomach growling.

"Fine, we'll eat quick, and then we'll..." For someone who mapped out the next several steps in her head, her mind was blank.

Trent touched her shoulder. "It's all right not having answers all the time. We'll get them."

She appreciated the sentiment, but she was screaming inside. *It would be nice just this once!* But she nodded and then went into the restaurant. They each got a coffee and a cheeseburger. Trent added a side of fries.

The woman at the counter was grinning at them. "Hey, it's you two again. Where's that sweet little girl of yours?"

She must have thought she and Trent were a couple, but Amanda wasn't in the mood to correct her. "She's with her grandmother tonight," Amanda told her.

"Good for her. Grandmas are the best." The woman turned

and scooped fries into a carton. She set them on a tray and grabbed their burgers as they came down the metal chute. Next, she poured out the coffee and added it to the rest of their order. "There ya go. Y'all enjoy."

"Thanks." Trent picked up the tray, and Amanda selected a booth in the corner.

The location was isolated and would give them privacy and some quiet. She took a bite of her cheeseburger and savored the comfort food, which her soul needed. Before she knew it, she'd inhaled her entire burger and was plucking a fry from Trent's wrapper.

"Please, just help yourself," he teased.

"Don't mind if I do." She took another one and popped it into her mouth.

He smiled at her and sat back.

"What?" she said.

"Nothing."

She felt her cheeks heat with him watching her. It made her uncomfortable not knowing what he was thinking because it left room for her imagination to take over. Was he thinking about what it would be like if they were more than colleagues, more than friends?

"I'm more than happy to do whatever you want, Amanda," Trent said.

"Ah, regarding?" His offer caught her off guard and paired with her stupid thoughts, her mind took a trip somewhere it had no business going.

"If you want to call rental companies all over the country, I will."

"I appreciate that. I just hate sitting still. Waiting."

"I know you do."

Her phone rang at the tail end of his sentence. "It's Malone. You good to go?" She looked at his food, and he only had a few fries left.

He nodded, and she shuffled out of the booth and answered Malone's call on the way to the door.

"We got a credible lead from the public appeal," he rushed out. "Guy's name is Travis Giles. He said he's renting a house he owns to Wilcox, only he knows him as Wilson Marsh."

What do you know... "Address?"

Malone gave them the ones for Giles and the rental. "Officer Brandt is watching the rental while a search warrant is approved, and SWAT is getting organized to move in. The latter could take a while. I want you and Trent to talk to Giles in the meantime. He's at home and waiting for you."

"Consider us there." Amanda's entire body trembled with a flush of fear and excitement. Trent had been right about grabbing a bite to eat. All hell had just broken loose.

FORTY

Amanda rang the bell, and the door cracked open. A man with silver hair was standing there in a light sweater tee and pressed pants. "Travis Giles?" she asked, flashing her badge.

"Yeah. Come in." Travis took them to a sitting room.

Once she and Trent were seated, she introduced them and said, "We understand you rent to Marshall Wilcox. What can you tell us about him?"

"The man not much, but he gave me a different name. Wilson Marsh, as I told the officer I spoke to on the tipline."

If Travis had done his due diligence before renting his place, he would have checked references. "Did he sign a lease?" She could inundate him with questions, but she'd start there.

"He did, and I've already dug it out." He grabbed paperwork from the end table and handed it over.

Amanda looked down at the page and noted it was signed on November thirtieth. "When did Mr. Wilcox reach out to you?"

"Last week of November. He said he got a new job and was eager to get situated. He paid for six months upfront. It's why I overlooked due process." Travis's gaze dipped to the floor.

"How much money are we talking about?" Trent asked.

Travis told them, and the math told her Wilcox was left with a healthy amount of spending money. She returned her attention to the lease agreement. References were provided, and two of the numbers looked familiar. "You said you overlooked due process. Did you call these people?" She pointed at the names on the page.

"No."

"Would you mind if I took a photograph of this page?" she asked him.

"Not at all." Travis sunk into the cushions.

She took a picture of the lease and handed the hard copy back to Travis. "How long was the rental for?"

"Just for the six months. Short-term wasn't what I preferred, but it was my best offer, so I accepted. He didn't seem to care it was furnished either, which is a no-go for some folks."

She flipped the pages to the front where Wilcox had listed his address in New York City. He'd left his phone number blank. Amanda got up and handed him her card. "If Wilcox shows up or calls, you call me immediately."

Travis nodded. "I will. What is he wanted for anyhow? The article just said he was a person of interest to the police."

"Trust me. You're better off not knowing."

Travis paled. "I better contact a lawyer to get that guy out of the house. I don't want to get caught up in this any more than I already am."

"And you don't need to." As of now, Wilcox wasn't his problem, he was hers.

FORTY-ONE

Amanda looked over at Trent from the passenger seat. "Trent, do you have those numbers Wilcox used with Mara? The one he used to pretend he was Jean Tanner and the one he gave her when he asked her out?"

"Yeah, it's on there." He handed her his tablet and told her where to find the information and got them on the road to the rental property.

She opened the file he'd directed her to. "All right. I thought they looked familiar. The numbers he provided for two of his references were those."

"This guy put in a lot of time planning, including lining up prepaid numbers."

"It's sickening." She couldn't give it much more thought than that. Instead, she'd focus on how this evidence solidified a case against him. No defense attorney could argue against premeditation.

"He only provided two references?"

"No, there is a third. Let me try that number." She took out her phone and tapped in the digits. The line went directly to voicemail. "Well, it's in service," she said, while listening to the automated greeting. She didn't leave a message and hung up. "No personalization to the voicemail greeting. Could this be Wilcox's active number?"

"We can't take the chance it isn't."

She got on the phone with Detective Briggs and explained the situation. He told her he'd get the authorization and track the number ASAP. She ended the call and updated Trent.

He turned down the street for the rental property and parked at the edge of the police cordon. Officer Traci Cochran was posted there. As they passed her, she gave them a nod.

The SWAT command vehicle was parked on the street near Malone's SUV. He was standing next to it. When he spotted them, he hustled over.

"SWAT's got this part," he rushed out.

"I understand that." His interception brought back a conversation they had more recently about her needing to hold off and wait for backup. In her defense, she only moved in earlier when she felt life was in danger.

"Have they breached yet?" Trent asked Malone.

"They're getting ready to." As Malone said this, SWAT officers in tactical gear approached the two-story house on the north side of the street.

The middle-class neighborhood was attractive to families with young children. The thought fired through and sickened her. The location might even be what led Wilcox to choose the house. They knew Wilcox planned ahead with the rental and the phones, so to think he'd scoped out the area wasn't a stretch.

A SWAT officer called out in the distance, announcing himself as PWCPD, just before the cracking of wood echoed in the air.

They would be inside. Now it was a waiting game. Would they find Eloise?

"Did any of the neighbors comment on seeing any young

girls going into the house or being around Wilcox?" she asked Malone.

"No, but the place has a garage. He could have had them in the backseat or the trunk, taken them in, put down the door..."

"With no one any the wiser," she finished his thought. It was terrifying what people could do when they set their minds to it.

"Do we know if the gray Kia is in the garage?" Trent asked.

"No way of checking that discreetly. The windows are slim rectangles and high in the door."

"Did anyone go around back? There might be a more accessible window on the rear side," she said.

"Officers checked that out. No window," Malone said. "The man door on the side has one, but a blind is covering the glass."

They didn't even know if this creep was home.

Time slowed down to a cruel pace. With each passing minute, Amanda became more anxious. After ten minutes, SWAT officers came out the front, and most headed back to their vehicle. The team leader started walking toward them. She, Trent, and Malone helped bridge the distance.

"No one's inside, but we found some disturbing things. There's a room in the basement with a padlock on the door. We broke it, and there's a child's bed in there with some stuffed toys and a play kitchen."

Amanda grinded her teeth. Her insides were pulsating.

The SWAT officer added, "Some girls' clothing was in the closet and a pair of unicorn pajamas on the bed."

"Eloise." The girl's name fell off Amanda's tongue, but she didn't give herself much time for sorrow. She turned to Trent and pulled out her phone. "We need the results on that number."

Malone held up a hand, and the SWAT officer angled his head.

"What number?" Malone asked her, and she told him about the lease agreement and her call with Briggs.

"Let's hope it turns out to be the break we need," Malone said.

"I want to go inside now," she told Malone.

"I get that. But just so you know, Crime Scene is on their way too."

She nodded and received his unspoken caution, even if it didn't need communicating. She could go in but had to be careful of what she touched to not contaminate the house any more. *The crime scene.* It was also likely the scene of Hailey's murder.

Just that thought had her moving toward the house, ready to strangle this Wilcox bastard. *I'm coming for you, you son of a bitch!*

Trent's footsteps sounded behind her, but she kept her pace fast and steady.

She gloved up and put booties over her shoes before entering the home and heading toward the basement stairs.

"Are you sure you want to do this?" Trent asked from behind her.

"I need to." She didn't understand the compulsion herself. An internal urge nudged her forward, as if by being there, she'd be brought closer to Eloise. She wasn't given the chance to save Hailey Tanner, and she wasn't failing Eloise. That girl had been taken on her watch, and she would make this right.

She reached the last step and let her instinct guide her. The basement was finished, and she walked through a family room to a doorway at the other end. This area housed the furnace, water heater, and laundry, but beyond that, another opened door led to a smaller space.

The sight of pink bedding made her head spin. She thought she was prepared to see this room... She reached out to the doorframe to steady herself as her legs became weak. Being here brought back the nightmares served up by a case they worked in February. Three months ago, but the imagery was still fresh. Though, she didn't think she'd ever forget that creepy house with its hidden room of horrors.

"Amanda." Trent reached out for her as her legs buckled.

She held up her hand, regaining her balance. "I'm fine." She wasn't. They both knew it. But surely, he must be having a bit of déjà vu himself. How these deviants could continue to draw breath after snuffing out the innocent was beyond her.

She let out a roar and drew back a fist to punch the wall. Trent caught her arm in the elbow.

"Just let me," she hissed at him.

"No. It's not going to help anything. It's just going to hurt you and contaminate the scene."

She was heaving for breath, consumed by rage.

"Amanda," Trent whispered. His soft tone drawing her back from the brink. "Save your fist for his face."

She met his eyes. "You always know the right thing to say."

He dipped his head. "We will get him. And Eloise."

"We have to." Her phone rang, and Briggs's name flashed on the screen. She answered before the first ring finished. "Tell me we have his location."

A pause, then, "I wish I could, but the phone's inactive."

She balled her hand into a fist. To be this close, yet so far away, felt like a cruel joke. "Okay, well, where did it last ping?"

"I can't tell you that either, unfortunately. I can tell you that number is also part of a prepaid block serviced by Universal. I also got authorization to look at the history on it, and the other one you provided me with. The one given to Mara from Wilson M. They were all activated the first of December and purchased at the same convenience store."

"Thanks," she said, despite wanting to punch the wall. The phone being offline might be her fault. She'd tried that phone about forty minutes ago. Had he seen the unknown number, freaked out, and turned the phone off?

"I hope you find this guy."

"Makes two of us." She said goodbye and turned to Trent, shaking her head. But she filled him in on the link.

"The evidence is just stacking up against this guy now." His phone rang. He pulled it out and told her it was the rental company he was waiting to hear from.

She listened in and could only catch so much, but what she could piece together sounded promising.

"Thank you so much. Goodbye." Trent cupped his phone in his hand. "We have our lead. We are going to find him, Amanda, and save Eloise."

This was his second time saying as much within a short time. Was he that positive or was he trying to reassure himself?

FORTY-TWO

Royal Auto Rentals confirmed that a Marshall Wilcox had rented a gray Kia K5, and a trace on its GPS was in progress. Amanda was leery about getting attached to a happy outcome. They could get Wilcox, but would they be too late for Eloise?

They returned to Central at eight o'clock and planned on sticking around to see what came back on the vehicle. Time wasn't slowing down, and Amanda's thoughts went from Eloise to her parents. She couldn't imagine being in their position, sitting around not knowing if or when they'd ever see their daughter again.

With nothing much to do but wait, Amanda caved and called home. Her mother answered.

"Everything's fine, before you ask." This time Amanda beat her mother to the question.

"Glad to hear it. What's up, then? Zoe and I are eating popcorn and watching a movie."

"Yeah!" Zoe called out in the background, and the sound of her voice lifted Amanda's spirits.

"It's going to be a long night, and I just need to say good-night to her."

"One second. Do you want to talk to Mandy?"

Mere seconds later, a rustling on the other end was followed by an exuberant, "Mom!"

Amanda's heart swelled. This would never get old, and she'd remind herself of this thought when Zoe was a teenager and saying it with a sarcastic groan and eye roll. "Hey, baby. Having fun with Grandma?"

"You bet. We had pizza for dinner, and now we're eating popcorn."

"I heard that, and you're obviously being a good girl."

"Always."

Amanda laughed. Forget waiting for her teenage years. Zoe was probably rolling her eyes now. She spoke with Zoe a bit longer, asking how school went that day and hearing all about how some boy in her class pulled her hair. "You know why he's doing that right?"

"He's an idiot."

Amanda resisted the urge to laugh. Such an honest and understandable assessment. "It's not nice to talk about people that way, remember."

"Fine. But I don't like him. And if he's not doing it to bug me, why is he?"

"He likes you."

"Yuck!"

Talking to Zoe was just what she needed to lighten her mood some and ground her emotions.

Trent stood in her cubicle doorway and was waving to get her attention.

"I've got to go, sweetie, but enjoy the movie and get to bed on time. School tomorrow."

"Yeah, yeah."

And she was gone. Amanda would have to work with Zoe on her telephone etiquette.

"We have a location," Trent pushed out.

She popped up and grabbed her jacket from the back of her chair. "Where is it?"

"Prince Park."

"That place is massive. It covers miles of woods and terrain." The park was also where a killer had buried his victims in a previous investigation.

"It does, and since we don't expect he'll just be sitting around in his car, the K-9 unit's already on the way and so are other officers."

"Let's go." Amanda's heart was pounding as she headed for the car.

Please, tell me we're not too late!

FORTY-THREE

Nothing much compared to a manhunt taking place in the dark, and in a wooded area, no less. The weak moon was intermittently suffocated by cloud cover, leaving them reliant on flashlights and headlamps. Amanda kept thinking how terrified Eloise must be if she was out here.

Marshall's rental car was in one of the parking lots, but there was no sign of him or Eloise. He could have left by other means. But with Eloise? That scenario seemed too risky. If Marshall had abandoned the Kia and called a car service, Amanda feared they'd be finding the girl's body in the woods.

Uniformed officers were directed by their sergeant to branch out and conduct a search. The K-9 unit had sent five handlers with their trained dogs, and they set out toward the deep woods.

Amanda hoped like hell they weren't too late for Eloise. Would her body be in a freshly dug grave, or on display somewhere like little Hailey Tanner? She held her breath as images of her laid out in her tutu and slippers struck with vivid clarity. She turned to Trent beside her. "Let's check out the play area."

He nodded, and they headed over.

The playground wasn't far from the parking lot, but it felt farther out at night. Amanda set the beam of her flashlight ahead of her and hurried as fast as she could, hindered by fallen branches and uneven ground.

Trent swept his flashlight over the play equipment, and nothing stood out. No lumps or unexplained shadows. But something about the playground sucked Amanda in. An energy? A hunch?

Amanda took cautious steps and rounded the sandbox. Directing her flashlight on it, she held her breath, but it hadn't been disturbed. She carried on past the swings to the jungle gym and the slide, illuminating each section as she went along. When the beam hit the top of the slide, she froze, paralyzed in place.

"Trent," she whispered.

"What is—?" His flashlight beam joined hers. "Shit."

"Yeah, this can't be good." She was going to be sick. "Eloise!" she yelled out as loud as she could. Her throat was throbbing after she pushed out the girl's name several more times.

It drew some officers over.

"Detective Steele, are you okay? Is everything all right?" Officer Traci Cochran asked.

Amanda felt her walk up next to her but never took her eyes off her discovery. She pointed at the top of the slide.

A stuffed unicorn, Eloise's favorite toy, was sitting there staring back at them. The beams from their flashlights reflected in the toy's glass eyes.

"Dear Lord. Does that mean what I think it does?" The whites of Traci's eyes appeared larger than normal when Amanda turned to her. Trent spoke before she could respond.

"Let's not jump to conclusions. All it means for certain is Wilcox was here," Trent said calmly.

Amanda couldn't understand how he was holding himself

together so well. "We could tell that by the Kia. This... *that* is a message, Trent. He's already killed her, or he's very close to doing so. This is his game, and he knew we'd track him down. This toy is like him telling us, we're just a little too late."

"You don't know that for sure," Trent pushed back.

Amanda admired how he was clinging to light in this darkness while she was struggling for ground. But his optimism was foolish and naive. She turned to Traci. "Report over the radios and loop everyone in on this." One of the other officers who had come over beat Traci to it.

Amanda set out toward the woods. She could hear Trent's footsteps cracking over small twigs in her wake. She stopped walking and turned around to face him. "What are you doing?"

"I'm not letting you go out there alone." He thrust a pointed finger at the woods.

"Time is running out for Eloise, Trent. I feel that. Let me go on my own, you go your way. We'll cover more ground, faster." Going off alone presented a risk, but it was one she was prepared to take. She had her gun, her training, and her wits. Even if she was being borderline obsessive about one little girl right now.

"I don't know. You seriously think that's a smart thing to do? You thought he was panicking when he thought Katherine was getting close. What do you think his mental state is now, with cops chasing him through this park? There's no telling what Wilcox will do if you run into him."

"Trent, please. If you fan out that way fifty yards and head toward the river like I'm doing, we'll meet up soon. This is our best chance of stopping Wilcox and saving Eloise."

He stood there, facing her. She could feel his eyes drilling into her through the night.

"Seconds count, Trent. Every. Single. One. As you just said, there is a lot of backup here. I'm safe."

"Tell yourself that. This guy is unhinged."

"He might be, but there's a little girl who needs us."

"Fine," he consented. "But one sign of Wilcox, and you yell like a freaking banshee. Got me?"

"Got you."

Trent set out east, and Amanda continued going straight. The river was a bit of a walk from here, and a thick forest stood in between. With Trent gone, it suddenly felt like the trees had eyes. The darkness closed in around her, but she kept moving forward with her flashlight's beam fixed ahead.

Taking one step at a time for Eloise...

But she stopped, holding her next breath at the sound of dogs barking in the distance. Had one of the K-9s found the girl?

She set out in that direction, hurrying her pace until her path was blocked.

Marshall Wilcox stepped out from behind a large tree. Eloise was limp in his arms, cradled like a baby. She couldn't tell if the girl was alive or not.

FORTY-FOUR

Amanda reached for her gun. She froze with her hand over her holster.

"I wouldn't do that, if I were you," Marshall seethed. "And I wouldn't call out either. Or I *will* kill her."

So she is alive... He must have drugged her. "PWCPD. Surrender the girl."

Marshall laughed. "And why would I do that?"

"You're caught, Marshall. Just let the girl go."

"I don't answer to you," he hissed.

"Please, we can talk about this." Why hadn't he just stayed hidden? Either he was feeling self-destructive or this fed into his game.

"No." He turned and walked away from her, exposing his back, giving her a clear target.

She reached for her gun, tempted to take it, but what if he detected the danger and her bullet struck too late for Eloise? No, she couldn't take that chance. She couldn't scream either. She took Marshall at his word. He was prepared to kill the girl. This left her with one choice. Follow him.

She kept pace with him, but he didn't glance over his

shoulder once. But why should he be anxious with Eloise in his arms? With her there, he was protected.

He reached the riverbank and stopped. The moon slipped out from behind cloud cover. Its light shone onto the dark still water, reflecting across its surface.

"Marshall, please, let's talk," she petitioned. She was wishing that she hadn't separated from Trent. Maybe together they could have devised a plan to take this man down. One of them could have distracted him while the other swept in for Eloise.

Marshall continued walking right into the river. The water must be freezing cold, but he showed no reaction to it at all. He just kept moving, taking deliberate steps. When the level reached the middle of his thighs, he turned to face her.

"There is nothing to talk about." He dropped Eloise into the water, and the child screamed. The shock of the cold water must have woken her. Her arms and legs thrashed as she tried to get away from him. To no avail. Marshall bent over the girl and held her under.

In a fraction of a second, Amanda reassessed her options. The chance she could put a bullet center mass without endangering Eloise was slim. She didn't trust her shooting skills to be precise enough to hit him between the eyes.

Amanda ran into the water. The cold soaked through her shoes, biting her ankles, then through her pants. She couldn't feel her toes. But none of this mattered.

She rushed Marshall, throwing all her weight against him. He toppled over, and she went with him. She struggled to get her feet beneath her, all the while thinking about Eloise. She turned and saw the little girl's head bobbing above the surface. Eloise was crying and trying to get away from Marshall.

"Swim to the shore!" Amanda screamed at the girl. "Get help!"

"You bitch." Marshall yanked Amanda's hair.

She spun around to face her adversary and went to punch him, but he caught her wrist and twisted her arm behind her back. Then he took the other. She tried to squirm loose, but all her strength wasn't enough.

He released her hands, just long enough to push down on her head.

She gulped a breath of air just before she was plunged beneath the water. Marshall was pressing down so hard, getting her legs under her was impossible. At best, the tips of her shoes brushed against the riverbed.

She flailed her arms, trying to gather momentum to propel herself upward, but to no avail. Her muscles weakened, and she needed air. She felt herself sinking farther down. Her fingertips grazed the bottom and slid across rocks, and the darkness tempted her to surrender. It would all be over soon, and she could succumb to peace. But as her consciousness drifted, she saw Zoe's face, heard her calling her *Mom*. She couldn't go out this way! Zoe needed her! Amanda had been so foolish thinking she could bring this man down on her own. She should have listened to Trent. Help might come too late. If she wanted to live another day, she had to save herself. Just muster enough strength to make an impact.

Her palm rolled over a sizable rock. *Grab it and hit him!*

But her lungs were starving for oxygen, and she was battling against instinct to open her mouth. If she did, she'd gulp nothing but water.

I can do this! I have to!

She wrapped her hand around the rock and got a toehold on the bottom. She thrust up, swinging as fast as she could. Her head still didn't break the surface, but she struck him hard. He howled, but his grip on her only weakened some.

She needed air. Now. She tried to hit him again. This time he caught her forearm and squeezed it in a vise grip. She cried out and swallowed a lungful of water. She started convulsing, her body wanting to purge the liquid, but every inhale kicked more river back into her lungs.

Her mind drifted to an inky blackness until there was nothing.

FORTY-FIVE

Amanda jolted awake, screaming. She was back in the river, everything dark and closing in on her. She greedily gasped for air, fearing her next inhale would suck in water. But it didn't. She was no longer frozen and submersed. Rather, she was somewhere bright and sterile. She then noticed a tube going into the back of her hand and other lines running from under the sleeve of a hospital gown to a heart monitor. She scanned the room. Another bed was across from her, but it was empty. Same too for a chair next to her bed.

"She just woke up." Trent came hustling into the room with a doctor at his heels.

"Well, hello, there." The doctor came over to her, eyes full of concern, his stethoscope dangling around his neck. At least it wasn't Dr. Paulsen with her looking the frightening way she must. *Such a ridiculous concern to have right now...*

Amanda watched as Trent walked to the other side of the bed. She reached out for his hand, and he took hers and squeezed it. She was safe.

The doctor cleared his throat. "How are you feeling, Amanda?"

She rolled her head to face him. "Ah, I'm—" She stopped talking, finding that her throat was sore. She tapped it.

"A sore throat and lungs are normal after the ordeal you suffered. Now, if you bear with me, I'm just going to check you over." The doctor checked her vitals and put a small flashlight on her eyes. When he finished, he smiled as he pocketed it. "You should be just fine. Nothing a little bed rest can't fix."

"Can't I leave? I don't have time to... just lie here." Her body was working against her. It felt like she was chewing glass to talk right now.

"Yes, but you're going to." The doctor gave her a tight smile. "Bed rest," he reiterated and left.

Trent turned on her. "*Can't I just leave?* Now I know the lack of oxygen has affected your brain. You could have died."

She felt his concern, heard it in his voice. "But I didn't." Images flashed of Trent hovering over her, of him leaning down and... The focus was hazy, but now she remembered coughing up water. "You're why I'm alive. You gave me CPR." It sank in that meant his mouth would have been on her mouth. Her cheeks heated, and she let go of his hand. "I'm sorry about..."

"No worries, and as for the CPR, it's nothing you wouldn't have done for me."

"True, but still—" A violent coughing spell wracked her, and the burning in her lungs intensified.

"Just take it easy."

"Just tell me we got Wilcox."

"We did."

She held eye contact, hoping he'd read her mind and continue talking. It would save her throat and her energy.

"Right, so Eloise screamed first, then Wilcox. I arrived first and found Eloise soaking wet and sitting on the edge of the river shivering and crying. Then I saw Wilcox in the moonlight. He was holding you under the..." Trent turned away for a second. "Yeah, well, it worked out."

"Keep going."

"I went in after him. It turned out holding on to you and fending me off was a lot for him. But once I hit him in the head with the butt of my gun, he relented."

He went in that cold water to save my life... "You could have just shot him from the shore and saved the court time and money." Saying all of that in one go made her throat feel like it was bleeding, but to hell with it. She had powerful feelings on the matter.

"Not at the risk of somehow hitting you. No way."

He didn't just administer CPR. He had been her White Knight. Her insides flushed with heat and softened.

"By then, other officers had shown up and Wilcox was apprehended. Paramedics tended to Eloise."

"And is she going to be okay? Was she..." Amanda swallowed roughly.

"She's receiving treatment down the hall and will be reunited with her parents. Paramedics said she will be fine. As for the other thing, the question you don't want to verbalize. Thankfully, the answer to that is no sexual assault."

Breathing became easier. Amanda had assumed the worst when she saw the girl's unicorn pajamas in that room. But what had prevented Wilcox from violating the child? Had he grown a bit of a conscience? Yet he was still willing to kill the girl.

"Eloise was in Hailey's clothes, though."

"And the other children's clothing in that closet. Do we think he abused other girls?"

"There's nothing to point us at any other victims. It turns out the clothing was brand new."

She nodded, and her head spun.

"I should leave so you can rest."

"No, not yet, please. What else have you found out? You didn't speak with Wilcox without me, I hope."

"He's been charged, but I haven't spoken to him. I thought

you had earned the honors. Far as I'm concerned the waiting will do him good. But in answer to your question, there are a couple of updates I can share. I tracked down the owner of the scarf pulled from Hailey Tanner's body. It turned out it belonged to Travis Giles's former tenant. I reached out to this woman, and she confirmed she had a scarf just like that one and hadn't seen it in a while, said she must have left it behind when she moved out in August. It makes more sense why Travis Giles was eager to take Wilcox's cash and not worry about checking out his references. The property has just been sitting there for months. But burying his active number in there was one way that Wilcox really messed up."

"Glad he did." She touched her burning throat.

"I should leave."

"No, please. Keep talking."

"Let's see. As you know, the entire rental house was searched. What you don't know is that CSI Blair found a printer which is a match for the toner used for the notes. She also recovered his laptop. His internet history showed that he stalked Katherine online."

"That's how he knew where she moved and where to go. Why he made himself a customer of the diner... All to get close to her and keep tabs on her. But speaking of all this, do we have any idea how he got here? We know he rented the car in town. Did he have another rental before the Kia?"

Trent shook his head. "Don't know, and I'm not sure it even matters. He probably used cash to get himself to Woodbridge."

"Anything else or...?"

"Oh, one thing. CSI Blair confirmed the apron from the Scoop has DNA that matches Wilcox."

"One more victory."

"All right. I should go. You need to rest. Everyone is worried about you though. Most of your family is in the waiting room, along with several officers from the PWCPD."

The thought of visiting with everyone was overwhelming, but for one person. "Is Zoe out there?"

He shook his head. "She's at your house with your mom. Everyone thought it was best she didn't see you like this. Guess your mom made it sound like she could play hooky from school."

Amanda's head was pounding. "School? What day is this?" He'd told her it was the next day, but her brain was too foggy to assign a reference point and get the answer.

"Thursday."

With that, flashes of the ordeal she'd suffered rushed through her mind. All the water, the bubbles, the thrashing, the hunger for air. Her lungs were still on fire. The recollections washed over her and wiped her out. She couldn't think about facing anyone right now.

The next thing she remembered was Trent's voice, sounding like it came from the other side of the world. "I'll leave you to sleep."

FORTY-SIX

Amanda checked out of the hospital Friday morning and went right to Central. Her family had come in to visit yesterday after she had gotten some rest. She insisted that Zoe be brought to her. She was still feeling horrible despite being medicated for pain, but there was no way she was missing out on facing the asshole who had killed two girls, almost a third, and tried to drown her.

Her spirits had been further lifted yesterday when Eloise had insisted her parents wheel her to Amanda's room. The little girl had wanted to thank Amanda for saving her in person. Her parents thanked her too, but Amanda couldn't claim all the credit. Either way, the wins made this job sustainable.

Malone was in when she reached the station, and he summoned her into his office from the doorway. Trent was in there seated in one of the visitor chairs. He looked at her over his shoulder and smiled. She felt her cheeks heat at the thought of him giving her mouth to mouth. He'd saved her life, and she owed him.

"How are you feeling?" Malone asked her.

She dropped into the chair next to Trent. "Ready to send this guy away for life."

Malone smiled and looked at Trent. "I'd say she's fine."

Trent was grinning.

"You have a knack for facing off with killers," Malone said.

"What can I say? It's a talent." It hurt to talk, and she'd prefer to preserve her voice for questioning Wilcox. But if she confessed this weakness to Malone, he'd send her back home. At least she hadn't given him any need to reprimand her. She hadn't gone against orders. Backup was all around her, even if they were too far away to save her from swallowing mouthfuls of the Potomac River.

"All right. Well, if you feel you're up for it..." Malone gestured at the door. "He's already waiting in Interview Two."

She didn't waste time hiking down the hall in that direction.

Upon opening the door, she was face to face with Marshall and his lawyer. Marshall had a gash on his cheek that had required stitches, and she took satisfaction in the thought she'd caused him some pain. He also had a line of stitches at his hairline. *From Trent...* It was the least of what he deserved.

He stared at her with defiance, and she pinned him back with her gaze. Somewhere in the last twenty-four hours, he'd lost his timidity.

She set down a folder she'd grabbed from her desk on the way here and pulled out some photographs. They were of Julie Gilbert, Hailey Tanner, and Eloise Maynard, and she set them down one by one in front of Marshall, rattling off their names as she went.

He looked at each photograph as it came to rest on the table.

"We can link you to all three crimes. The assault and murder of Julie Gilbert and Hailey Tanner and the kidnapping and attempted murder of Eloise Maynard. Let's start with Julie. Why?"

Marshall glanced at his lawyer, who nodded.

"She was a spoiled brat. She had everything handed to her and looked down on everyone else."

"Did she look down on you?" Trent asked.

"Every female looks down on me."

It seemed Amanda was spot on with her earlier thinking. "How do you figure that?"

"You get kicks out of dominating men, using your sexuality to keep us loyal and in line. If it's not for that, it's just because you can. All females are bossy and loud-mouthed. Arrogant." He leveled his gaze at her.

"You're saying *I'm* arrogant?"

"All of you are. I'm finished being made to feel like shit."

Amanda was piecing together all he'd said and recalled what Katherine had told them about Wilcox's former boss. "Did Leslie Gallagher mistreat you?"

"She thought she was better than me, just like my mother."

And there it is... How little it took to get there. She pointed at the scar on his lip. "Did your mother do that to you?"

"If we could stick to the point, Detective," the lawyer chimed in. "What evidence do you have against my client?"

"I'll circle back to your mother. You took Eloise Maynard from her bed. Why not Hailey Tanner?" She hadn't heard if Marshall's shoes were a match to the scuff marks found on the trellis outside of Hailey Tanner's window, but it seemed likely. That's why she ran with it as fact.

"Whatever you say."

The lawyer shook his head. "Evidence against my client, Detective?"

"All right. How about this..." Amanda laid out everything pertaining to Eloise, including the incriminating video that showed Marshall walking down the Maynards' street with the girl in his arms. She summed up with, "Not to mention he was found with Eloise Maynard."

"Any evidence against my client pertaining to Hailey Tanner?"

She mentioned the marks on the trellis now and the fact Eloise was dressed in Hailey's clothes. Then added, "The reason I asked why you didn't take Hailey from her bed is because I know you were in her bedroom." She paused there, but neither Marshall nor his lawyer said anything. She continued. "You might have planned to take her but were interrupted. You ended up taking one of her tutus and a pair of ballet slippers from her closet, though, didn't you? The ones you dressed her in to dispose of her." Amanda set out a photo of the crime scene, and the lawyer turned away.

Marshall looked at the picture, and a smile tugged at his lips.

She resisted the urge to reach across the table and throttle the bastard. Instead, she'd hit his ego. "But you didn't carry off the abduction that night. You chickened out, got spooked."

He met her eye with a defiant gaze. "I wasn't scared. I was biding my time, waiting for a bigger impact."

"Not buying it." Amanda sat back, and his eyes set ablaze. "Go ahead. Tell us what happened when you were in Hailey's room."

"Someone was in the hallway and peeked into her room. I ducked into the closet to hide. That's when I got the idea to take her clothes. It would make for a beautiful scene."

Amanda recalled thinking that with the way Hailey was posed, the person responsible felt remorse or affection for the girl. But it was only about making a perfect scene. "Is that why you chose Heroes Memorial Park? Because it is beautiful?"

"I knew about the carousel and how perfect she'd look there."

Or the big impact it would make... "So you planned to kill her all along?"

He shrugged. "I returned for her. On my schedule."

"How long did it take you to build up the courage?" She was trying to rile him. Let him build the case against himself.

"Two days."

"When did you first lay eyes on Hailey?"

"At *The Nutcracker* in December. I knew right away that she was the one."

"Then why wait so long to take her?" Amanda leaned forward, clasping her hands on the table, showing her interest. Such indulgent body language would feed into Marshall's need to feel powerful and important.

The lawyer turned to his client and back to Amanda. "My client refuses to answer."

"I enjoy watching for a while," Marshall admitted.

The lawyer sat back and flailed an arm.

Marshall went on. "I learned her routine, and when taking her from her own bed didn't work out, I thought snatching her from the studio would be the next best thing. It turned out that it was." He smiled, and Amanda assumed he must have received tremendous pleasure from witnessing the chaos he'd caused.

"And how did you get her to go with you?"

"Easy. I exploited her trust. I met her on the day of the show when she was with Mara. All I had to do was tell the girl her nanny was running behind and sent me, her friend, to pick her up."

It was along the lines Amanda had figured. "You love watching so much, was that how you became obsessed with Julie Gilbert? You watched her from a distance, and then when you saw her at the family home you couldn't help yourself?" Amanda recalled that photo of Dickson. Only it was never about him. The focus of the shot was Julie.

The lawyer faced Marshall. "I recommend you don't respond to that."

"He doesn't need to. We have these." Amanda pulled out

photocopies of the notes he wrote taunting Katherine. "Forensics have confirmed they match the printer in your rental house. One has Marshall's fingerprint. But why leave a note in the hem of Hailey Tanner's dress calling out Katherine Graves? You had to know this would connect Hailey's murder to Julie Gilbert's. And you had to know Hailey's murder would be investigated. By doing this, you implicated yourself in two murders."

"Katherine had to know I was calling the shots. She should have minded her own business," Marshall seethed. "She's not even a cop anymore."

"This isn't on her," Amanda hissed. "*You* molested and killed those girls. You traumatized another one and her family."

"Whatever."

"Help me understand. Was it your ego that tripped you up? Your need to feel powerful and in control for a change?"

He met her eye but didn't say a word.

I hit a bull's-eye... She decided to continue beating on the matter. "It makes no sense at all. And to come forward and identify Hank Dickson through Katherine's website when you could have just stayed silent... There's no logic in it. But it's a good thing you did. Not for you, but for us." Briggs could never tie the email to Marshall, but he didn't have to know that.

Marshall grimaced. "You don't know everything."

"Please, enlighten me."

"I just wanted to take her focus off me."

Amanda scoffed laughter. "Katherine never knew you existed."

"You're lying."

"Nope."

"I don't believe you."

"It doesn't matter to me if you do. You killed Hailey Tanner for the same reason you killed Julie Gilbert. You wanted to. It had nothing to do with Katherine Graves. If anything, this is about your mother, isn't it?"

Marshall balled his fists, nostrils flaring. "Shut the hell up right now."

Amanda turned to Trent. "I touched a nerve."

"I'd say," Trent agreed.

"My old lady was a demon. She never wanted me and blamed me for everything!" Marshall roared. "I was worthless because I had a penis, and she made me feel inferior until her last breath. I couldn't do anything right, and to punish me she'd tie me up and do things to me. Is that what you want to hear?" Marshall tossed this out with such vehemence, Amanda pulled back. "You wanted to know about my scar? Yeah, it was her. She sliced me with a knife one day. Just for fun, to see how much I'd bleed. I hope she's burning in hell!"

Time passed in silence before the lawyer spoke. "I'd like a few minutes with my client."

"He's all yours." Amanda walked to the door and turned around. She made eye contact with Marshall. "Are there other girls we don't know about?"

The corners of his mouth twitched. "Wouldn't you like to know?"

Amanda walked out with Trent and slammed the door behind them. She told the officer at the door to take him to the cells and went to the room next door. Malone was there with Katherine and Detective McGee.

Katherine came over to Amanda and hugged her. "I can't believe this is finally over, that the man who killed Julie is finally going away."

"If there's justice, for the rest of his natural life. We couldn't have gotten him without your help." Amanda touched her friend's arm.

"I like to think I contributed, and while he deserves a heavy sentence, there is a small part of me that wonders where his justice is. It sounds like his mother put him through hell as a kid and messed up his mind."

"Emasculated him at every turn from the sound of it," Trent said.

"As tragic as that is," Amanda began, "in the end we all must make our own choices. He made his."

"True. If you would allow me"—Katherine turned to Malone—"I'd love to notify the Gilberts that we caught Julie's killer."

Malone glanced at Amanda and nodded at Katherine. "That's fine."

Amanda regarded her friend and hoped the closure would bring her some peace. "If there's anything you need, call me."

"I will. After I deliver the news to the Gilberts, I'll be spending some time with my aunt May. I told her about Julie, but nothing about all this." Katherine turned to Amanda. "And I suggest that as soon as you can, you get home to your beautiful daughter."

"You can bet I will." Before that could happen, she and Trent would have the pleasure of letting the Tanners know they'd captured their daughter's killer.

Malone left the room with Katherine, leaving Amanda with Trent and McGee. She faced the detective. "I'm surprised to see you here."

"I told you I care too much."

Amanda caught a flicker in his eyes. "This happen to someone you loved?"

"*Love.* Well, not a child. But my wife went missing seven years ago. It's why I got transferred to Missing Persons."

"Sorry to hear that. Any idea what might have happened to her?" Amanda tiptoed.

"Nothing but dead ends so far, but I won't give up."

"I hope you find her," Trent told him.

"Thanks. I was wondering if it's not too much to ask if I can accompany you to the Tanners'."

"That's fine with me," Trent said and looked at Amanda.

"That works for me. How about we go right now and deliver some good news for a change?"

She, Trent, and McGee did just that, bringing the Tanners some comfort in knowing their daughter's killer would be brought to justice.

About an hour later, they returned to Central, and McGee went his way.

"The paperwork can wait until Monday. I'm heading home. You?" Amanda asked Trent.

"You bet. I'm going to make the most of this weekend."

"Oh yeah? Big plans?"

"If that's what you call sitting on the couch with Kelsey binging movies and drinking wine?"

Amanda laughed. "That sounds glorious. Have fun." She got into her car and called Libby to stitch up a loose end.

"Amanda?" Libby answered. "I heard about what happened. You were already out of the hospital at that point but—"

"Not to worry. I'm fine. I'd like to know if you're engaged or not. So...?"

"She said yes," Libby burst out.

"Congratulations."

"Thank you."

"You know the family is having a gathering tonight at my mother's. You and Penny are welcome to join."

"I'd love that. Let me talk to her."

"Sure. Six, if you can make it. There will be food and drink, so there's no need to bring anything. I'll text you the address."

"Thanks." Libby hung up, and Amanda started pecking out the message to her when her phone rang.

She took a deep breath upon seeing the name Carter Paulsen and answered, "Dr. Paulsen."

"Huh. I thought *I* was Dr. Paulsen," he said, a smile lighting the line.

"A smart-ass, I see."

"Just to confirm, this is Detective Steele?"

"Amanda," she clarified.

"I see. Well, that correction makes my question easier to ask. I was wondering if you'd like to go out for a coffee sometime?"

She could think of a million reasons to turn him down, including her job and Zoe. But Carter was a doctor. He'd understand unpredictable working hours. But she may be getting carried away. Friends went out for coffee. No big deal. And even though there was the promise of a new beginning, she'd take life one day at a time. "Sure. Why not?"

A LETTER FROM CAROLYN

Dear reader,

I want to say a huge thank you for choosing to read *Three Girls Gone*. If you enjoyed it and would like to hear about new releases in the Amanda Steele series, just sign up at the following link. Your email address will never be shared, and you can unsubscribe at any time.

www.bookouture.com/carolyn-arnold

If you loved *Three Girls Gone*, I would be incredibly grateful if you would write a brief, honest review. While writing this book, it drilled home how influential the past can be and how it can have a powerful hold on us. But that doesn't always have to be a bad thing. Grief and injustices fueled Katherine, Amanda, and Trent. And just as Amanda decided to take one day at a time, we can do the same, in the best way we know how.

On another note, if you'd like to continue investigating murder, you'll be happy to know there will be more Detective Amanda Steele books. I also offer several other international bestselling series for you to savor—everything from crime fiction, to cozy mysteries, to thrillers and action adventures. One of these series features Detective Madison Knight, another kick-ass female detective, who will risk her life, her badge—whatever it takes—to find justice for murder victims. Then there's my latest series, featuring Sandra Vos, a top negotiator with the FBI. These reads are fashioned to be pulse-pounding thrillers.

If you enjoyed being in the Prince William County, Virginia, area, you might want to return in my Brandon Fisher FBI series. Brandon is Becky Tulson's boyfriend alluded to in this book. You can be there when they meet in *Silent Graves* (book two in my FBI series). This is also where readers get to meet Trent Stenson for the first time. The Brandon Fisher FBI books are perfect for readers who love heart-pounding thrillers and are fascinated with the psychology of serial killers. Each installment is a new case with a fresh bloody trail to follow. Hunt with the FBI's Behavioral Analysis Unit and profile some of the most devious and darkest minds on the planet.

For those familiar with the Prince William County, Virginia, area, or who have done some internet searching, you'll realize that I've taken creative liberties. This also includes the parks and businesses named in this book, which are all fictional. (Though, there is a Heroes Memorial Park in Texas.)

I'd like to thank everyone who helped me with this book. George, my husband and best friend, my editor, Laura Deacon, and Jonathan Perok with the Public Information Office of the Prince William County PD. He helped me with some procedural questions on missing persons cases. There are many others, too, and I appreciate everyone. And you, my beautiful reader, thank you for your support.

Before I sign off, please, don't underestimate the power and influence of word of mouth. Talk to your family and friends about my books, your local bookstores and librarians, your neighbors, the people at the checkout counter, your dentist, your... well, you get the point. Thank you!

And last but certainly not least, I would love to hear from you if you're so inclined to drop me a note. You can reach me via email at Carolyn@CarolynArnold.net. You can also follow and interact with me on Facebook and X at the links below. To investigate my full list of books, visit my website by following the link below.

Until the next time, I wish you thrilling reads and twists you never saw coming!

Carolyn Arnold

Connect with CAROLYN ARNOLD Online:
www.carolynarnold.net

f facebook.com/AuthorCarolynArnold
X x.com/Carolyn_Arnold
g goodreads.com/carolyn_arnold

PUBLISHING TEAM

Turning a manuscript into a book requires the efforts of many people. The publishing team at Bookouture would like to acknowledge everyone who contributed to this publication.

Audio
Alba Proko
Melissa Tran
Sinead O'Connor

Commercial
Lauren Morrissette
Hannah Richmond
Imogen Allport

Cover design
Head Design Ltd

Data and analysis
Mark Alder
Mohamed Bussuri

Editorial
Laura Deacon
Imogen Allport

RAISING READERS
Books Build Bright Futures

Dear Reader,

We'd love your attention for one more page to tell you about the crisis in children's reading, and what we can all do.

Studies have shown that reading for fun is the **single biggest predictor of a child's future life chances** – more than family circumstance, parents' educational background or income. It improves academic results, mental health, wealth, communication skills, ambition and happiness.

The number of children reading for fun is in rapid decline. Young people have a lot of competition for their time, and a worryingly high number do not have a single book at home.

Hachette works extensively with schools, libraries and literacy charities, but here are some ways we can all raise more readers:

- Reading to children for just 10 minutes a day makes a difference
- Don't give up if children aren't regular readers – there will be books for them!

- Visit bookshops and libraries to get recommendations
- Encourage them to listen to audiobooks
- Support school libraries
- Give books as gifts

There's a lot more information about how to encourage children to read on our websites: **www.RaisingReaders.co.uk** and **www.JoinRaisingReaders.com**.

Thank you for reading.